MW01616773

PRAISE FOR VIVIAN AREND

"If you've never read a Vivian Arend book you are missing out on one of the best contemporary authors writing today."
~ *Book Reading Gals*

"A Rancher's Heart was a spectacular start to this new series and I am very excited to see what comes next for the rest of the Heart Falls crew."
~ *Guilty Pleasures Book Review*

"Brilliant, raw, imaginative, irresistible!!"
~ *Avon Romance*

"This story will keep you reading from the first page to the last one. There is never a dull moment..."
~ *Landy Jimenez*

"Arend became a favorite author of mine because not only does she write about sexy cowboys, she gives us families who love and take care of each other."
~ *SmexyBooks*

"This was my first Vivian Arend story, and I know I want more! "
~ *Red Hot Plus Blue Reads*

A RANCHER'S BRIDE

THE STONES OF HEART FALLS: BOOK 3

VIVIAN AREND

ALSO BY VIVIAN AREND

The Stones of Heart Falls

A Rancher's Heart

A Rancher's Song

A Rancher's Bride

A Rancher's Love

A Rancher's Vow

Holidays in Heart Falls

A Firefighter's Christmas Gift

A Soldier's Christmas Wish

A Hero's Christmas Hope

A Cowboy's Christmas List

A Rancher's Christmas Kiss

The Colemans of Heart Falls

The Cowgirl's Forever Love

The Cowgirl's Secret Love

The Cowgirl's Chosen Love

A full list of Vivian's print titles is available on her website:
www.vivianarend.com

This is a work of fiction. Names, characters, places, and incidents either are the product of the author's imagination or are used fictitiously, and any resemblance to any persons, living or dead, business establishments, events, or locales is entirely coincidental.

A Rancher's Bride
Copyright © November 2018 by Arend Publishing Inc.
ISBN: 9781989507698
Edited by Anne Scott
Cover Design © Damonza
Proofed by Angie Ramey & Linda Levy

All rights reserved. No part of this book may be used or reproduced in any manner whatsoever without written permission except in the case of brief quotations.

1

For the umpteenth time that day, the ground rose up and slapped Luke Stone silly.

The initial moment of contact knocked the wind from him, but the smack to the bruise already forming on his hip was the real kicker. He stayed in motion, rolling instinctively to his hands and knees. Lying on his back on the cold January snow and groaning in pain wasn't an option unless he wanted a hoof print branded onto any vital parts.

The world was still spinning when he shoved a hand in the air to indicate he was breathing and somewhat alive.

The signal gave his brothers permission to jeer.

"I swear you bounced that time, bro." Walker marched across the arena to offer a hand. He hauled Luke to his feet, not even attempting to hide his smirk.

Luke brushed the snow and dirt from his jeans, forcing a good-natured response, although it was tough with all the faces eyeing him with amusement. Even his kid brother, Dustin, wore a grin.

The three of them had shown up to watch him work the new mare he'd offered to train. It was the way they'd always done things at Silver Stone ranch—since the death of their parents they'd worked together, played together, fought together.

And yes, laughed together, occasionally at each other.

Caleb was the oldest by a couple years and had been in charge since that fateful day. Luke had no problem when his big brother winked over his shoulder then headed after the mare to bring her back for Luke to try again. And Walker, while a couple years younger than Luke, was a champion bull rider. He'd earned the right to laugh at anyone who came off the back of a beast unwillingly.

Dustin, though? Hell no.

Luke pointed a finger at the twenty-year-old. "Laugh it up. You wouldn't last two seconds on her."

The youth was smart enough not to argue. "Still entertaining to watch you land on your ass."

His wide smile was taunting but one hundred percent family, and when Dustin swung over the railing to join Caleb as he walked Chili Pepper, Luke decided this time he'd let the kid off easy.

Walker laid a hand on his shoulder. "Ready to call it a day?"

Luke shrugged, eyeing the filly carefully as his brothers paced her around the arena. "I'm not going to get her trained if I give up the first time she throws me."

"First time? Math never was your strong suit," Walker teased gently before folding his arms and checking him over with an experienced eye. "You're hurting, Luke. I can tell from the way you're moving one of those landings scored a little too hard."

"Maybe. Doesn't matter—I can go for a bit longer."

Walker seemed about to say something more but then shook his head, glancing at his watch. "You'll be black and blue tomorrow, but the truth is, you need to stop because we all have other things to do. And you know the rules—you're not working a wild ride without backup."

Caleb and Dustin had reached them by that point, the mare

standing like an angel at the end of the lead line. The cantankerous creature that had bucked him off a dozen times running was now all sweetness and light. She moved forward and crowded him with her head, batting at his belly to push him toward the barn.

Luke wrapped his arms around Pepper and patted her nose. "Bossy creature."

"See? Even she knows it's time to call it quits." Caleb offered a satisfied grumble, his gaze fixed on something outside the arena.

Luke turned to discover Caleb's children making their way across the snowy path from the ranch house. "It's time for you to stop, at least," Luke admitted.

"Ivy is expecting me, as well," Walker added. "There's some kind of 'past New Year's, but as close to it as we could get' fundraiser meet-and-greet for the school board, so I have to go put on a suit and tie."

All four of them groaned at the same moment, three of them in sympathy. Walker's fiancée was the vice principal at the local elementary school, which meant she was pretty involved in all sorts of community activities.

Big brother Caleb was now happily married to Tamara, and while she was eating crackers and drinking ginger ale, they were thrilled to be adding another kid to go with the two mischievous girls approaching the arena.

Luke was glad his brothers had found partners who made them happy. Still kind of dug a knife into his gut considering his failed relationship had been over for only a few months.

Even Dustin chortled with glee as he shared his evening plans. "I have a date tonight."

"Really?" Walker's tone turned serious. "I heard you were going over to Ivy's parents' house. Are you seeing one of her sisters?"

Dustin's eyes widened for a brief second before he turned all nonchalant. "None of your business if I were."

Luke and Caleb glanced at each other, exchanging an *oh shit, he didn't go there* look.

"Death wish?" Caleb asked Luke drily.

"Brain dead. It hasn't registered yet that the body is soon to follow."

Walker glanced at them, his lips twitching before he pulled his serious expression back in the line. "Spill the beans," he ordered Dustin.

Their youngest brother rolled his eyes. "Number one, you guys have zero sense of humour. Just thought I should point that out in case you were under some misconception. Number two, it really is none of your business, but because you look as if you're ready to draw and quarter me, no, I'm not dating one of the Fields sisters. Not because they aren't awesome, but two of them are way too old for me and Rose is a good friend. But Rose's best friend, Kandi with a K, is damn hot."

Luke was going to develop an eye twitch trying to keep a straight face while enjoying a side-eye exchange with Caleb and Walker. "*Kandi?*"

"...with a *k*. Awww, that's sweet—" Walker began, only to be interrupted as their nieces climbed on the fence, shouting for Caleb.

"Daddy, Daddy, Daddy."

"Papa. *Paaapaaa*."

Caleb smacked a hand on Luke's shoulder. "The summonses have been pronounced. I'll see you all tomorrow."

Walker took off in one direction, and Dustin and Caleb in another, and suddenly Luke stood alone in the arena with Chili Pepper nudging his pockets, looking for treats.

"Looks as if all the Stone boys have hot dates tonight," Luke teased at his own expense. He slid a hand along Pepper's neck and gave her a pat as he led her toward her stall. "You and me, we're doing fine. Only we need to talk about this habit you have of wanting control. I don't mind sharing the reins now and then, but when a guy says he wants to be in charge, he means it."

He twisted on the spot as he opened the gate, and the creaking floorboards beneath his boots fell silent for a brief moment. Long enough to let a light snicker reach his ears.

He sighed mightily, shaking his head in exasperation as he looked up into the hayloft. "Your eavesdropping is going to get you in trouble someday, Kelli James."

"Maybe, but in the meanwhile, it sure is damn educational." She swung into view, slipping past the railing to drop to her jean-covered butt on the outer edge of the loft. Her well-worn cowboy boots hung toward the floor, kicking lazily as she smiled down. Her dark-brown hair twisted in two braids over her shoulders, brown eyes snapping with mischief.

Luke leaned a shoulder against the pen. "Since you're here, make yourself useful. Grab a couple of brushes and you can help give Pepper a rubdown."

What the woman should've done was get to her feet and head to the side wall where the ladder was. Not Kelli. She gave him a quick nod then flung herself headlong, falling from a height that was enough to break her fool neck considering she was nearly a foot shorter than his six-foot-two.

Luke lurched forward involuntarily to catch her. No matter that he'd seen her do this dozens of times over the years, it still caught him by surprise. At the last second, she caught hold of the pipe attached to one wall and used it to guide her to the floor.

She smacked down with one heck of an impact, but at least her feet were the first to land and not her head.

He bit his tongue and refused to give her the pleasure of cursing or scolding her. She already knew he thought it was a reckless move.

Kelli was light on her feet—he had to give her that. And she didn't dawdle as she grabbed what she needed.

Luke headed in the other direction to scoop up feed for the

mare, tossing some oats in a nosebag before joining Kelli at Pepper's side.

She handed him a brush. "Any orders, boss?"

He deliberately loosened his jaw to keep from grinding his teeth. "You're exceptionally annoying tonight," he said calmly. "I'm not your boss, and you know it. Ashton is."

"You're still in charge more than I am, so technically I can call you boss. *Boss.*" She glanced at him judgmentally before giving his butt a firm smack with the stiff brush bristles. "And my good day just got even better because you have shit on your ass, and I don't."

Luke sighed. He hadn't gone unscathed during his time bouncing off the ground thanks to Pepper's lack of enthusiasm for him as a rider. "Comes with the territory," he muttered before getting to work. "Glad you had a good day, though. What were you doing?"

Kelli went on to tell him what she'd been busy with, helping their foreman Ashton deal with some of the rowdier stock. As she spoke, her hands kept moving, the bristles sliding smoothly again and again. Confident and sure, just like always.

She'd been a part of Silver Stone ranch for nearly as long as they'd been running the place without their parents. And it didn't surprise him to hear that Ashton was using her for some more delicate tasks, although it did worry him at times that she was out the middle of the herd with animals big enough to crush her with a thoughtless move.

But even now as Pepper adjusted her stance, Kelli slid forward, almost as if she was dancing with the horse. She slid an arm around her neck and used Pepper's momentum to reach up her withers.

"I think tomorrow you should let me help," Kelli said firmly.

Luke blinked, not sure where the conversation had gone. "Help? With what?"

Kelli slid the rest of the way around to stand beside him,

smirking as if she knew a secret. "Is it past your bedtime?" she teased. "Awfully late for somebody old like you to be up."

He folded his arms over his chest and glared. "Don't be rude. What're you talking about?"

Pepper chose that moment to complain. While he and Kelli were still standing in the pen with her, neither of them was giving her any attention. Like horses the world over who wanted to criticize, she made her point by shifting her balance and pressing her considerable weight toward them.

Luke twisted out of the way before he could be trapped against the stall boards. Kelli ducked under the horse's belly, popping up on the other side and climbing until she sat on the top divider.

They grinned at each other.

Then Kelli got that look in her eyes. The one that said she was getting ready to ask for a favour—also known as *tormenting him until he gave in.*

"I want to help with Pepper. You know I can do it. I bet she'd love for me to train her."

Luke examined Kelli closer. The petite woman was perched on the wooden barrier like some kind of barn pixie. After eight years of working at Silver Stone she was as much a part of the place as the rest of the crew, and as familiar as his brothers. She *was* good with the horses. Damn good.

Considering the goal of training Pepper was to make her a good mount for the owner's daughter, who probably weighed about what Kelli did—

Only he was still responsible. "Yes, you can help, but not yet."

The excitement on her face flashed and faded quickly as he spoke. "What does that mean?"

"It means you have work to do for Ashton, so you're not going to be available all the time, anyway. Plus, as much as you insist Pepper likes you, she's not ready for different people to be getting on her back."

Kelli nodded, thoughtful agreement in her expression. "But you'll let me help when she hits the next stage?"

"I'd love your help," he told her honestly.

"Super." She flipped backward into the empty stall behind them and once again his heart did this strange *stop-start* jolt.

"Dammit, woman," he muttered, patting Pepper farewell before rejoining Kelli in the main walkway.

"I promise I'll do good job," Kelli assured him.

"Just don't go skipping out on your other tasks trying get to helping me sooner," he warned.

The eye rolling commenced again.

"As if," she snarked. "You really think Ashton would let me get away with that? Even if you think I'm dumb enough to try it in the first place, which I'm not."

He wouldn't have been surprised to see her stick out her tongue at him like his niece Sasha.

But, no, even though at times she seemed younger than the twenty-six years he'd seen on their payroll record, Kelli wasn't given to high drama. Probably part of why he liked her so much.

Of all the hands who had been around Silver Stone over the years, Kelli was rock-solid. Good sense of humour, good work ethic—

Damn good with horses. Even now she was blowing kisses at all the stock as she walked ahead of him, pausing to say hello and offer pats and treats to every beast she passed.

Then she was gone, headed off to her rooms on the west side of the bunkhouse. Luke glanced around, but it was pretty much him and the ranch dogs that were waiting to see if he did anything exciting.

He offered them a pat on the head and a scratch behind the ears but kept walking, headed away from the main ranch house and toward the place he'd been building for the last couple of years. The house that had taken so long because his fiancée Penny had been shit at making decisions and sticking to them.

Their relationship had finally fallen apart back in late August, to his unconfessed relief. He still didn't know what Penny really thought about him calling their engagement off, but he doubted she was pining for him or anything. They hadn't had that type of relationship.

Still, it felt weird to think he nearly had a finished house of his own. Over the past four months, since he hadn't needed to spend time with his fiancée, or get everything approved by her, or change things because she'd changed her mind, he'd been able to get tons done on the place.

Funny how that worked. Time on his hands, no one else to have to run decisions by. It made the work go a heck of a lot faster.

That was about the only positive thing he could think of—

And this wasn't where he wanted his brain to go. He didn't want to dwell on the fact he'd spent a lot of time and energy on a relationship that had failed.

Didn't want to think too hard about building a house on land that, unless things turned around, might not belong to the Stone family by the end of the year.

Luke stomped through the door of his almost finished mudroom. He was starving. Plus, Walker had been right. His body ached from head to toe after getting bucked far too many times.

He was also filthy, which Kelli had been so eager to point out. But the roar emerging from his belly said it was food first, then a shower. Then he'd have to figure out something to pass the rest of the evening.

It was just not right that the rest of his brothers had people to spend the evening with and he didn't—*he* was the charming one in the family, dammit.

Luke walked through the kitchen, plugging in his phone and turning on his laptop. He grabbed leftover pizza from the fridge, pulling a stool over with a foot and dropping onto it to check his emails. He ate one piece of pizza cold while the rest reheated in the microwave.

It was incredible how much crap email a person got daily. There were a couple of messages from his sisters that he marked to read once he had cleared out the mess when his eye fell on a far more interesting subject title.

Triple Crown Gala.

A laugh burst free, and he nearly choked on the piece of pizza in his mouth. "Yeah, me and a gala. Good one."

Except something twigged in his brain. Why did this sound familiar?

The message was from a trusted friend. Bertram Cooper was a go-between. He found horses for buyers, or suggested stud placements or training opportunities. Silver Stone had been lucky to count Bert as a friend, and some of their top deals over the years had been brokered by him, so Luke opened the message, curiosity, suspicion and that echo of importance he just couldn't remember vying for top billing.

With Bert's twisted sense of humour, the man was probably setting Luke up for an all-you-can-eat chicken-wing night and pulling his leg.

Yet when the microwave beeped another reminder the time was up, Luke continued to ignore it because the email was not a tease or a joke or bullshit.

Bertram had gotten wind of a spectacular event happening in the area and had wrangled Luke an invite. It *was* a gala. A buyers-and-sellers, by-invitation-only gathering of the elite in horse breeders of North America.

Not a time with actual horses and cash exchanging hands, but a meet-and-greet with spouses and families, and—

Luke's mind raced at the possibilities. For the past while, Silver Stone ranch had been going through some rough weather. They were nowhere near out of the woods yet, even though Walker had topped up the family coffers last fall after some amazing rodeo payouts. The ranch had to take the next step, which should involve the horses Luke had been working on diligently over the years. It was their best shot, and this invitation was a golden ticket falling into his lap.

He glanced through the information more thoroughly, shuddering at the price tag attached to the event. Thank God it was being held just hours away in Kananaskis Country, which meant they'd be able to drive and not have to fly to Texas or Kentucky.

A few quick calculations and it was clear that even one new sale would cancel out the oversized price tag, and this gala wasn't likely to trigger a one-off transaction. These events were king makers.

Holy shit.

That's why this sounded familiar. His ex-fiancée, Penny, and her family had been in a similar situation years ago. The right place at the right time at a gathering very similar to this—and they'd never looked back.

The gala was exactly what Silver Stone needed.

The message from Bert was clear and concise.

Got word of this shindig. Organizers asked me for a couple of recommendations of up-and-coming breeders, and I thought of you. I don't have to tell you this is a Big Deal event. If I had an operation like yours, I'd be drooling at the opportunity. Feel free to send me a bottle of the good stuff down the road.

Heads up on a couple of things: the group is a bit old school, which doesn't mean they expect you to bring a wife, but a fiancée is better than a girlfriend. And while they're up-to-date enough they won't make you sleep in separate rooms, they do want to deal with family operations. So for fuck's sake, be sure you bring your fiancée. Don't let her give you grief on this one.

Best of luck, and I'll see you soon. I've got a couple of requests I'll send your way come the spring. Touch base if you need anything sooner.

Part of his brain was analyzing and considering, but Luke's hands were already moving because this wasn't something he needed to think about too hard. The gala could save the ranch, so he absolutely had to be there. It wasn't his fault Bert wasn't up-to-date on the fact he and Penny had called off their engagement.

The tip about *family* operations, though—that was a good piece of intel.

Luke clicked through the invitation to a Google doc to fill in the required information. The name of the ranch, their top horses and studs to date.

He got a lot of pleasure out of being able to list animals he'd been instrumental in raising. He wasn't just blowing smoke out his ass. Silver Stone was one of the top ranches at their size of operation. They just needed a break to move to the next level.

He filled in his personal history without blinking. It was only when he got to the section that asked for the name of his spouse/significant other that Luke paused.

Bert's message had been received. Luke was not going to this gig as a single male even though that's how everything had been until recently at Silver Stone. Just because they hadn't been a family with spouses didn't mean that they weren't *family*, but he wasn't about to argue with already-set prejudices.

Caleb and Tamara were out. Caleb didn't like the schmoozing, and Tamara was so sick due to her pregnancy that she'd spend the entire time in the bathroom. Walker and Ivy were out...

He could contact his ex and ask her to do him a favour, but that was risky. Part of the reason their engagement hadn't worked was Penny was unpredictable, and he didn't trust her. A family event meant they would have to at least pretend to like each other.

They didn't hate each other. It's just that they were kind of indifferent, which had always been the problem in their relationship. At least outside the bedroom.

Nope. There was a far simpler solution, especially when he started thinking about the whole concept of *family*. Maybe it wasn't what the organizers were thinking, but as far as he was concerned she was as good as family. He filled in the blank space without a qualm, tapping the computer keys happily.

Kelli James.

Luke hit send then got up to add another minute to the pizza in the microwave.

Hell, Kelli would love to come with him. The honest truth was she'd done a lot over the years to help create what Silver Stone had going, and it would be a great opportunity for her to get to know some key people.

Plus, it was a holiday. Who wouldn't want to go hang out at a fancy hotel in the middle of the Rocky Mountains for a few days with no chores?

Energy surged through him. Getting a new lease on the future did that to a man, it seemed. After he got cleaned up, heck, he might have to head out dancing for the night.

Luke sent off a quick message to a friend, then settled in front of the TV, clicking through channels until he found something borderline interesting to watch while he ate his pizza.

Funny how fate could step in and change your entire world when you least expected it.

2

Kelli James kicked a clod of dirt down the path in front of her in frustration. It was totally unfair how her body had turned into one enormous compass.

Anytime Luke Stone was around she all but quivered in his direction.

She meandered back to the bunkhouse, stomping along the snowy trail to where the light outside her porch shone cheerfully. Her space at the end of a long row of identical motel-like rooms had been home for a long time. Other ranch hands had come and gone in the time she'd been working here, so it wasn't being the only woman on staff that gave her rights to the best location.

Even Ashton Stewart said she was basically their senior hand, and the responsibilities that came with that title were something she was pretty proud of. She'd taken on a huge task, and found a place for herself where she was appreciated and useful.

Although there were moments she longed for more, having a place to lay her head and be a part of something important—it wasn't a bad gig for a girl who'd been a runaway.

She grabbed her shower kit and slipped outside, off her porch to the back side of the building.

"Heads up," she warned as she stepped into the steaming warmth of the outer change area.

"Nearly done." The masculine reply echoed from around the corner. "You can wait inside where it's warm if you want. Although, if you want to join me, I won't complain."

Kelli ignored the suggestion as she got her things ready, hanging up her towel and prepping her shampoo and soap. "Alex, you're not only an optimist, but you're an optimist who thinks the *top* half of the glass is full."

A low chuckle escaped from the other ranch hand who'd been working at Silver Stone since the summer. "I'm using all the hot water. Just saying."

"Bullshit on that," Kelli retorted. "You're taking cold showers and crying into your beer over me."

The water turned off, and he laughed, deep and hearty. "I might have to head to Rough Cut tonight for that beer. You plan on going?"

"Yeah. I'm meeting my girls," she told him.

"Nice."

"It's too snowy to do anything else," she pointed out. "Rough Cut is a warm place to hang out on a cold evening."

"I'm headed your way," he warned. "In case you want to take pictures of my magnificence."

She pretended to gag, deliberately turning her back to give him privacy to towel off.

It was the only area where they hadn't figured out a perfect solution with her working at Silver Stone. Kelli insisted she didn't want preferential treatment. No way did she want the Stone family to face the expense of building a separate shower house just for her. It took a little juggling to make things work, her sharing space with all the guys, but the common shower house had never worried her.

The guys were like brothers, teasing moments aside. She figured the occasional bit of dirty talk was natural. She didn't feel uncomfortable or harassed by the guy chatter that went on around the ranch.

It helped that one of the first talks any new hire got was "keep your hands off Kelli or lose your nuts."

"Is Rose going to be there tonight?" Alex asked far too casually.

Kelli laughed. "Maybe. You want me to put in a good word for you?"

"Hell, yeah. Dance with me first so she'll let me take her for a spin."

Which made her laugh harder. "You guys figured out how we run things on the dance floor, did you?"

"I'm decent," Alex told her. "I mean, I'm dressed. And yes, it doesn't take a genius to notice you decide who is safe to dance with, and your friends follow suit."

Kelli twisted to look him up and down. He'd pulled on clean jeans, but his feet were still bare and his chest was uncovered to expose olive-brown skin, water droplets clinging to his broad shoulders as he toweled his hair dry.

He wasn't bad looking at all, and she could appreciate the muscle show as much as the next girl. Only that was as far as it went—appreciation. There were no sparks, nothing that set her belly tumbling in a wild dance.

Not like when Luke Stone accidentally bumps my side.

She shoved away the annoying truth and gave Alex a raised eyebrow. The man *was* talking about one of her besties, and so had better know more than one person had an eye on him. "*Are* you safe?"

He dropped his towel to the bench beside him and tugged a T-shirt over his head before offering her a broad smile. "Safe as a kitten. Plus, I know how to dance."

"So her feet won't get crushed, that's what you're saying?" She folded her arms over her chest as he draped his towel around his neck and gathered his things.

"Just put in a good word for me, please?" Alex asked, this time a little more seriously. Holding her gaze until she nodded. "See you later, Kelli."

He slipped out the door and she followed him, hanging up the sign she'd made years ago to announce she was occupying the space. Then with *Kelli's Private Spa* as a warning for any of the rest of the hands that they'd have to wait, she locked the door and stripped.

Steam lingered in the main shower room, which meant it was warm as she flipped on the nearest tap and let the forceful spray run over her aching shoulders.

While she had a few privileges, like getting to lock the door to have the shower house to herself, and the best room in the bunkhouse, her work responsibilities were no less because she was a woman.

Over the years the guys had slowly stopped giving her easier tasks because of her size. It might take her a couple extra trips to move heavy equipment, she still got it done.

But at the end of a long day where she'd moved her weight in bales a number of times over, the forceful massage on her shoulders felt damn good.

Hands raised in a long stretch, she snickered for a second. It would probably seem weird to a stranger looking in that she was so comfortable chatting with Alex like that, but this was her reality. She'd lived on the ranch for long enough that whole "just one of the boys" thing worked ninety-nine percent of the time.

She lathered up and rubbed soap over her body, efficient and quick, undoing her braids then working her fingernails against her scalp as her hair plastered down against her torso nearly to her butt.

She really was one of the boys, which was good—

—until it wasn't. The whole "keep your hands off Kelli" thing had made it damn difficult to do any experimenting of a sexual nature. Not that she'd been chomping at the bit, but she had been curious, and sexual frustration wasn't exclusive to the male portion of the population.

Kelli tipped her head back to rinse off the shampoo, amusement drifting in as she remembered the shower house was where she'd tried sex for the first time.

The ranch hand she'd hauled in with her had been cute enough, she supposed. And they'd been hot for each other, but neither of them were looking for more than casual, so it was pretty much a one-off deal. Stealing away time in the shower had been a way to scratch an itch. One that she really didn't get that often. It had been time, that was all.

You're a liar, her brain told her.

Kelli did the mental equivalent of sticking out her tongue and blowing a raspberry at herself. "Yeah, because I'm just gonna up and confess I had sex with somebody else because Luke got engaged."

She *had* liked the guy, but her conscience was right. It had been more about trying to wipe out the cravings she had for Luke than the other dude being super-special.

Having a long-term, unsatisfied crush was something she was far too familiar with.

Kelli figured for the first years the emotion had been nothing more than puppy-love. She'd been way too young to do anything except keep her distance and hope Luke never got a clue that walking past him made her heart rate jump.

Instead she'd focused on the fact she was living her dream in so many other ways. Getting to do what she loved—working with horses, and living on a ranch—heck, it was the closest thing to paradise she could imagine.

When she finally hit twenty-one, though, she figured there was no reason not to make a move. Luke wasn't the high-and-mighty type who would look down on getting involved with someone just because she was a ranch hand. Besides, they were already friends. She'd needed to convince him they should move the friendship into something more hands-on. Short-term would be fine.

Then he'd gone off and met Penny, and before Kelli could say "lost-opportunity," Luke was engaged and off-limits.

Three damn years she'd been forced to put her cravings aside and behave. Three long years where she'd held her tongue—mostly—as a woman who was all wrong for Luke got to be in his life and his bed.

Kelli had shown amazing restraint, really. Three years, and not once had she accidentally shoved Penny into a dung heap.

She still felt the sense of relief that had struck when Luke suddenly called off the wedding and Penny was no more. Thank. God.

Kelli finished up in the shower house then marched double time back to her room, sliding into a well-worn pair of jeans and a soft cotton top. She braided her hair so it would stay out of the way, slipped on her dancing boots and was ready to roll.

Luke Stone might be back on the market, but she didn't want to move too fast and be nothing more than a rebound fling. But she wasn't going to move too slow either and lose out again.

Just like working with jittery horses, it was all about the timing. Right now, Luke wasn't ready for her to show her hand.

Which meant tonight? She was going to have a rip-roaring good time, kicking up her heels and pretending the man she wanted more than anything didn't exist.

Maybe she'd do Alex a solid and dance with him first.

"You're shitting me. You got an invite where?" Josiah Ryder shook his head in disbelief. "I don't know if I should be jealous or offer you high-test tranquilizers to deal with the stress."

"I'm pumped," Luke admitted, "but it's not a done deal, so don't go passing that information on yet. And that means not even to Caleb, because I don't want to get anyone's hopes up if my attendance doesn't get approved."

Joshua raised a hand in understanding. "Smart move. I know about this in real time because someone in my circle at veterinarian school got an invite to one of these gigs then got *un*-invited."

Luke turned toward their local pub, the bright lights of the leftover holiday decorations reflecting onto the snowy main street of Heart Falls. "That's harsh."

"The guys who organized the event were serious about the family-positive focus of the event, and it turns out the invitee had a few too many skeletons in her closet."

That sounded like a load of bullshit. "Right. Because your average farmer who decides to go into veterinarian training has links to the Mafia or some other nonsense."

"Gang related—her dad was involved in moving pharmaceuticals. When they found out about his record, her invitation was rescinded." Josiah shook his head even as he reached for the door of the truck.

"It's not her fault what her dad was up to," Luke pointed out.

"He paid for her training. She knew."

Luke joined Josiah on the wooden steps leading to the entrance of Rough Cut. He'd been spending more time with the man in recent days even though it used to be Caleb who hung out with Josiah.

Caleb having the girls and Tamara to keep him busy had put a serious damper on his social life. And yet his big brother had never seemed happier. Luke was honestly thrilled for him.

And as Josiah pushed through the doors of the pub and was greeted cheerfully, Luke had to admit it wasn't a bad situation, getting to spend time around the popular man.

They paused to the side of the door. Josiah glanced around, checking who was already on the floor. "Perfect. I see at least a half-dozen women who are craving my attention."

Luke smacked him on the shoulder and sent Josiah rocking. "Hound dog."

"That implies I'm following them around, sniffing for a chance. Nothing of the sort," Josiah told him, raising his voice to be heard over the chaos.

"It implies that you keep sinking your teeth into a new bone every time, and at some point, they're going to turn around and rattle *your* bones."

Josiah shared a wide grin as he ran his fingers through his blond hair. "*Grrrr.*"

Luke stood where he was as Josiah wove his way across the dance floor. He stopped and tapped the shoulder of a tall man who was enthusiastically two-stepping with a shorter woman. The man stepped back with a shrug, and Luke recognized him as one of their hands.

It was a little less entertaining when he realized the woman Josiah was now twirling quickly across the floor was Kelli, her long braids flying as she twisted, smiling at the veterinarian.

Luke watched for a minute. He could certainly understand why Josiah wanted to dance with her. They moved smoothly with none of that awkward back-and-forth that happened when a woman figured she knew how to dance better than her partner.

It was one thing when a guy couldn't dance, but the bullshit thing Penny used to pull on him, trying to subtly lead when he didn't need any help—chaos. And fucking annoying.

Josiah was definitely the one in charge, his leadership apparent when he changed directions at the last second to avoid crashing into a less competent dance couple. The rapid motion twirled Kelli closer, her braid flying out like a helicopter blade, her body snugged against Josiah as she laughed.

A moment later they were farther across the floor, talking as they moved. She was definitely light on her feet on the dance floor.

A strange twitch hit the back of his brain. Why did that seem so surprising? Luke thought it over hard until the truth struck.

Had he really never danced with Kelli?

Then again, why would he? He'd never danced with any of the other hands, but as he watched them, something tugged at his insides.

It didn't sit right to see them cozied up and chatting happily.

It was nerves, Luke decided. It was thinking about Josiah's comments and the possibility that even though the gala had been offered, it could still be taken from his hands.

Heck, what was he worrying about? Silver Stone was squeaky clean, and always had been. From the time his parents had established it with their best friends, all the way through until now, there'd never been a peep of gossip.

He supposed Caleb's disastrous first wife could be considered a blunt on the *strong family values* chart, but considering he'd recently re-married, and he and Tamara were expecting a child— Plus Tamara's family were rock-solid members of their community. There were no skeletons in the Stone closet, so Luke could push that worry aside.

Yup, it was nerves and restlessness.

That had to be why he found his feet moving toward Kelli. He didn't have any concerns about her dancing skills, or his own, but it'd be a good idea for them to practice a bit as a couple.

The music changed as he reached their side.

Kelli's chest rocked as she took deep breaths. "Damn, that was fun. Thanks, Josiah."

He bumped knuckles with her and offered a wink. "No problem."

She turned to walk away, ignoring Luke and the fact he was right there, waiting his turn.

What the hell?

"Kelli. Stop." He pushed past Josiah and stepped closer. "Let's dance."

Her jaw dropped slightly, and something flashed across her face before she rolled her eyes. "Smartass."

She whirled on her heel and kept walking, dodging between couples who'd started a fast-paced reel swirling around them. He would've damn near had to run to catch her.

Someone cleared their throat behind him. Luke turned to find Josiah staring at him as if he had mud on his face, both of them standing motionless in the middle of the crowded dance floor.

"What are you doing?" Josiah asked.

Luke thought it was apparent. "I asked her to dance."

Confusion lit Josiah's face. He tilted his head toward the side of the room before marching away so rapidly Luke had no choice but to follow. They found a place at a table with two chairs and barely any room.

It was like cloak-and-dagger bullshit as Josiah leaned in to speak quietly. Well, as quietly as he could, considering the volume of music. "*Why* did you ask her to dance?"

"Because—" *Oh.* He hadn't mentioned this part. "I said Kelli would be coming with me to the event. I figure at some point we'll have to dance, and I figured a practice run would be good."

Josiah looked shocked. "Kelli. With you. To the gala."

His exasperation was rising. "Do I need to use smaller words? Who else would I take? Neither Caleb or Walker can go, and Dustin would be fairly useless. Ashton would kick my ass if I asked him to attend something like this. Kelli will do awesome."

His friend was staring as if he was still working on the first part of Luke's statement. Then Josiah shook it off, amusement spreading over his face. "Fine. You're right, Kelli will do awesome. But...you didn't tell her about the gala yet, did you?"

"Of course not. You pointed out not even thirty minutes ago that's not a good idea until I get the official acceptance."

Josiah nodded slowly. "Then take a word of advice. Don't start any weird shit until it's time."

Luke thought about it before sighing in exasperation. "Oh."

"Yeah, *oh.*" Josiah raised a brow. "You do know what you're doing?"

"Look. I need somebody with me who will impress the hell out of people who know horses, and Kelli fits the bill. We can make up the rest of it as we go along."

"Just seems to me— Never mind." The twist to his lips said Josiah was holding back some sarcastic comment.

Luke folded his arms over his chest, now thoroughly annoyed. "Kelli and I have spent tons of time together. We get along like a house on fire."

His friend raised a hand, motioning for one of the waitresses to come take their order. "Yeah, because burning shit down is definitely the way to impress people."

Luke laughed, staring across the room at Kelli a little more intently than before. Josiah had made a good point about waiting.

But as soon as Luke got the official word, he'd make sure she was fully on board. It shouldn't be too difficult. Kelli was fun to be with, and they would have a ton to talk about with all the rest of the horse-loving crew.

Josiah poked him to get his attention. Luke gave the waitress his order, then he and his friend fell into a friendly debate over which were better, red-hot wings or sweet Thai chili.

His gaze drifted over the room, keeping an eye on things. And if he happened to end up checking where Kelli was a few times, there was no harm in that.

The itchy sensation at the back of his neck was nerves. That's it, nerves. He lifted his beer and drank deeply, while over the edge of the glass rim his gaze returned again to a slim cowgirl who never seemed to stand still.

3

Something was seriously wrong. Kelli peered around her friend Tansy, jerking back before he spotted her, but there was no denying the truth. Luke Stone was watching her.

"Girlfriend, if you bump my beer arm one more time, you'll be wearing it," Tansy warned.

"Sorry." Kelli peeled her eyes away from the tempting man, twisting her body toward the other side of the room so he was nowhere in her line of vision.

Tansy's sister Rose leaned in close to examine her. "You feeling okay? You look flushed."

Good grief. The two of them were like bloodhounds wanting to sniff out everything Kelli definitely did *not* want to talk about. She deliberately raised a brow and gave Rose a dirty look. "You seemed flushed when you finished dancing with a certain tall, dark cowboy."

Rose smirked but she didn't look away. "Dancing is a vigorous exercise if you do it right."

"So's sex," Tansy quipped. "Oh, I'm sorry. I forgot who I was talking to."

A snort escaped before Kelli could stop it.

Rose turned an evil eye on her sister. "Do you mind?"

Tansy just grinned then turned her attention back on Kelli. "Don't spill my beer, but if there's anything on your mind you want to talk about..."

An opening Kelli was unwilling to take. Her obsessive thoughts about a certain man would not see the light of day until she was ready to move. It had been the only way to survive the years of shattered hopes—she didn't need her friends knowing she was a hopeless romantic.

She scrambled to find something else to distract them. "Luke says he might let me help train Chili Pepper."

The sisters exchanged glances before letting out huge sighs and turning back to the dance floor. "And on that change of topic, Kelli is once again back to discussing all things horsey."

"Horses are awesome," Kelli insisted.

"They are, but you don't need to talk about them twenty-four/seven," Tansy pointed out. "I don't talk nonstop about the red-hot chili peppers in *my* life, do I?"

Kelli gave a smirk. "You're a chef. I expect you to talk about food."

"And you're a cowboy, but good grief, girlfriend, you need something outside of Silver Stone and those horses to keep you entertained."

Rose nodded in agreement, and the two of them dove into an old argument, suggesting different things to broaden Kelli's horizons. It was kind of entertaining.

Definitely distracting, and not wanting to turn around and check out where Luke was improved her mood. Kelli leaned back against the wall and let her gaze drift as her friends suggested activities they could try at their upcoming girls-night-out gathering.

Not all of them sounded terrible, but Kelli wasn't about to apologize for loving horses. Working with them had been her dream since she was young. The ranch where she'd grown up was similar to Silver Stone, although her mom had been on staff as a cook, not a hand.

Hanging out near the horses had been like breathing to Kelli. And the day she'd climbed on the back of her first horse had been a revelation. The creature had looked over his shoulder at her, and it had been love at first sight.

Her daydreaming was interrupted as Alex returned, another tall cowboy at his elbow. He winked at Kelli before the two of them turned their gazes determinedly on her friends.

Tansy checked with Kelli before answering the cowboys' request. "You okay on your own?" she asked. "Because we can say no."

Kelli made a rude noise. "Good grief, go dance. I'm good." She stepped back and let amusement slip in as she was temporarily abandoned.

She watched as Rose and Tansy slid into strong arms and were twirled away. Something satisfying stole in at seeing people she loved enjoying themselves.

Her gaze drifted onward, over familiar friends and neighbours until she noticed something across the room less happy-making than dancing and drinking was going down. Voices were raised briefly, loud enough to be heard over the music. A woman ducked her head and slid back from her date, out of fist range.

Kelli moved instinctively, her feet carrying her through the crowd. Her smaller size made it easier for her to weave through the narrow gaps between bodies all the way to where the couple now stood.

Not being foolish, she paused before rushing in. It took a single glance to realize the woman's forearm was being held so tightly her knuckles were going white. Kelli shot forward the final distance.

She smashed the side of her hand sharply on the man's wrist, twisting her body and knocking him off-balance as she pushed the woman behind her to safety. A second later she was back up on her toes, twisting her mouth into a lopsided smile, playing it up as an accident.

"Sorry. I'm a little tipsy," she offered, backing against the woman who was whimpering softly.

The man in front of her glared. "Chelsey, get your ass over here."

Kelli twirled on the spot, rocking slightly as she grabbed hold of the other woman as if she were hugging her simply to find her balance. "If you need help," she said quietly, "go to the bar and order a white angel."

She squeezed the woman's shoulders briefly before staggering back, angling her body so she slammed into the angry man, blocking his path.

He caught her by the arms, his grip tighter than polite.

"You don't look very happy," she slurred at the man, raising her voice and swaying drunkenly. In her peripheral vision, she saw Chelsey slip safely into the crowd.

The man tried to look around Kelli, but she raised her palms to his face to keep his attention focused forward. "Grumpy man. You need to smile more."

"Don't mess with things that aren't your business," he snarled, shoving her aside.

Or at least that's what he intended. But Kelli had spent too much time dealing with beasts that outweighed her to be put where she didn't want to go. She caught hold of his arm and used momentum to swing around his bulk, feet raised before driving them against the back of his knee.

As he staggered, Kelli climbed upward, the change of weight sending him farther off balance until his feet slipped from under him. He landed with a crash, taking out a couple of nearby dancers.

Kelli hit the dance floor as well, rolling to take the impact. Bouncing to vertical as quickly as she could, her fake smile gone.

Chelsey had vanished, but the asshole who'd been manhandling her was on his feet, glaring at Kelli with anger in his eyes.

His gaze slipped behind her, rising higher.

The noise faded slightly in the area directly around them. Kelli was street smart enough to realize what was happening, so when a hand landed on her shoulder she was able to hold back the instinct to jab an elbow into whoever had moved up against her back.

The jerk in front of her edged away slowly after sending one final snarl her direction.

Kelli didn't look away. Didn't give the idiot a chance to make a lunge, because bullies like him were the type who could be stupid right up to the final second.

When the side door closed behind him, that was good.

Bad—? Even as the asshole left the vicinity, the owner of the bar was fast approaching, and the good looking Asian-Canadian was scowling hard.

"Shit." Kelli took a deep breath and straightened, easing away from the oversized presence at her back far enough to twist her head and confirm her suspicions.

Yup. Luke was glaring at her. "What the fuck were you doing?" he demanded, pulling her toward an open space at the side of the room.

"Kelli." Ryan Zhao addressed her sharply as he intercepted them. He lowered his voice as he looked around, making sure no one was close enough to overhear. "We set up safe words for a reason."

Kelli threw her hands in the air, snapping her head back and forth between the two of them. "Hey, I'm not the bad guy here." She glanced over Ryan's shoulder. "Did Chelsey get away okay?"

"She's in my office," Ryan confirmed. "But that doesn't answer the question of why you were acting as my self-appointed bouncer."

Luke folded his arms across his chest and glared at her as if she were a leftover pile of manure in a stall.

"I didn't do anything wrong," she began.

Luke pressed a hand to her lower back to guide her from the room. "I'll take care of this, if you don't mind, Ryan."

"Fine. Kelli, call me later," Ryan snapped, and then Kelli couldn't see anything because she was being ushered out the front door with zero recourse. Her overreacting protector wasn't being rough, but she couldn't turn around unless she wanted to pull some self-defense moves.

The fact Josiah left the building hard on their heels made the whole situation that much more awkward.

"Good grief, you guys. We don't need to empty the dance floor." She checked the area quickly, but the overgrown ass from the bar was nowhere in sight.

"Shut up, Kelli," Josiah said softly before turning to Luke and laying a hand on his arm. "Take a slow breath," he warned. "She doesn't need you going off the deep end."

Luke's hand was plastered to her lower back, and he was damn near vibrating. "She deliberately stepped into a situation where she could've gotten hurt."

"*She* knew what she was doing," Kelli snapped. "Come on, Luke. That guy was hurting her."

He tugged her to face him, pivoting her so fast her braid whirled over her shoulder. "Which is exactly the type of guy who could have hurt *you*. If I hadn't been watching, what do you think he would've done?"

"What any bully does when confronted by a woman in a crowded place. He would've made some rude comment and then left. Mean words won't break me," she told him forcefully.

The two of them glared daggers at each other until Josiah broke the standoff. "You both need a timeout. Luke, she did it for a good reason, although, honey, your acting needs a little work. Drunks can't turn off a stagger that fast."

Luke glared at his friend, finally peeling his attention off Kelli. "You're not seriously giving her an acting critique."

"I'm saying Kelli helped somebody tonight, and while I might not approve of how she stepped in, giving her shit is not going to change her impulse. Plus, it's not what she needs right now." Josiah reached for Kelli and tugged her against him, hugging her tight.

She took a deep breath and let it out slowly. A shudder shook her from head to toe. She pressed her forehead against his chest and took a second to calm herself.

When she finally managed to get her racing heart to slow, she gave him a squeeze and he let go.

Kelli looked up with a grateful smile. "Okay, point made. I will work on less dangerous impulses, *and* my acting."

Josiah tweaked her nose and turned to Luke. "What about you?"

"Gee, do I get a hug too?" Luke snapped.

Good grief. "And on that note, I'm going home. You can stay here and be Mr. Cranky Pants without me."

She really didn't care why Luke had such a stick up his butt right then. She'd done the right thing, but as Josiah had somehow realized, the adrenaline rush was fading and she was close to crashing. It would be far better if she was in her room before that happened.

"Fine. I'll take you home," Luke grumbled.

No way. "I have my truck."

"I said. I'll. Take. You. Home." He bit out every word as if they were torturous.

She glanced at Josiah, hoping for his support again.

Only this time, he shook his head. "I think you should go with him," Josiah offered softly. "I'll drop your truck off in the morning."

Irritating males, all of them. Kelli growled out her frustration, but she handed over her truck keys before glaring at Luke. "Fine.

Let's go, sunshine."

~

LUKE DIDN'T TRUST himself to say anything as they walked. It was dead quiet as he guided her across the road and down the alley to where he'd parked.

Him carting her off like this left a bit of a mess for Josiah and Kelli's friends, ferrying vehicles back and forth. But as he yanked open the passenger door and waited for Kelli climb in, he realized he didn't really give a crap.

Most women would've sensed his level of frustration and kept silent, at least for the first part of the journey.

Not Kelli.

She twisted in her seat, arms folded over her chest, and started up the instant he opened his door. "If you want to yell at me, you can do it right here. Then no one has to worry about getting my vehicle home."

He stared at her long enough that she twitched, but she didn't look away, matching him glare for glare.

It took forever until she flopped back in the seat and did up her buckle, staring straight ahead as if her eyes were laser beams that let her blow up shit. Probably imagining he was standing in front of her.

Fine by him. Because he was imagining more than a few explosions himself.

He made it onto the main highway before his temper eased enough to speak in a reasonable tone.

"You know, I'm the Stone brother considered to be levelheaded and cool. Caleb could go off the deep end and get far too protective. Walker was always throwing himself off of something dangerous. But I was the one who could calm the waters. I could talk everybody off the edge and get the world back on track. Would you agree with that?"

He was doing it now, the calm and cool thing. Or at least faking it well enough that she shifted her attention and instead of mainlining the road, she glanced at him for a few seconds. "Yeah, I guess."

Luke pulled off on the side of the road in a section that had been cleared of snow and ice. The plows were using it as a turnaround, because the drifts were well over the top of the truck.

A few deep breaths later he put the truck into park then adjusted position so he could partially face her across the bench seat. "So, this is me being calm and collected and telling you if I *ever* see you pull that sort of stupid, impulsive act again, I'm going to lose my ever-loving shit, and someone will get seriously hurt."

Her mouth dropped open slightly as she stared at him, her dark brown eyes dancing over his face in a decidedly un-Kelli fashion. She didn't seem nearly as in control as she had when facing down the bastard at the bar.

Her body trembled, shaking slightly even though she was putting on a tough act.

It pissed him off she was ignoring the truth here. She was probably going to write this all off as a blip on the map, and sure enough, when she spoke it was with a slight lift of her shoulders.

"I don't go around answering bat-signals, and I won't accost someone that size in a dark back alley. But I'm not about to let some guy be abusive in a public place without letting the woman know she's got options."

"Even if it means you could end up on the floor?" He caught her wrist, keeping his grip loose even as he raised her arm toward him. He pushed up her sleeve, and sure enough, as he'd suspected, faint red marks marred her skin. "Even if it means you're the one who gets hurt?"

Her shoulders had gone as rigid as two by fours, and she stared at the rising bruises on her forearm as if utterly surprised to see them there.

She quivered even more noticeably, still focused on her arm.

That's when he finally clued in about what Josiah had tried to tell him earlier.

"Shit." Luke unlocked his seatbelt and reached over to hit the release on hers. "Come here, baby girl. You're having a reaction."

He hauled her across the seat and scooped her up like he would've one of his nieces, pressing Kelli's head against his chest and holding on tight. It was the same thing Josiah had done briefly before, but for a man who prided himself on his smarts, it seemed Luke had a wide gap in understanding when it came to figuring out what made this woman tick.

She was like a scarecrow in his arms at first, arms sticking out it awkward angles, her shoulders as tense as if there were straw stuffed up her sleeves.

He made soothing noises and tried his best to relax, which was hard since he was still freaked the hell out over the danger she'd thrown herself headlong into. The same way she threw herself off things in the barn.

"Nobody got hurt too bad," he assured her. "Your white-hat routine helped someone, and I won't shout at you anymore tonight."

She wiggled in his arms, rocking slightly, and he realized the damn woman was laughing softly. "No more shouting tonight? Good to know. That means you'll save the shouting for later?"

No use in lying. "Probably."

He patted her on the back, turning the motion into a slow rub between her shoulder blades. "Take a few breaths and try to relax. You're wound up tighter than Chili Pepper when she first arrived at the ranch."

Another snicker escaped. "Good one, boss. Compare me to a misbehaving horse."

"If the shoe fits—"

They sat in silence until Kelli let out a long breath and finally relaxed against him. He held on to her for another moment, debating which way the conversation needed to go next.

Drop the topic for now? Distract her with something else?

Maybe it wasn't the wisest choice, but then again, he could be totally upfront with her about this being only a possibility. "You good to move to the next subject?"

Her head rubbed across his chest as she placed a hand against him to wiggle herself free. Strong fingers lay over his biceps as she levered herself back to the passenger seat.

She still looked tense, but he didn't blame her. Not after what had gone down tonight.

Distraction was definitely in order. "Do up your seatbelt. I've got something to tell you. This is not one hundred percent going to happen, but Silver Stone got an invite to an important event happening soon in Kananaskis. No horses present, but a whole lot of people who like spending money and earning money from horses—"

All the tension drained away instantly as Kelli lit up like a firecracker. "Silver Stone got asked to the Triple Crown? Oh. My. *God.*"

That was borderline creepy. "How the hell did you do that? I know you've got ears attached to the walls in the barns, but I haven't told anybody about this except Josiah. Heck, I only found out a few hours ago."

She did up her seatbelt then faced him again, enthusiasm back on high. "It was just a guess, but am I right? Because, jeez, Luke. The topic came up on one of the blogs I keep an eye on. They did a couple reports about previous attendees from that kind of event. If Silver Stone got an invite that's stupid fantastic."

He buckled up and headed onto the highway, his distraction working better than he'd planned. "I forgot you're knee-deep in a bunch of those online groups."

"Stop being so righteous. You go online just as much as me, only in different places. TCG got mentioned because it hasn't happened yet," Kelli admitted. "Nobody is connected enough to be headed there, of course, which makes Silver Stone getting to go even more incredible."

"Invitation-only at this point," Luke warned her. "I sent in my registration, but I haven't heard back yet."

"You'll get in," she said firmly. "Hell, I'm shocked you've never hit their radar before. Especially two years ago when a couple of Nemo's offspring grew up enough to start placing on the circuit."

That had to be a factor in their favour. Having a good strong horse was one part of the equation, but when a stud's foals grew up and started winning races, it made a huge difference to a breeder's bottom line.

"You helped broker a couple of those deals," he reminded her. "That was you chatting him up at the Stampede."

"Didn't do anything out of the ordinary," Kelli insisted. "I didn't even know who the other owners were when I started bragging on him."

"Still, Nemo's stud fee keeps rising steadily. If this keeps up, the income will make a huge difference in the ranch's bottom line." He glanced over at her. She was smart enough to know what was going on, especially considering how much she learned with her damn eavesdropping.

Kelli fidgeted. Twisting her fingers together on the strap of her seatbelt. "So, if you're gone, I guess it'll be a good time for me to take over Chili Pepper's training."

Luke chuckled. "Nice try."

She gave him puppy-dog eyes. "Please? You'll be gone for a few days, maybe more. Someone will need to take care of her while you're away."

"It's a full six days, and you're right. Someone will need to take care of her, but it's not going to be you."

"Luke. That's not fair." All of her indignation and energy was back to full force. It seemed she'd gotten over her upset from earlier in the evening. "You said that I could—"

"I want you to come with me," he interrupted.

That shut her up fast.

"I think you're the perfect person to help represent Silver Stone. You know just about everything there is to know about our horses and our breeding program. Plus, you're not intimidating, and you get along fine with people."

"With cowboys," she pointed out. "And with the ranch hands and ordinary, everyday people. Not with the highfalutin' moneybags who'll be hanging out at that event."

He made a rude noise. "They're just people, Kelli. The fact they've got a little more money in their pocket isn't a reason for you to think less of them as people."

She didn't answer. This time it didn't seem to be shock, but embarrassment. So be it. It wasn't right to judge anyone except on what was in their hearts and came out in their actions.

He filled the quiet rattling around in the cab as quickly as possible, keeping his tone light. "Hey, as we just remembered, you talked to some of those people a couple years ago, and they liked you plenty. And you liked them, and this is something I could really use your help with."

A low groan escaped her as if she were being tormented. "Okay, fine. I will come with you to a fancy hotel where I don't have to shovel shit for nearly a week. And I will eat donuts for breakfast and steak for supper, and I will talk nice to everyone while I pretend that they have nothing more than a couple of toonies in their pocket, same as me."

"That's my girl," Luke said with a grin as he turned down the drive and headed toward the bunkhouse. "Keep your lips sealed until I find out more, and that goes double for your online community. Not a word, before or after."

She rolled her eyes. "I don't post private stuff online. I just read the articles."

"Yeah, right."

Kelli grinned. "Thanks for giving me the opportunity. I promise if this goes ahead, I will do everything I can to make sure

Silver Stone sounds bright and shiny so we can impress all those ordinary people."

The other topic of discussion—her acting like a masked vigilante—was also better to drop for the night. Leaving her happy now meant when he approached the topic tomorrow to get her promise to not do it ever again, she should be more receptive.

He pulled up outside her bunk. "I'll let you know as soon as I can."

"Thanks." She hopped out.

Luke was in the middle of backing up to change directions when she tapped on his window, guilt painting her features. "I acted irresponsibly at the bar and scared you. You're right. That wasn't the proper way to go about helping, and I'm sorry."

She was stronger than just about anyone he knew. The confession had come far quicker than he'd have been able to spit one out. "I'm sorry I went all stubborn and made you leave without your truck."

She shrugged, a glimmer of mischief back in her eyes. "Eh. I'm used to you being a stubborn overlord. It's okay. I would never expect a donkey to change their nature overnight."

Bam. Apology and insult, just like he'd expected. "Good night, Kelli."

"Night, boss."

4

Sheer willpower got her into her room without flipping out with excitement. Or was that panic rushing through her veins?

The entire evening had been one rush of adrenaline after the next, and she knew better than to slip into bed without dealing with it.

She was pumped to the max. Between the bully at the bar and Luke being all alpha dude, and then him hugging her out of the blue—

Not to mention the gala.

If she crawled into bed now she'd end up staring at the ceiling for hours, buzzing.

Kelli stripped out of her dancing gear and pulled on a worn set of sweatpants and a loose T-shirt, dragging out her yoga mat and plopping down in the middle of her floor to try and find some Zen.

Being all guru-y wasn't something she'd ever aspired to, but the Stone family's foster sister, Dare, had sworn by it. If there was anyone who Kelli trusted to know ways to successfully deal with a mass of bullshit in their lives, Darilyn Hayes was one. The woman was now married and living elsewhere, but she'd passed down this legacy.

So Kelli sat on her brightly coloured mat, legs tangled like a pretzel as she took deep breaths and worked on relaxing. Breathing in peacefulness and breathing out all her stress.

The way her insides had tangled so hard the instant she saw the bully—*breathe out.*

The way her heart rate picked up when Luke Stone gazed at her with those dark brown eyes—*breathe out.*

Breathe out.

Breathe out.

It took a few more breaths before the tension eased just from the thought of him. That was the first time he'd ever wrapped his arms around her in a way other than a friendly clap on the back. It sucked that she'd been on the verge of tears.

No, that was a good thing, her brain shouted. *That was* not *the moment for him to look at you like anything other than a friend. Definitely coworkers would be the limit.*

Competent—at least he believed she was competent enough to be invited to the gala with him, and good Lord, *that* thought took a good dozen breaths to relax her way out of as well.

Silver Stone ranch was in trouble. Kelli knew it, and not just because people liked to speak where she could overhear. She'd been around for long enough to see the signs. It felt as if the whole ranch was at a tipping point.

The troubles were through no fault of their own, just time and circumstances, which was really unfair considering the family's positive presence to the community.

Breathe out.

It took an hour to loosen up, slowly moving from sitting in one spot and working on her breathing to moving into her relaxation routine. Upward dogs and downward dogs and twisting rotations that worked out the kinks from not just her long day but her impact with the floor at the bar.

Thankfully, by the time she slipped under her quilt she was relaxed enough to fall asleep almost instantly, eyes popping open five minutes before her alarm was set to go off at six a.m.

The next day passed quickly. Kelli timed the end of her first shift to coincide with chore time so she could visit with Caleb's little girls as they cared for their pet goats.

"Come here, Meany," Emma said firmly as she pointed to the ground in front of her, grinning when one of the dapper creatures danced over and batted his nose against her side. "Good boy."

"He doesn't know you're talking to him," Sasha said authoritatively to her younger sister. "He just wants food."

"Don't say that," Kelli interjected. "You can teach goats their names. Even train them to come when they're called."

Sasha twirled toward her, jaw dropping.

"Yep." Kelli slipped off the top railing as the girls moved in closer. "Lots of animals are smart enough for that, but goats especially. They were one of the first animals people tamed—domesticated—way back when. Of course, some of that wasn't just so that they could be enjoyed as pets," she admitted.

Emma wrinkled her nose. "People eat goats. But not *our* goats."

"No. Eeny, Meany, and Miney are not on anyone's menu, but that doesn't mean eating goat meat is bad. We respect people's choices."

Sasha was nodding slowly. "Daddy says that, lots, because some of my friends are vegetarian." She looked around before lowering her voice conspiratorially. "I like hamburgers."

"Me too," Kelli whispered back. "With bacon."

Emma's little-girl snicker carried over the sound of her dropping grain in the feed trough. "You put bacon on nearly everything."

Kelli was about to deny it when she gave it a little more careful thought. "Pretty much."

That got both of them laughing. Kelli joined them in the pen to help clean the sleeping straw.

The girls worked hard, or as hard as easily distracted kids could, pausing only when a cheerful voice broke in. "I can't find my cookie testers."

"We're in here, Auntie Lisa," Sasha called, poking her head out of the shelter. "Wanna help?"

"I'll wait until you're done," Lisa said. A moment later, the three of them joined the dark-haired woman at the gate, her pleasant smile encompassing Kelli without a blink. "You have time for a snack?"

"Kelli says there's always time for snacks," Sasha announced cheerfully as she climbed over the gate instead of opening it. She and her sister took off for the backdoor of the house at a full-out run, leaving Lisa chuckling.

"The Kelli-isms she spits out sometimes kill me," Lisa offered. "That kid's got a full-blown case of hero worship."

Which made no sense whatsoever to Kelli, but ever since it had been pointed out to her, she'd been doing her best to make sure she watched her p's and q's around the girls. "I like them. I guess she knows that."

Lisa tilted her dark head toward the house, tucking her bare hands into her pockets against the moderate cold of the January day. "Join us. Tamara's feeling well enough she's sitting in the living room. She'd love to see you."

Kelli checked her watch, but she didn't have anything dire that needed to be done. "I'm on late chores. Setting up a base of cookies to get me through until supper sounds like a great idea."

"I always find a mess of cookies in my stomach makes just about any task go easier."

They turned and walked side by side, silence falling between them.

Lisa had been around Silver Stone since the middle of

December, but she and Kelli were still feeling their way around a relationship.

Tamara had settled in at Silver Stone ranch in a very finite and determined way. Now wife to Caleb, and a better mom to Emma and Sasha than their birth mother had ever been, Kelli had silently given her stamp of approval to the not-so-recent newcomer.

But in her book, everyone had to show their own colours before they got to be one of the *Silver Stone* family. Lisa might be Tamara's sister, and she might be here to give a hand, but Kelli had been reserving judgment until everything proved to be on the up and up.

The funniest part about it was Lisa seemed to know exactly what was going on, and furthermore didn't have any problems with being on probation. Nope, she just took it in stride and kept smiling.

That alone was endearing her to Kelli far quicker than if Lisa had tried to ingratiate herself.

"I'm glad you're here to help Tamara since she's still not feeling a hundred percent with this pregnancy, but don't they need you back in Rocky Mountain House?" Kelli asked before realizing that came out wrong. She quickly added, "Not because I want you gone. I'm just curious."

"I'm not offended," Lisa said as they strode through the snow to the ranch house. "Truth is, a year ago I wouldn't have been able to take off like this. The Coleman holdings amalgamated a lot over the past twelve months. Means instead of just my dad, my older sister and me, plus hired hands running Whiskey Creek land, we've now got the resources of the entire Coleman clan."

"Nice. I wondered how it was working. Sounds a great idea."

"It was a *brilliant* idea," Lisa said, a grin spreading across her entire face as she pulled open the back door. "Just took an awful lot of convincing to make it happen."

Kelli didn't have a chance to ask what that meant before they stepped into the warm, chocolate-scented air of the only place she'd ever really considered home.

Her gaze went across the room, smile at the ready to greet Tamara, who was curled up in her favourite spot on the couch.

Kelli slipped off her boots and made her way forward. "There's the boss of the house. How's the baby building going today?"

Tamara adjusted position slightly so Emma could crawl beside her and curl in, leaning against her hip. "On a scale of one to ten, where ten is me ready to take on anything, I'm thankful to report that today is about a six."

"That means she doesn't need to throw up." Blonde curls bounced as Emma shared this tidbit with great seriousness.

Tamara rolled her eyes, but she draped an arm around her daughter's shoulders and squeezed her close. "Remember our discussion about how even though you don't mind talking now, there are some things that are better left unsaid?"

"But, Mama, it's Kelli. She knows about throw up."

Kelli happened to be watching Lisa at that moment, and the two of them fought to keep from bursting into laughter.

Lisa grabbed a plate full of cookies and held it out. "On a completely different topic, chocolate chip or walnut?"

"Both," Kelli said at the exact same moment as Sasha announced, "Kelli says cookies need both chocolate and nuts."

Tamara stared at the ceiling, fighting her own amusement. "Put the kettle on, Lisa, and Kelli can come and tell me what's happening in the barns, because going out there is a three out of ten these days."

It was good to get caught up. As Kelli shared the latest gossip, Emma snuck off to join her sister. They sat at the table with glasses of milk to go with the fresh, warm treats. Lisa wandered the room, tidying and working on something in the kitchen between moments of joining the grown-up conversation.

Another sensation drifted through Kelli as they visited. As

much as she loved Silver Stone and her work in the barns and with the horses—

This part, this family-like connection with another woman, was special. It was something she'd never had until Tamara had shown up. She'd had the guys, and Ashton, but someone almost sisterlike? Never.

"Girls-night-out gathering is Tuesday," Kelli reminded Tamara.

Her friendship with Rose and Tansy had grown over the years, and they had another woman in the community, Brooke, who often joined them. But recently their pack of four had welcomed others in, like Tamara, Ivy, and Hanna.

Kelli glanced over at Lisa and considered.

Lisa had already been in attendance at a number of unofficial events, but maybe it was time to formalize her presence a little more.

Tamara caught Kelli's eye, nodding slowly as if she'd already figured out what Kelli was considering. "I can't commit now, but if I'm feeling up to it, I want to go."

"We're not doing anything too wild," Kelli said. "It's Rose's turn to pick an activity, so chances are it'll be something artsy-fartsy that doesn't involve too much gyrating."

"I'll take care of the girls, so you don't have to worry about them," Lisa offered, pouring water into the teapot.

"Nope, I think you have to come out, even if Tamara doesn't make it," Kelli insisted. She raised a hand like a stop sign when Lisa blinked at her in surprise. "You haven't done anything fun that didn't involve certain adorable little people under the age of twelve since you got here. That's not how we do things at Silver Stone. All work and no play—that sets a bad precedent. If you keep it up I'm pretty sure they'll expect the rest of us to fall in line, and no way. Just, no way."

"Work hard, play hard, drink 'til you drop," Sasha piped up, not even aware of what she'd said before she sank her teeth into a cookie and continued reading her book.

Lisa slapped a hand over her mouth. Tamara's eyes widened.

Kelli dropped her head into her hand and took a deep breath before looking up. Part of her wanted to apologize, but... "I don't *think* that's my fault."

Laughter danced in Tamara's eyes. "Sasha, honey. That quote is not to be repeated in front of *anyone*, understood?"

Her daughter glanced up, thinking hard as if mentally repeating what she'd just said. She made a face, then shrugged. "Okay, Mommy."

She went back to reading, and Kelli considered how lucky she was to be a part of something so special. This house of warmth and happiness. God, she wanted this, and so much more.

Tamara gestured her over, and Kelli sank to her knees in front of the couch, shocked but pleased when the woman leaned in and gave her an enormous hug.

It was easy to hug her back, but after Kelli slid away, sitting on the coffee table as she eyed Tamara with suspicion. "Pregnancy hormones acting up again?"

Laughter burst free from both Tamara and Lisa before Tamara gave Kelli's fingers a final squeeze and answered softly. "I appreciate you so much."

Kelli shrugged. "I'm glad. I like my job a lot."

The other woman shook her head. "No. I'm not talking about the you who works in the barns and tells me the gossip about what goes down. Although that's entertaining, and I'm going to have fun teasing Caleb about the stuck door you mentioned. What I love even more is that you show up and spend time with my kids. They adore you. I can see you care about them, and I'm glad for it beyond being grateful for your help while I'm under the weather. I don't blame you for that quote that popped out earlier at all, just to be clear."

That warmth inside kept growing. "They're great kids."

"You're more than just a ranch hand to them, and to me. We all feel that way." Tamara took a deep breath. "You know Silver Stone is your home, no matter what, right? Like, I'm never letting you leave."

"That sounds slightly creepy," Kelli joked to cover up the knot forming in her throat.

"Right? Our own Hotel California." Tamara winked.

It was Kelli's turn to take a moment before she could speak. "I promise everything I do is because I love Silver Stone. I really want the best for her, and for all of you. You guys *are* my family."

"That's how I feel too. Honestly," Tamara admitted, laughing quietly as she wiped at her eyes. "And we need to stop this because pregnant women are water spouts at the best of times."

"Cookie?" Kelli suggested, rising to her feet.

"You enjoy. Someone needs help with her homework." Tamara welcomed her second daughter into her arms, and together they opened a book for Sasha to read out loud, cuddled at her side.

A few farewells later Kelli was wandering over the snowy ground, the warm cookies Lisa had tucked into her hand a sharp contrast against the chilly air. Across the frozen water of Big Sky Lake, lights reflected against the early-winter darkness. Luke's frame was visible moving slowly though the kitchen of his house. Dreamlike and perfect.

Almost perfect.

The feelings bursting from inside her were as loud as a shout. Family, and more, all of it so much what Kelli had always wanted. To be a part of something bigger than herself. For Tamara to welcome her in so warmly, even though she was just a worker—it had to be a sign.

This was what people meant when they talked about the stars coming into alignment. It had to be. As long as the gala went ahead, Kelli would be able to finally take the next step.

The trip with Luke would give her the perfect opportunity to let him know she had a mad, wild crush on him, and had for years. She'd have to move slowly, but this was an opportunity she would not let slip through her fingers.

As if the heavens themselves were agreeing with her, a shooting star dashed across the sky, a silver shimmer against the deepening black.

Kelli made a wish—or started to, but she suddenly wasn't sure exactly what she was hoping for anymore.

Luke? To be with him? To be a part of the Stone family for real? That seemed too lofty a goal. Tangled needs and desires taunted her, and she tossed her confusion to the stars and made a wordless wish for happiness.

If the gala went ahead, *that* would be her sign it was time to act on her attraction to Luke. Short term or long term, she'd leave that up to fate to decide.

~

WAITING to hear back was going to kill him.

Luke wandered between the barns and his house for the next two days in a mindless haze, worried about what had gone wrong. It wasn't until he realized he'd filled in the application on a Friday night and chances of anyone getting back to him until Monday morning were slim to none that he decided he wasn't screwed. There was still hope.

Didn't make him any less grumpy as he worked with his family.

Caleb's warning looks were coming far too often by the time Sunday afternoon rolled around. "Somebody giving you trouble?"

"No," Luke rumbled.

His brother swore softly, pausing in the middle of his task to fold his arms over his chest. "Want to talk?"

Since this wasn't something he could discuss yet, "No."

Caleb moved in closer. "Something happen with Penny?"

Instant reaction. "*Hell*, no."

His brother shook his head. "In other words, there's nothing wrong and you're just being a jackass, or something's wrong and you don't want to talk about it."

Luke thought about it for a second. "Pretty much."

Caleb gave him a raised brow then laid down the law. "Get your head out of your ass or go find something to do that doesn't mean the rest of us have to put up with you grumbling like you swallowed a beehive."

It wasn't his goal in life to make things more difficult for his family, so Luke coiled up the rope in his hands and hung it outside the stall. He stepped past his brother, patting him on the shoulder as he went. "Doing as ordered. I promise I'll tell you as soon as I can."

As he kept marching toward the exit, his brother's words offered a final assurance. "Tell me sooner if you need to."

His family was the best, which is why it was even more important for this event to be successful. *If* they got to go.

Damn it.

Since he couldn't talk about secrets with just anyone, it made sense that his feet carried him to Kelli's bunkhouse. When there was no answer there, he walked the rest of the way around the corner to their foreman's small cottage.

As he guessed, Ashton knew exactly where the woman was, and ten minutes later he'd tracked her down at the front entrance to Silver Stone.

Kelli paused as he approached, the dogs running alongside the ATV he'd grabbed instead of saddling his horse. She had a warm woolen band covering her ears, with her cowboy hat firmly jammed on top. Head to toe in sturdy Carhartts, she tucked her hands into her pockets to protect them while she waited for him to turn off the vehicle.

"Need something?" she asked.

Luke suddenly felt stupid, because there was no reason for him to interrupt her work. He went with honest. "I'm antsy waiting for news, and I can't tell anyone why I'm jittering like a twelve-year-old boy on a double shot of espresso."

She grinned, bright understanding flashing across her face. "You and me both. I had to bite my tongue a dozen times this morning. Alex was teasing me at breakfast that I must have a hangover because of the faces I was making. Did you know that a couple years back both Lightning Arabians and Sweet Sugar Pie ranch had invites to this kind of event?"

He gaped at her. "Are you serious? And how did you find that out?"

Kelli rolled her eyes. "There's this thing called the World Wide Web..." She pulled a screwdriver out of her pocket. "You okay if I keep working while we talk? I have this real exacting boss who will give me shit if I don't figure out how to fix this before I head to the chow line."

"Let me help." He stepped closer and eyed the gate. "I didn't know you dealt with electrical fixes."

"I don't do the tricky stuff, but Ashton said this one was my speed." She pointed to one side of the rolling gate. "It's less about fixing the electrical and more about making sure the pathway is clear. Tamara doesn't need to be getting out of the van every time the gate needs closing."

Luke moved forward and helped the way he would have with any of the hands, lifting and passing tools, working around each other in an easy rhythm. He rose high over her, though, and took control when the gate decided to come off its tracks.

The entire time they talked their heads off about the possibilities that could arise from attending the event. Plus, they talked about the inane, which was just as comfortable.

"I know no one asked my opinion, but I have to say Sweet Sugar Pie is a terrible name for a ranch," Kelli criticized.

Luke shrugged. "Pet name for somebody?"

"Yeah. Her name for him, according to the news article."

Luke grunted as he lifted the heavy metal back into place. "Bullshit."

She made a rude noise. "What? Doesn't it get you all hot and bothered to think about getting called *Sugar Pie*?"

"*She's* the one with a honeypot—" He slammed his lips together.

What the hell was he thinking? This was *Kelli*. He and his brothers were pretty damn careful to *never* push the line with rude talk when she was around.

Kelli kept working intently with the wiring system, staring down at it, her lips twisted in a smirk. Only her cheeks were pink, brighter than the mild winter temperatures called for.

He'd embarrassed her. "Sorry, Kelli. That was uncalled for."

"Not untrue, though," she pointed out, sending him rocking back on his heels in surprise. She kept talking and her words hit him like a slap upside the head. "Besides, if a guy is doing things right, I can't imagine *any* woman having enough mind left to toss out cutesy names. Orgasms should leave you mush-brained and boneless."

He stared at her, *his* brain dribbling out his ears.

Kelli twisted the screwdriver and adjusted a few lines without saying anything more except about the job. "Put it in the track and shove it back and forth a few times to see if it needs lube."

He knew she was blunt-spoken, but *damn*. That sounded dirty.

Luke cleared his throat and blinked hard. It was his own fault for letting his mind start down this road.

"Luke? You need a written invitation?" she teased.

He stood and adjusted the heavy gate until she told him to stop. He lowered it into place, suddenly feeling a little more awkward than the usual comradery and competitive spirit between them created.

"I should get back to work," he said.

"I'll be a few more minutes finishing this up. Let me know when you hear about the gala, but I'm pretty sure you're a shoe-in for this." She glanced at him quickly then back at her work.

He took off a lot slower than he'd arrived, feeling something strange in the pit of his belly.

It *had* to be nerves over waiting to hear. That was it—that was causing everything to feel so out of joint. Discomfort with his brothers, strange sensations brewing while talking to Kelli.

This wasn't him. This wasn't the organized and easy-going person he was.

It was almost anticlimactic when midway through Monday the official email arrived. Dates and times for checking at the Grand Palisade in Kananaskis Country. An agenda for the event.

Link to payment options—he didn't hesitate. Half an hour later, he was out the door and headed over to Caleb's to let him know the good news.

Come Friday, he and Kelli would be waltzing through the doors of what could be the turning point for Silver Stone ranch. It was going to be perfect.

What could go wrong?

5

Kelli looked over the notes scrawled on the two-by-two-inch Post-it note in her palm "I should just kill him now, because chances are before the week is over, I'm going to commit accidental homicide."

Lisa considered. "I don't think that's possible. The fact you mentioned the possibility to us means you've given it some forethought, so you'd either get a second-degree murder or voluntary-manslaughter charge. Unless you're talking about *justifiable* homicide, which I totally understand."

Kelli wasn't the only one who fixed her gaze on Lisa. The entire room fell silent, seven women staring until Lisa realized what she'd done.

The dark-haired woman raised her brows and attempted to look innocent. "Oops?"

"CSI addiction?" Hanna Lane asked.

"Don't mind my sister, she reads the encyclopedia for fun," Tamara teased. "Come on, Kelli. What horrible things has my brother-in-law jotted on that teeny note that's making you grimace so hard?"

He'd handed her the note when he'd told her they were going

to the gala. She'd nearly fallen over between the rush of panic and hopefulness that had slammed her.

He'd grinned then left immediately to deal with scheduling, which was probably a good thing because she'd been tempted to grab hold of his plaid shirt and climb up him to plant a kiss right then and there.

Which would have been awkward, to say the least.

She focused on the issue at hand, which seemed to be that girls-night-out had become "let's figure out how to send Kelli to a shiny event without embarrassing herself" night.

It seemed her guess about artsy-fartsy activities hadn't been far off.

She looked over the note again so she could give an answer, but the mess didn't become any clearer. "That's part of the problem. His handwriting is the shits, always has been. One time he left a note for Ashton that looked as if we were supposed to get the cattle out from the far lane. We spent all day hunting for invisible beasts only to discover he wanted us to move the *cats* out of the far loft." She waved the teeny bit of blue paper in the air. "I can make out the words swimming pool, dancing and formal, but if that means we're going to a ball, he's taking the wrong person with him."

"I think he's taking exactly right person," Tansy said, tossing her head cheekily. "Honey, you know how to dance, and you know horses. Bullshit your way through the rest."

Tamara was on the phone even as she nodded her agreement. "Exactly. I couldn't agree with Tansy more."

"Bullshit I can do," Kelli muttered.

Tamara held up a finger as someone at the other end answered. "Luke, we've got a couple questions. We're helping Kelli get together clothes for the trip, and I want to make sure we've got everything covered." She listened for a minute. "Okay, we can deal with that. Do you need anything? I don't know if

Caleb's got anything fancier in his closet than what's hanging in yours."

She listened, nodding in silence. She said goodbye before looking up at Kelli with a long-suffering expression. "Good thing we checked. Luke talked to a friend who will be there. There's only one formal event. The rest of it is business casual, and there is a swimming pool."

"What the hell is business casual?" Kelli demanded.

"It means you can't wear jeans," Hanna informed her.

There had to be some mistake. "How is that even possible? Is that something people do on a regular basis?"

The only description for the expression on Tansy's and Lisa's faces was *smirk*. "They really do. It's only one week," Lisa offered in consolation. "Just think, you can eat all the steak you want. The Palisade has a really good restaurant. I looked it up online," she said before Tansy could make some smartass comment.

Kelli dropped into a chair and rested her head in her hands. "Nothing is worth this much hassle."

"Sure it is. By the way, what's Luke giving you for helping him?" Tansy asked.

"Not enough," Kelli responded, hauling out her phone and finding his number. She hit call before she had time to think it through.

Seduction 101 might be on the books, but some atrocities were pushing it a little too far.

Luke didn't even bother with the niceties. "What?"

"Hi to you, too. When we get back, I am in charge of *all* of Pepper's training," she demanded, turning her back on the rest of the room as the girls pretended to get busy. They were probably writing down lists of tutus and ballerina slippers and other horrible things she needed to pack. "You didn't tell me I couldn't wear jeans."

His chuckle carried over the line. It was annoying how the sound alone was enough to make her skin quiver as if he were in the room, stroking her body. "If it makes it any better, I don't get to wear jeans, either."

Okay, her brain was really not being her friend, because the options it slapped up involved him, a pair of boxers, and nothing else. Probably not business casual, but something her imagination had dreamed up far too many times for it to be healthy.

"Kelli? You still there?"

She shook herself alert. "I'm glad we get to suffer together, but I mean it. That's what I want for payment for attending the event. I'm going to do the best job possible, just like you know I will with Pepper's training, but I want you to promise."

He let out a long sigh. "Yes. Anything else?"

She wasn't fast enough on the uptake to come up with something terrible on the spot.

"I'll let you know." She hung up then turned back to others, smiling sweetly. "Okay, now that I have that settled, gird my loins, girls. I'm going into battle."

It wasn't the first time the differences between her and her friends became clear. As they suggested outfits, Kelli felt as if she was listening to them speak a different language. Rose got out a notebook and started drawing pictures, adding notes of the few things Kelli already had in her closet that the girls remembered would be appropriate. Things like tank tops and a few skirts she'd worn during summertime dances.

Tansy and Rose raided their closets, and slowly a pile of borrowed items was stacked on the coffee table.

Hanna snuck away after her phone rang. She came back into the apartment with a bag in her hand and a flush on her cheeks.

"You just got kissed," Tansy guessed.

Hanna lifted her chin and blushed harder. "Thoroughly, and there wasn't any mistletoe in sight." She made her way over to Kelli and offered the package. "See if this fits. You lent me clothes after I lost everything. We're pretty much the same size, and it's really a gorgeous dress. I'm not going to have too many opportunities to wear something that formal, so you might as well enjoy it."

Kelli peeked into the bag and found a creamy froth of white fabric. "Oh my God."

Tansy leaned over her shoulder and peeked in. "Sweet. That looks fancy."

"New Year's Eve we had a formal thing to go to with the Fire Chiefs from all over Alberta. I told Brad I didn't need anything special, but he insisted." Hanna offered a secretive smile, twisting a very shiny engagement ring on her finger as if she was still getting used to it being there. "We went shopping for a few things while we were in Calgary."

Tansy pushed the bag against Kelli. "You'd better try it on and see if it fits."

There had to be something else Kelli could demand of Luke to make up for this. Still, it made no sense to show up at the hotel with nothing to wear.

She hauled Hanna with her into one of the back bedrooms. "You have to help, because I do not want to rip anything."

Hanna stood quietly as Kelli removed her flannel shirt and tank, then slid out of her jeans. But when she grabbed the dress and went to step into it to put it on, Hanna shook her head.

"I promise I won't look, but you can't wear a bra. Or at least not that one. And the dress goes on over your head, not stepping into it. Trust me, I got that lesson taught to me very firmly in the salon."

It wasn't Hanna who deserved her rumbles, so Kelli kept them in. Stripping down to nothing but her undies, and with help from her friend, they wiggled the feather-light material over her head.

It dropped into place. She felt as if she was waiting for it to land. Kelli glanced down, expecting to have to shimmy things into place, but the material lay wrinkle-free over her breasts and torso, flaring over her hips before coming to a halt mid-thigh.

Hanna stepped behind her and did up the zipper that stopped barely above her ass. The dress size was right, amazingly enough, and the shiny garment seemed whisper soft. Kelli was afraid to touch the fabric for fear her rough fingertips would snag the material.

"I'm scared to wear this," she admitted.

Hanna stepped in front of her, shaking her head as she looked Kelli up and down. "You should be scared of the reaction of absolutely everyone who sees you in that. *Wow*. Now I know why Brad couldn't keep his eyes off me, if I looked half as good as you do in it."

"I can't wear this," Kelli said hurriedly, tempted to reach behind herself to undo the zipper and escape. "The dress is special to you. What if I rip it? What if I spill something on it?"

Her friend laid a hand on her arm. "Kelli, I lost absolutely everything in a fire a month ago, and I have never been happier in my life. Do you really think I'd be upset if something happens to a *dress*? Even a special one? I have the memories, and they're not going away."

Kelli took a deep breath, squeezing Hanna's hand. "Okay. You're right." She stepped back, trying to see herself in the small mirror on Tansy's hutch. "Does it really look okay?"

Hanna pushed her toward the door. "You won't believe me no matter what I say, so go ask Tansy. You know she won't lie."

Even walking was wrong, the fabric sliding over her thighs in an unfamiliar way.

When she stepped through the doorway and all of her friends turned to gawk at her, conversation coming to a complete stop, Kelli felt extremely uncomfortable.

She stood there for a moment before folding her arms in frustration. "You're not being very encouraging."

"Don't jump to conclusions," Rose said. "It's just really hard to talk when you've swallowed your tongue. "

"Wow." Tamara sat up straighter in the corner of the couch. "So many things I want to say, but I think *wow* pretty much sums it up."

Kelli slid farther into the room to try and catch a glimpse of her reflection in the window, the darkness outside turning the pane into an uncooperative mirror. "Don't say things just to make me feel comfortable, because as long as I don't make a fool of myself, I'm okay. But since the whole point is to make Silver Stone shine, there's no use putting a load of manure up on display."

"Stop that. You've never put yourself down before, so I don't know why you're starting now." Tamara glared in annoyance.

Because this wasn't just about making Silver Stone look good? Kelli's pulse was far faster than normal.

"You look good," Tansy told her softly. "*Really* good. Except you need different undies."

Kelli was torn between accepting the compliment or picking up the gauntlet regarding the continued attack on her poor, defenseless undergarments. "I'm already mostly naked under this. Don't push it. Also pointing out, horses don't give a damn what I wear on my ass, unless it was armour. Then they might bitch."

"The equivalent to chain mail for females is a chastity belt, and honey, I don't think you want to wear that under anything, jeans or a slinky dress."

"The undies I have on are as dressy as I've got," Kelli admitted.

A soft cough came from the quietest member of their group. Ivy Fields adjusted her grip on a cup of tea. "I might be able to help you with that."

Kelli was torn between absolute rejection of the idea and extreme curiosity.

Curiosity won. "What naughty secrets are you about to confess?"

Ivy shrugged. "I have a bit of an obsession with silk. But because I can't get out to the shops that often, I've been ordering online. Anything that doesn't quite fit gets put in a side drawer to be returned all at once. Come over tomorrow and we'll see if there's anything there that will work under this. Because the girls are right. It would be a travesty for you to not go all the way and look like a million bucks."

Kelli twirled toward the window and eyed herself critically. Hell, it wasn't what she usually wore, but from what she could see, it seemed pretty enough wrapping. And the idea of having slinky underthings to try…

Well, seduction was supposed to involve underwear, wasn't it?

"I do look decent," she admitted. "Only don't expect me to wear makeup. Can't do it."

Tansy stepped behind her, wiggling her brows. "There will be lots of good-looking guys at this event, all of whom love horses as obsessively as you."

Great. Meanwhile she'd be standing next to the only good-looking guy who seemed to turn her crank. Good Lord, she'd been such a fool the other day, thoughtlessly slipping into as close to flirting as she knew how.

The utter horror on his face when she'd made a dirty comment was a clear warning to wait until she had time to explain what was going on.

Still, as Kelli turned to admire her reflection, this wasn't the time to start feeling uncomfortable with her body. She was strong, no matter whether she was draped in fluff or her usual working gear.

"Only thing you need to finish up is a bit of advice." Hanna stepped in front of her, planting her fists firmly on her hips. "Trust me on this one, because I saw it at that New Year's Eve party. This kind of outfit? You can't move like your ass is on fire, if you'll excuse the work-related joke."

Heads were dipping all around the room. "Pretend they're a bunch of skittish horses," Tamara suggested. "No sudden moves, then sweet-talk everyone, the way you do every day down in the barns."

Kelli laughed out loud before she realized they were serious. "You just told me to treat a bunch of billionaires like horses. You're not speaking very complimentary about powerhouses in the industry."

"She's not saying it to be insulting," Hanna insisted. "It's about the right tool for the job. Same with clothes. You wouldn't wear rubber boots out on the dance floor, would you?"

"Of course not."

"And you wouldn't stomp through a stall with a pregnant mare…"

Okay. Now it made sense. Kelli nodded then glanced around the room. Seven pairs of eyes were looking at her with admiration and happiness. "You guys are the best. Thanks for taking care of me."

Hanna squeezed her hand, and Tansy came in to wrap her up in a bold hug. "You're worth it. Also, damn, that fabric is nice. Don't mind me. I'm just going to stay here and pet you for a while."

Kelli slapped her hand away.

Tansy snickered, and as Kelli went off to get changed into her normal clothing, she carried the warmth of friendship with her. She was ready for this. She had the clothes and a game plan that would help her impress the important people.

Now all she had to do was figure out the best time to start.

FRIDAY HAD NEVER TAKEN SO long and yet arrived so quickly. With his brothers' help, Luke had pulled together everything he needed to make a good impression while he and Kelli were gone.

He'd repacked his bag a dozen times, and wasn't that just the kicker considering Kelli had been the one to give him hell about the dress code. He'd had to scrounge around to find enough things to wear, and in the end, Josiah saved his butt by providing formal wear that fit.

Damn monkey suits. One of the reasons Luke loved working the ranch was because he didn't have to dress up. He had a few outfits from his time dating Penny, but none of them were in good enough shape for this event, and he didn't want to add expenses on top of what he'd already laid out. Borrowed gear made the most sense.

He dropped his bags at the main house in the morning before heading into town to deal with some final banking with Caleb. Kelli had obviously already been there because her well-worn hockey bag rested inside the back door.

Lisa came forward when he called into the house. "Hey, Luke. Caleb is saying goodbye to Tamara. She's in bed again."

Damn. He felt terrible for her, but also helpless. "I thought morning sickness only lasted three months."

A slight motion lifted her shoulders. "There are no hard and fast rules when it comes to pregnancy. She's healthy, just feels like crap. I'll bet she's having a boy."

Luke snickered. "Because men make women ill?"

"Oh, honey. Testosterone is the cause and the cure for so many ailments." Lisa eyed his packed bags, wrinkling her nose. "That's everything you need?"

He'd packed most of his closet. "Doesn't it look like enough?"

"Never said that."

Caleb came out of the master bedroom and closed the door carefully behind him, pausing to wrap an arm around Lisa's shoulders to give her a brotherly hug. "She's feeling better, but I convinced her to take a nap before trying to get vertical again."

Luke checked his watch. "We'd better get going to make our appointment on time."

"Go on," Lisa insisted. "I'll take care of everything that needs to be done here."

"You're a lifesaver," Caleb told her.

"That's what family does—they take care of each other." Her grin widened. "Even when they don't want to be taken care of."

"Damn right," Luke agreed. Tamara was stubborn, so it was good to see her sister and Caleb were keeping her under control.

They got everything done in town pretty quick, but Caleb sat in silence as they headed back to the house.

"I'm gonna do my best," Luke assured him.

"Oh, I don't doubt that. Glad you're the one going and not me." He glanced over at Luke before putting his gaze back on the highway. "Think you'll run into the Talismans?"

His ex-fiancée's family. "Possible. I don't think they'll make trouble, though. Penny and I called it off pretty mutual."

"There's no lingering plans to reignite that, then," Caleb stated.

Soft curses escaped before Luke shut them down. "*Definitely* no. Not a thing you need to worry about. That was a different time and place, and I learned my lesson."

"That's what I'm afraid of," Caleb muttered.

Jeez, he didn't need any bull right now. "Cryptic much?"

"Just feels as if the lesson you learned was to not get involved with women, period. They aren't the enemy."

Yeah, not the conversation he wanted to have before heading into a stressful situation. "I hear you, and I agree one hundred percent that women are wonderful creatures, but you took a breather after your wife left. Give me the courtesy of doing a reset myself."

"Okay. Only tell me you'll go with your gut," Caleb

encouraged. "Because it took me far too long to work up my courage to try again. Doesn't mean you have to."

"And on that note, drop me by my place. I'd better get changed. I'm supposed to meet Kelli in about thirty minutes so we can get on the road."

His big brother still seemed to have something to say, but he closed his mouth and nodded. "No problem."

Caleb dropped him off then headed back to the house.

Luke didn't bother to do anything except change. He grabbed his phone charger then hurried to the main house. He left his truck running so it would warm up, stepping to the front door to grab their bags.

He stopped, staring at a set of three matching pieces of luggage in confusion. "Hey. Where's my stuff?"

Lisa poked her head around the corner from the kitchen. "What's that?"

Luke looked around. "Did you move my bags?"

Tamara stepped from the master bedroom, a soft blue robe wrapped around her slim form. She blinked at him.

Damn. "Sorry I woke you."

She shook her head. "I was awake. It's my fault—I told Lisa she could. Your things are in there."

She pointed at the smart blue suitcases waiting at the front door.

He paused for a second before it registered. Fancy hotel, making a good impression. Not the place for his worn gunny sacks or Kelli's ancient hockey bag. "Damn. Okay, that's rather brilliant."

Lisa joined them at the front hall as the door opened behind Luke, and Kelli stepped in.

"I transferred your clothes, but I didn't look at any of it," Lisa promised.

Luke rolled his eyes. "I promise I won't faint at the thought of you handling my socks."

Lisa picked up the third, smaller square and pushed it into Kelli's hands. "This one has your things that didn't fit in the other case. Don't bother looking now, you can figure it out when you get to the hotel. There are travel advisories being posted for this afternoon, so you'd better get on the road before the snow stops you."

"What are we doing?" Kelli asked, eyeing the bags with suspicion. "Where's my bag?"

Luke put a hand on her shoulder and twisted her toward the front entrance. "We're leaving in five minutes flat. Take a pee break if you need, and let's go."

He picked up the two matching suitcases, tipped his chin toward the girls, then stepped outside.

Tossing the bags in the back of the crew cab, he paused. He didn't know which one was hers and which one was his. No problem. They'd get everything straightened out when they opened them in their hotel room...

Their hotel room.

Understanding of how intimate this situation was struck Luke out of the blue. He'd honestly been blind to the implications, and now the truth rushed in and slammed him with the force of a tsunami.

Jesus, he was in so much shit.

6

Hands down, this was the most awkward road trip Kelli had ever taken.

It hadn't started that way. For the first forty-five minutes or so she'd spent her energy chatting up the training techniques she'd been reading about that could help Chili Pepper.

Talking her fool head off was the only option. Either that or she'd have fallen into twisting her fingers in her lap like some shy miss as she fought to start this seduction business.

It wasn't fair. Kelli's education in sex had been ninety percent animal husbandry, and horses didn't need invitations to get on with the deed. Nope. When the opportunity arose, they took it. Enthusiastically.

And the guys she'd fooled around with, while not an extensive list, were all heat-of-the-moment, gotta-do-it-now events.

This slow, deliberate bullshit was for the birds.

When she realized Luke was doing nothing more than making noncommittal grunts and *uh-huh* noises, she started giving him some side eye.

Kelli thought back, wondering if she'd been unintentionally

rude or out of line. Nope, she couldn't think of anything out of the ordinary.

She fell silent for a bit, glancing at his hands on the steering wheel. It was probably the whole gala thing reeling inside her gut, at least to some degree. They were about to show up where she didn't feel comfortable, and he couldn't either. She'd cut him slack for that in the hopes that he'd do the same when it came to her acting awkward.

Maybe she should take Josiah up on those acting lessons. She wasn't sure anyone else in the community was aware he actually did have a background in the arts.

Secrets.

She closed her eyes and rested her head back, stretching her spine and trying to relax. When it came down to it, all of them had secrets.

Secrets were not necessarily terrible. They just were. Never in a million years had she dreamed as a fifteen-year-old sitting on a bus to the middle of nowhere that at some point she'd have the opportunity she had today.

Suddenly the need to tell Luke that grew bigger than she could hold back. She sat upright and faced him. "Thank you. Thank you for trusting me, and for bringing me along. I promise I'm not doing it just to get to work with Chili Pepper, but because I want the very best for Silver Stone, and for Emma and Sasha. I want this week to go really well."

That was all true. It wasn't all she had on her agenda, but... she couldn't make herself continue. Not with him acting so weird.

His fingers tightened on the wheel, knuckles going white. "I know you do."

He seemed about to say something else before his lips pressed together.

Okay, then. Someone *else's* stress level was a wee bit out of control.

"You're totally going to rock this. I mean, you know how to

talk to these people. If I wasn't already head over heels with Silver Stone, hearing you talk about her would impress the hell out of me every time."

Babbling. She was babbling.

"Thanks, but I'm not looking for a pep talk."

Kelli adjusted her position to stare out the front window as huge snowflakes swirled through the air. The next time she spoke, she wasn't quite as cheerful. "Then you might want to take a couple Xanax before we get there, because right now you are not chill. Not at all."

"I've got something on my mind."

"Obviously."

He growled.

Kelli glanced at him, and in spite of her own worries, a snicker snuck out. "Wow. I thought my nose was out of joint about not getting to wear jeans for the next week, other than the ones we've got on right now. Which, thank you very much for figuring out there was one event we needed to dress down for."

He ignored her chatter and slid over to the side of the road, pulling into a rest stop. Then he jerked open his door and got out, slamming it shut behind him as he paced off a few steps into the whirling snowfall.

Well, it appeared *somebody* was more than stressed. Considering it wasn't anything she'd done, it certainly wouldn't hurt for her to try cool him off.

Kelli got out, and by the time she joined him, he'd stomped his way back. "Spit it out. I've never seen you this cranky."

He dragged a hand through his hair before jamming his hat back into place. "I thought this was going to be no big deal, but the closer we get to the hotel, the more I realize I jumped to a few conclusions. And now we're stuck, and I don't know how to tell you."

Okay, that was not sounding as positive as she'd hoped. "You're starting to freak me out."

He planted both hands on his hips and took a deep breath. He looked her straight in the eye. "I think you're the best person to come to this event with me, I truly do. But I might have told the registration team that you and I have a slightly different relationship than what we've got in real life."

She was doing her best to keep up, but he was not making it easy. "What kind of relationship did you tell them we have?"

"You got the part about me saying you're the best person to come to this event, right?"

"The fact you're emphasizing that makes me suspect whatever you said equals me wanting to kill you."

Unflinchingly, Luke confessed. "I told them you're my *significant other.*"

Kelli maintained eye contact. It was probably the most difficult thing she'd ever done in her life. Not even leaving her old life behind, abandoning everything except what she could fit into a backpack, had been this tough. That had been her and her alone. Doing what was right to make a better life.

Having him look at her, truly *look* at her, with such utter misery— The first sensation in her gut was to want to fix it for him...

The second sensation was not quite so generous.

She'd spent years—*years*—hiding her attraction. Keeping the lines firmly in place because it wouldn't have been right to step beyond them, and he went and lied without blinking and turned them into a...*them*?

"Is there a reason you need a *significant other*?" That couldn't be her voice. It was far too calm and cool.

He nodded. "Family businesses get a leg up far quicker than some flighty dude who is solo and still sowing wild oats. We *are* a family business, but I'm the only brother who could go. And I had a fiancée, but that's over now—"

"Just don't. *Don't* talk about Penny," Kelli snapped.

Okay, that was rude on her part, but seriously? The guy was in enough trouble right now. Comparing her even remotely to that cold-spirited woman was not going to make this go easier on him.

Kelli's heart pounded. She deliberately uncurled her fingers from where they'd squeezed into tight fists. Not that she wanted to plant one in his face, but...

Well, okay, that option wasn't completely off the books.

She took a deep breath, pulling back to her yoga Zen. She still wanted him, damn him anyway, but this thoughtless act of his was wrong. So very wrong.

"You fucked up big time," she told him.

Luke gave a quick nod. "I know. I mean you're right. I mean —" He sighed heavily before twisting to stare up at the Rocky Mountain range that rose to the west of where they stood. "Damn, I'm sorry. I was doing the logical thing. I didn't think this through."

Her thoughts darted like river trout on a caddis-fly hatch day. "Then you can think it through with me now. We're supposed to act as if we're a couple around a bunch of people we need to impress with the quality of our stables and our skills with horses. And since I work for you, if I *don't* do this, and thus screw up the event before we even get there, then potentially, there's a threat hanging over me because you could fire me."

Luke blinked. "What? I'm not going to fire you."

"What if I told you I wasn't comfortable lying about our relationship? That I didn't want to go through with this?"

He opened his mouth. And wisely closed it.

"What if the only way I would do this was if I didn't work for you? You know what, maybe you should just go ahead and fire me."

His eyes flashed.

She moved in closer. "Do it. Say, *you're fired, Kelli.*"

"What the hell are you talking about? I'm not going to fire you."

"But you have to, because this isn't a work event, is it?"

"It is— I mean, it isn't."

"Just fire me, Luke," she ordered.

"No. Not even if you tell me to turn the truck around and forget the gala." As he said that, though, he looked sick. His face had gone white, and she was one second away from forgetting the whole thing.

This was killing her, too, it really was, but he needed to *know* what he'd done was wrong, dammit. "Fire me. *Do it*," she shouted.

"Fine, you're fired," he shouted back.

She grabbed him by the jacket front, dragging him close enough their faces were on the same level. "Too bad you're not my boss. You don't have the authority to fire me, only Ashton does. Besides, Tamara said I'm never allowed to leave Silver Stone, so there."

Her fingers were still tangled in his jacket, their bodies inches away from each other. Luke looked as if she'd shoved him through an old-fashioned wringer.

"Then what the hell did you make me say you were fired for?" he asked far more quietly, more of the old Luke looking back at her instead of the haunted, worried stranger.

She loosened her grip a little, staying close enough to use him as a wind block. "To prove that I *don't* work for you, so no one can say that you forced me into this. And because you're twenty kinds of asshole for not knowing this was a fucked-up idea. And because you deserved to suffer a little."

"Thought I was having a freaking heart attack a minute ago," he admitted.

She wasn't done with him. He still might keel over before their conversation was finished.

"Aren't I your friend? Why didn't you come to me earlier and tell me what was going on?" she demanded.

"You are my friend, and I didn't say anything because—" He stared over her head for a second before confessing, "I didn't realize. I mean, I already considered you family when I wrote your name down. It honestly didn't hit me until I saw the suitcases how intimate this whole thing could be, and that's when it clicked."

Intimate. A shiver raced over her skin. He had no idea. No idea at all what she'd wanted and dreamt of and hoped for so long.

And he thought of her as a...sister?

Luke straightened his shoulders. "I stand by what I said at the beginning. You really are the perfect person to help me represent the ranch."

She did a quick reshuffle inside, doing her damnedest to shove away the part that was saying she was crazy for not picking up something heavy and bopping him over the head with it while she had the chance.

This not just being a work-event changed things. A *lot*, and now it was her turn to have to pull a balancing act. It was one thing to have hoped to start something sexual—that would have been two grown adults having fun behind closed doors. No one would have known.

Being connected for real...

For fake real...

God, she didn't even know what to call this nonsense. Other than complicated. Very complicated.

A layer of snow was building on both their shoulders as the white-out conditions increased. As much as she'd like to have it all out, here and now, that wasn't going to happen.

Besides, he'd probably like to be hanging on to something when she tossed her final grenade.

"Get back in the damn truck," she ordered. "We'll figure out the rest while we drive. No use in freezing off limbs before we have to make friends and influence people."

He stared at her in near shock before his smile spread, and as usual, warm molasses heat drifted through her belly. "You're not going to call it off?"

"Nope, but I am going to up the ante. You've got one hell of a bill to pay."

HE'D ALWAYS PRIDED himself on being one of the smarter of the Stone boys, but getting back in the vehicle and heading on to their destination gave him plenty of time to reassess.

On the good side of the ledger: Kelli had not instantly taken his keys and run him over until he was dead. Although he *was* smart enough to know that was still a high possibility.

She grabbed the printout he'd made of the actual events and was staring at the sheet intensely. Again, something he should've done with her if he'd been smart enough to discuss this a few days ago.

"So they're impressed by family-run stables. Silver Stone definitely has that. Caleb and Tamara would've done a great job attending if she was up to it. So it's not a lie, not really. I can do this."

He couldn't help it. A laugh escaped. "You really have to do that bit of mental aerobics in order to be able to pull this off?"

She glanced up at him, her face innocent. "D'uh, *yes*. I don't lie."

"Kelli, have you been interfering in dangerous situations for the last six months without telling anyone?"

She was quiet for a moment before shaking her head. "I did tell someone. I told Ryan, and we set something up to help the women who need it. I didn't tell *you* because you didn't need to know, and when you asked me, I didn't lie. I just refused to answer."

He made a rude noise. "You spend more time figuring out how not to tell the truth than it would take to just spit it out."

"Says the man who could've told me at any moment in the

past four days that we were marching into this situation pretending to be lovebirds," she snapped.

"I didn't tell you because I was an idiot," he snapped back.

The truth was enough to get her to shut up.

At least for a few minutes, and then she was at him again, waving the piece of paper vigorously. "There are only two events where we're going to get to talk about Silver Stone and what we've got going on. And even that is a stretch."

"Because the gala is not specifically about the horses. It's about building relationships with other people."

She let out an enormous sigh and damn near collapsed on the seat. "Relationships that are built on a lie. Gee, I don't see how this is going to end poorly at all."

"You just said the truth is there. Caleb and Tamara are rock solid. Heck, so are Ivy and Walker, but there's no way Ivy could deal with this kind of event. Not with her social anxiety. And *you're* not a lie."

She made a really rude noise.

"I mean it. You are family to Silver Stone. You're just not...family."

Kelli glanced at him, a pretty forlorn expression on her face. "I'll do my best, but, dude, you should have hauled in someone like Rose who at least would have worked as arm candy."

Luke took a second to register what she was talking about, and when it did, all he could think was *bullshit*. He'd never expected to have to reassure Kelli about her appearance. "You look fine. You're cute, and you make people happy. I don't know how you even do it. Just be natural and everybody will love you."

She dipped her chin slowly. "Okay, what's our story?"

"What story?" She hit him on the shoulder. "Ouch."

"Luke, you're the stupidest genius I know. I'd swear you were being deliberately dense." Kelli shook out her fingers. "If I'm your fiancée, how did it happen? Us meeting, and the rest? I mean, obviously at the ranch, but you were engaged to Penny until the end of August."

Oh, that kind of story.

Wait. *What?* "Fiancée? You can be my girlfriend."

"Nope, I'm your fiancée."

She said it straight up, and if he wasn't certain she'd hit him again, harder this time, he would have laughed. "I thought you had trouble with lying."

"I have trouble with not doing everything we can to make this work. You *were* previously engaged. You said you had to bring your *significant other*, and considering how important this event is, there's no way you'd haul along a casual girlfriend. Also, first girlfriends after being engaged for years tend to be considered a rebound relationship. I'm not signing up for that."

He shouldn't find this so entertaining, but...

It was *Kelli*, and now that he'd established she wasn't going to castrate him—which he knew *she* knew how to do since he'd trained her, God help him—it felt more like a co-conspirator situation. "Isn't it awfully quick for me to be diving back into the whole love thing?"

"It happens. Although we don't want anyone to suspect you and I were fooling around while you and Penny were an item. Because that would not slip into a family-friendly file folder, now, would it?"

For fucks sake. "We weren't fooling around," he snapped.

She snorted. "Perfect, your indignation is totally buyable. Make sure you keep that mindset. When did you send off the registration, boss?"

"Don't do that," he said, snapping up a finger. "I know we work together, but it's best to not emphasize the fact too much. And as you've firmly established, I'm *not* your boss."

"Fine, sugar pie."

If he hadn't been driving, he would've planted his forehead against the steering wheel. "This is going to be so much fun."

Kelli damn near giggled. "If you say so. Pumpkin."

He ignored her teasing as best he could and got back to the more important part of the planning. "We've only got fifteen minutes before we arrive, so let's keep it simple. Yes, we've worked together forever, but there was nothing between us until recently."

"Because you were engaged. Plus, our official thing had better have happened really recently, considering I don't have a ring."

He was such an idiot. "New Year's Eve?"

"Too romantic. You asked me last week between currying the horses and cleaning stalls."

The hell? He glanced over, but Kelli was examining her nails and totally ignoring him. "I don't think so."

She twisted toward him, one brow arched high. "I didn't say yes at first because I thought you were kidding. Then you got called out to deal with something and didn't track me down until the next morning."

"You're having way too much fun with this," he grumbled. "There's no version of this story that doesn't make me look like a fool, is there?"

"Nope," she agreed. "But you'll be happy to know that when you did find me in the morning, I said yes. Then I pointed out that you should've looked where you knelt, because I hadn't finish cleaning that stall yet."

"Kelli James, you are one lump of trouble."

"Who is going to do everything in her power to make sure all those bigwigs want to come and see our horses." Her voice had gone far more serious. She laid her hand on his arm. "I'm teasing now because I'm still a little mad, and a little spooked, and a lot worried. Yet if I come back to that core part—to where I think about how strong our stable is and what kind of magic could be made—that part is absolutely true. I can work with that."

He rested his fingers over the top of hers, warm and heavy.

Basically, holding her hand in a way that he never had before. Not ever, not even once over the past eight years.

They'd worked together. They'd pulled each other out of stinking wet holes and through piles of mud. They'd helped lift each other over snowdrifts, but it was the first time they'd ever made contact like this. Just a hand touching another hand for a reason other than work.

It was a different kind of connection. Luke liked it.

"Thanks, Kelli. I agree. I know this might be awkward at moments, but what you said is the biggest thing for us to focus on. Let's bring it back to what we know is true. Silver Stone deserves to shine."

Her eyes were bright again, and for the first time since he'd realized what an asinine move he'd made, Luke Stone took a full breath. He wasn't out of the woods yet, and frankly he didn't deserve to be, but he was going to make it up to her. Somehow.

Together, though, as a team going forward. He liked the sound of that.

He liked the thought of that a lot.

7

As a man in a fancy uniform rolled forward with a cart and piled their luggage onto it, the matching bags taunted her.

She'd chickened out.

Kelli wiped her palms on her thighs then tucked an errant strand of hair behind her ear. The place in front of her was enormous. As close to a castle in a movie as anything she'd seen in recent history.

The circular carpark they'd pulled into was covered overhead by a rock and wrought-iron balcony. Floor-to-ceiling windows were tucked to their right. Luke was handing his keys to someone, so Kelli followed behind the luggage, through the massive doors and into the grand foyer.

The ceiling went up to forever, with massive log beams suspended overhead in arches and flying buttresses. River rock graced all the walls, the smooth surfaces as awe-inspiring as any jagged granite. Massive tiles lay underfoot, with rich carpets centering each of four collections of leather couches arranged in comfortable gatherings.

An arm hooked around her shoulders, and she jerked

upright, glancing to the left as Luke's chuckle surrounded her. "It's incredible, isn't it?"

"I can't stop staring. Tuck me in a corner so I don't look like a complete greenhorn, but it's too pretty to pretend I'm not in awe."

He squeezed gently then tugged her to the side. "Let's both find a wall for a minute, because I'm pretty gob-smacked myself."

She pressed her shoulders against the rocky surface he found them, letting her head fall back to take in the mass of heights. Closer by she spotted a fireplace that took up nearly an entire wall by itself. "That's big enough for people to walk into," she said with a whisper.

"Just like in the fairytales, darlin'," he assured her. "Over there is the dining room, and I think that path leads to the swimming pool and spa."

"Wow. We aren't in Kansas anymore, Toto."

Luke stepped away from the wall and moved in front of her. "Stay here and I'll check us in."

"Sure thing, bos—*buster*." Her lips twitched as she fought for a straight face. "Sorry, old habits."

He gave her a warning glance then strode away.

She really shouldn't, but as he marched off it was impossible to keep her gaze from his ass. He wore brand-new Levi's, with a crease running down the front of the legs. They cupped his ass like the seamstress had sewn them onto him, and she sighed happily.

She was some kind of masochist to be enjoying this so much. Not to mention her plan to go full steam ahead as soon as possible was going to take a lot more courage than she'd expected.

Considering she'd planned to make her move on the final part of the drive and then utterly failed.

Kelli was still staring after him when feminine laughter drifted over, drawing her attention away from the massive beauty of the lodge and the man.

A slightly heavyset woman with a massive amount of dark curly hair stood by politely. Her smile was bright, and her dark eyes danced with amusement. “Sorry for being so forward, but I assume you know that fine representation of manhood?”

And so it began.

Kelli held out a hand and gathered her chutzpah. “Kelli James. Yes, I’m with Luke. Luke Stone.”

Her mysterious woman arched a brow. Brightly painted full lips pursed slightly, not in a judgmental way, but in an intrigued and *going to get to the bottom of this mystery* way. “Well, now, this week is going to be far more exciting than expected. I’m Diane Jakarta. I’m here at the Triple Crown with my boyfriend, Jack.”

“Nice to meet you. Sorry you caught me gawking. It’s pretty incredible.” She gestured at the over-the-top lodging.

Diane smiled and stepped in closer, wrapping an arm around Kelli’s waist and guiding her toward the check-in counter. “Sugar, you were not gawking at the wainscoting, and we both know it. There are things in life far more worthwhile to stare at than a bunch of pretty rocks.”

Kelli could agree with that. “Have you been here long?”

“Got in about five minutes before you, I think. We drove from the Calgary Airport. Glad we made it ahead of the storm.”

Diane’s accent was something southern and sweet, and Kelli could have listened to her talk all day long. “It wasn’t as long a trip for us. Silver Stone is just over an hour from here. At least it is right now with the pass open. If this snow keeps up, we’ll have to drive all the way around, through Calgary, to get home.”

Diane shivered. “I tell you the snow was nearly a deal breaker. I’m not sure why they decided to hold the gala this far north in January. At least I hear there’s a good spa where we can get the chill out of our bones.”

Kelli had been watching Luke out of the corner of her eye. A lanky black man about Luke’s age had exchanged handshakes with him, and they patted each other on the back the way guys did who knew each other.

But as Diane led her to a couch with soft cushions near the sign-in desk, both of the men had their full attention on the woman behind the check-in counter.

It didn't appear things were going as smoothly as any of them hoped.

Diane glanced the same direction, clicking her tongue in concern. "Seems there's a bump in the road."

There was certainly some arguing going on. Polite, but still arguing, with very serious expressions on the check-in attendant's part.

Jack laid a hand on Luke's shoulder and turned him to face the room, his eyes shifting in a search pattern until he spotted Diane.

His smile widened. It was rather astonishing how easy it was to read the delight in his eyes. That expression was not fake, *that* was one hundred percent in love.

It made something inside Kelli tighten a notch as if a rope were being coiled up tight enough to shove in a small compartment.

A slightly haunted look shuttered Luke's eyes as Jack guided him forward, but he hauled his best smile into place and held out a hand to greet Diane as she was introduced.

"Luke and I spent a weekend together in tight quarters a couple years back," Jack told her.

Diane lifted an eye. "Is this something you want to talk about in mixed company?"

Kelli snorted before wiping her hand over her mouth as if she'd been caught in the middle of a sneeze. "Excuse me. Dust."

A low rumble of amusement rose from Jack. "It was that time I got caught by a snowstorm, if you remember that story. And if you don't, we'll remind you later." He turned his attention to

Kelli. "And you're the mysterious woman Luke's been telling me about."

He took her hand, turning it over so he could kiss her knuckles.

Kelli hauled her jaw off the floor. "Damn. Can you teach Luke how to do that?"

Delighted laughter rose from Diane. "Tell us, boys, why the long faces?"

Luke slid sideways, his hand coming around to rest gently on Kelli's hip. Keeping her by his side without pulling her in too closely. "Trouble with the room bookings for the gala."

"It's nothing we can't deal with," Jack said with a hand wave before turning to Diane. "Burst pipes or something, but for a couple of days they're short on rooms. Luke here was going to get shoved off into a double somewhere far from the action. I said there was no problem with them taking the second part of our unit. We've got one of the penthouse suites."

"Of course, we don't mind." Diane laid a hand on Kelli's wrist. "There's plenty of room, so we won't be underfoot with each other, but when we do want some company we won't have to go hiking through the wilderness to find each other."

Kelli glanced at Luke. She got zero clues from looking at his face. She assumed he desperately wanted her to turn down the offer, but then again, maybe this was one of those *take advantage of the opportunity* moments.

It certainly was for her. Sliding into the next stage of her agenda would be far easier if they were shoved into close proximity.

Speaking of which...

May as well begin the way she meant to go on.

Kelli leaned against him and slid her hand into his back pocket, ignoring the way he stiffened up like she'd poked him with a cattle prod. "That's really generous of you. If you're sure we won't be putting you out...?"

"We wouldn't have offered if we didn't mean it," Jack insisted. "If you're good with that plan, Luke and I will go tell them so they can give us a full set of wristbands and take your luggage up."

"Meanwhile, I'm starving," Diane said, grabbing Kelli by the hand and tugging her toward the restaurant. "It's only a couple times zones different, but I swear we missed three meals already today."

Kelli glanced over her shoulder. Luke was still standing there, seemingly in shock as he twisted his gaze between Jack and Kelli.

She widened her eyes and pulled her lips back into a patently fake smile, making sure neither Jack or Diane noticed.

Luke's lips twitched. Then he shrugged before offering a firm nod and a thumbs-up. Which she supposed meant whatever chaos they'd just stepped into, he would deal with.

She didn't have time for butterflies to develop because Diane was tugging her toward the most wonderful aromas.

"I hear they have triple decker hamburgers," Diane shared conspiratorially, guiding Kelli down a side passage that held a discreet plaque that said Triple Crown and nothing else.

"With or without bacon?" Kelli asked.

Diane squeezed her arm. "I can tell we're going to get along just fine."

~

THE DAY HAD STARTED with a bit of nervous energy in his belly, but Luke completely in control. That was hours ago, and with every minute that ticked past, control became more of an illusion.

How the hell had this happened? It was a good thing Kelli seemed to have gotten past the stage of wanting to rip his guts out, but he wasn't sure how long that would last, considering they were now being forced to share a room.

He kind of doubted the suite ran to Jack and Jill beds.

Kelli had made her point clear. She had agreed to come and

play along on this gig, but he bet being forced to share a mattress was pushing it a little hard.

Add in the fact she was acting weird...which in turn made him react like a hyperactive hare. She'd never been so touchy-feely before, and while her cozying up against him wasn't out of line with them being a couple, it had set off an uncomfortable reaction.

A whisper of heat that was completely unexpected. Luke wasn't sure what to blame it on, but he knew he needed to get it under control as quickly as possible.

By the time he and Jack had settled everything with the front desk and sent the luggage on up, Diane and Kelli had already ordered for them.

Or more accurately, Diane had ordered with Kelli's approval.

Jack slid into the bench seating next to his girlfriend and placed an arm around Diane's shoulders. "There we go, all set up."

Luke settled next to Kelli, suddenly uncertain where he should put his hands.

"We really appreciate it," he started again, but Jack waved it off.

"It's been a couple years since we got to talk. And while I know we've got the week ahead of us, you're going to be busy chatting it up with everyone else." Jack squeezed Diane's shoulders as he glanced at her with affection. "This way we're guaranteed to get some of their attention, right, darlin'?"

"See? We have selfish motives for our generosity," Diane offered with a wink. She stared intently across the table at Kelli, one brow rising the longer she focused. "I haven't met you before, have I? Because you look familiar."

Kelli shook her head. "Unless you've been out to Silver Stone or the Calgary Stampede, it's doubtful. I don't get around that much."

Then she messed with his mind, leaning against Luke's side

as she wrapped her fingers around his biceps. With her cuddled up against him once again, that hitch in his belly shot back to high.

She was acting like they were a couple, and he couldn't fault her on that, but every time she moved he was far too aware of her strong grip on his arm. Her thigh under the table brushing his.

The food arrived, and the temperature in the room seemed to skyrocket. He thoughtlessly pulled off his jacket, not realizing that the next time Kelli touched him, her fingers would brush bare skin.

It was hard to concentrate on the conversation, and the only thing he truly remembered about lunch was admiring the way Kelli slid into her comfort zone the instant Diane brought up the topic of horses.

Somehow they made it to the end of the meal, transitioning to the next thing without him making a single decision as well.

That whole out-of-control business—yeah, still in play.

"The food filled the holes, but now I need a chance to wash those travel hours off me." Jack glanced at Diane, mischief in his eyes. "Ready to join me?"

"Hmm, now that you mention it, the trip was rather exhausting." Diane slipped her hand into Jack's before turning to Kelli. "Don't worry. I promise we'll behave and not make you uncomfortable while we're sharing space."

Jack and Diane were obviously very into each other. But the questions and the conversation had stayed low-key and generic throughout the meal. Out of all the people they could've ended up having to room with, Jack was as solid as they came.

"You guys go enjoy some privacy," Kelli suggested. "Luke and I are taking a walk. We need to stretch our legs a little."

"This is supposed to be a holiday from your chores," Diane reminded her, "but we'll get time to chat later. Enjoy your exploration and the snow, and I will enjoy checking out the shower facilities with my man."

The smile stayed firmly on Kelli's face until Jack and Diane had vanished in the distance, then she grabbed Luke by the hand and tugged him straight toward a set of exterior doors.

Once outside, she released him, marching across a wide expanse lined with spruce trees wrapped in twinkling white lights. The landscape nearby was a mess of gardens and what would be grassy areas in late summer, now covered by a beautiful blanket of pristine white.

"Slow up," Luke ordered.

"Too public for my purposes."

That sounded ominous. He went for distraction. "Lunch went well."

They'd reached an area set up as a skating rink. To one side, ice walls rose vertically to create a windbreak. Kelli stepped behind it and he followed.

It wasn't just one wall, it was three, set up in a rectangle to form a fantasy garden, with ice statues on carved pedestals around the perimeter. The effect was stunning as the final rays of the day shone over the nearby mountain and lit up the western ice wall. Small alcoves were tucked along the east side, with fuzzy blankets draped on the seating areas.

In the middle of the space was a heater, somewhere to warm hands and toes—

—then he couldn't see anymore because Kelli had grabbed hold of his face and turned him determinedly toward her.

"We need to talk."

There was fire in her eyes again, and considering the tightrope line he'd put himself on with this whole disastrous event in the first place, Luke hesitated to jump to any kind of assumption regarding what she wanted to talk about. "Okay."

"We're sharing a room." She swallowed hard.

Before she could speak again, Luke hurried to reassure her. "I'm sorry, but I was doing my best to figure out a way to give you space, and then Jack showed up, and one thing just kind of led to another—"

Instead of getting all indignant and flashing him righteous fire, she rolled her eyes. "Two ears, one mouth. Shut up and listen."

"Listening." Although he had thought apologizing was the more important thing.

She pushed him backward, and he was forced to move or fall over. His feet hit the edge of a seat and he tumbled back into an alcove. A little more privacy was probably a good thing, though, as another couple wandered into the space, arm in arm.

Kelli stepped closer, that determined expression of hers that he knew far too well back in place. "We are no longer having the discussion we had on the road while headed here. Got that? We agreed this is about us— You as just Luke, and me as just Kelli. Both of us adults who represent Silver Stone. Correct?"

"That's right." A huge sense of relief raced through him. She was being so amazing in spite of his foolishness.

"Adults. Who are not related in any shape or form, which means there is no problem with us sharing a room."

Tension was building inside far too quickly. He was on a damn emotional roller coaster between one second and the next. He hurried to reassure her. "Nothing will happen, though. Just because we have to share a room—"

"What if I want something to happen?" She lowered her voice and leaned in as she spoke, her face inches away from his. Eyes fixed forward so there was no way he could ignore how serious she was.

Only his brain was a jumble, and nothing seemed to be firing in order. "*Wha...what?*"

Her gaze dropped to his lips, drifting over his body before rising back to meet his eyes again boldly. "I'm giving you a green light, Luke. Hell, I'm telling you if something doesn't happen between us

I'm going to be disappointed. But just like you should've talked to me and not tossed that *significant other* at me last-minute, I've realized I can't storm in and demand we jump into bed."

She'd laid her hands on his shoulders, and the light pressure was the only thing keeping him from falling over. "Wait. You're saying—?"

Kelli didn't offer any more explanation. Her lips pressed together in a serious smirk. One brow rose as she waited for him to clue in.

Oh, he'd heard every word, but he was having a hard time processing. Until today he'd spent so much time and energy making sure he didn't think about her as a woman, tossing that aside was the equivalent of picking up an entire truck.

"You want to sleep with me." The whispered words sounded far too shocked, like an indignant turn-of-the-century virginal maiden.

"I assume sleep will be involved at some point, but I am talking about sex." She straightened, her expression only the slightest bit embarrassment, but instead mostly determination. "I planned to seduce you, but I obviously have zero skills. And to demand sex be put on the table would be wrong, because I don't want you thinking we *have* to fool around. If you're not attracted to me, I'm not about to get mad. I know I'm not the most feminine—"

"Dammit." He caught her by the hand and tugged, rotating so she ended up on the seat next to him.

The shock of the movement stopped her ramble, which was a good thing. If she'd kept talking, his brain would get fuller, and there was zero space left between his ears to begin with.

"Two ears, one mouth," he repeated.

"Shut up?" she asked primly.

He nodded, taking a deep breath and examining her closely.

She wasn't pulling his leg, which meant sometime in the past few minutes he'd entered the twilight zone. Which explained why the number-one thing racing through his brain had nothing to do with the tangled knot she'd tossed his direction.

"What are you putting yourself down for?" he demanded.

Kelli tilted her head to the side.

"Not the most feminine—? Total load of bull right there. What the hell does that even mean?"

Her brows popped up. "It means I've been around the ranch for a long time, and you've never once looked at me like I'm a woman. And I get that part of it is the whole 'working together' thing. But just because I've had the hots for you forever doesn't mean you feel the same way. And that's okay."

It was a good thing he was sitting down, or he would've fallen over.

A snicker escaped as she adjusted position on the heavy blanket, curling her legs up and sliding in a little closer. "Your face is hysterical right now."

"You're messing with my mind," he confessed.

"I feel a little giddy," she returned. "I'm not drunk, but I may as well be considering I'm spilling all the beans I've held back for so long."

Luke shook his head. "I had no idea."

"That was the whole point," Kelli informed him. "And honestly, I'm not telling you this for any reason other than if it's something that you want as well, I'm saying this would be a pretty awesome time to have a bit of a fling. You know, if there's any chemistry. But no harm, no foul if there's not."

The words were beginning to register, but inside, he was still a mess. "I can't—"

"And don't think you have to jump me right now, or tell me no. Just... Green light, that's all I'm saying. If nothing more comes of it, I promise you will never hear another word from me about this."

"I—"

"And if anything *does* happen, I don't expect it to last beyond the gala. We go home, it's over and will never be mentioned again."

Luke nodded because she was still talking, and he couldn't really speak right then anyway, but it seemed polite to acknowledge he was sort of comprehending.

"Only, one thing? Nonnegotiable." She twisted, half-launching herself off the seat.

Instinctively, he threw his arms out to grab her and when the dust settled, Kelli was sitting in his lap, her arms draped around his shoulders.

Face to face.

His turn to swallow hard.

She stared at his lips again. "If we're supposed to be a couple, you can't jerk away every time I touch you. Just like I can't react as if it's the first time you've ever touched me. I know that's a little out of our comfort zone, so we'd better practice."

Her sitting in his lap, staring at him intently, was doing wicked things to his system. Luke had been aware Kelli was a woman, but he'd deliberately not thought about her in a sexual way before.

Being given a green light—stupid how parts of his brain had switched paths almost instantly. The more animal-based parts.

Her sitting in his lap now was not remotely like the other day when he'd hugged her, offering comfort. Nope, feeling her slight weight resting against his body sent a whole different sensation roaring through him.

"You're right."

Jeez, was that his voice? Far too low and far too needy.

She tipped off his cowboy hat, gingerly stroking her fingers through his hair, and a shiver shot down his spine. A second ago he'd had an enormous knot in his throat, and now his mouth had gone dry, and as she slid a finger down the side of his neck to the top button on his shirt, heat flared.

Shocking in its intensity. Devastating in the speed of its arrival.

"I'm going to kiss you," she warned.

He should be warning her off. He should be stopping her, turning this entire train around before they went out of control, but the track had already been set.

"Tell me no," Kelli whispered. "Or tell me yes. This is up to you."

His heart pounded, and the heat gathered in his belly had nothing to do with impressing people or making Silver Stone look good. It had everything to do with the fact he was suddenly, shockingly aware of the woman in his arms. The strong, confident and *desirable* woman who he had never even thought of being with, and yet here she was.

A woman who had clearly told him she wanted him, no strings attached. No demands, no fallout. Just desire.

He still wasn't sure where the train was going, but there was no way he could stop this part of the journey.

Luke leaned in and slid his hands around her body as their lips connected.

8

This was really happening. She was sitting in Luke Stone's lap, kissing him.

Being kissed, because even as she leaned in to make the connection, it was clear Luke had made his choice.

This was not a man sitting passively while she pressed hesitant kisses on him. Which was what she'd worried about in the first place, and sometime when she was alone, she and her confidence were going to have a firm talking to because the whole "maybe you don't want me, but I'm going to tell you how I've been drooling over you for years" confession had been a little over the top for someone who was used to keeping her cool.

That had not been cool at all. Nor flirtatious or seductive.

No, what it had been was honest, which was pretty much where Kelli's head and heart were firmly stuck. So be it. Just like when she had refused to tell Luke about her situation that had led to helping Ryan, it hadn't been her lying. Just keeping silent.

It seemed those were her two choices: shove down her emotions or let them spew.

Didn't seem to have harmed her so far, though.

And then she wasn't thinking anymore because their soft,

gentle exploration was heating up. Luke's hands fell to her hips, sliding down her thighs slowly as their mouths explored. Lips moving, teeth nibbling. The connection was still delicate, but instead of a slow, single drip from a faucet, pressure was building.

Her hands were in his hair, stroking and playing, the soft strands teasing her palms. His thumb rubbed back and forth just above her knee, his other hand easing up her spine until he wrapped his hand around the base of her braid. He tugged lightly to pull their lips apart.

Luke swore softly, gazing into her eyes for a split second before his lips returned to her skin, brushing over her cheek, making contact below her ear.

A shiver took her, shaking her entire body and making her ache. Heat flashed between her legs, and she pressed her hands to the tops of his shoulders so she could shift position.

Kelli intended to rearrange herself to straddle his thighs, only at that exact second a polite but firm cough sounded behind them, and Luke jerked his body the wrong direction. She was already in motion, unable to stop the firm connection between her knee and his groin.

Luke made a soft sound of distress, then in spite of the fact she'd just canned him in the nuts, he rose awkwardly to his feet. He hauled Kelli up with him, and when he shifted her to stand half in front of his body, she went willingly.

She was particularly grateful that female anatomy, while annoying in some ways, didn't announce arousal as vigorously or visually as for males. Except nipples, and that's what padded bras were for.

"Sorry to interrupt." The older gentleman was mostly serious, but amusement danced in his eyes. No way could he have missed that they'd been fooling around. "I thought I recognized you in the restaurant earlier. Someone suggested I might find you out here."

Luke held out a hand, reaching around Kelli's shoulder. "Luke Stone."

"Timothy Carlyn," the other man responded.

Holy little cats in the milk jug. That was a name she'd heard mentioned in some big-time circles. Kelli shoved out her hand as well. "Kelli James. It's a huge honour to meet you, Mr. Carlyn."

"You as well. I assume you're here for the Triple Crown Gala?"

Kelli nodded. "Representing Silver Stone ranch. You've probably met Luke before at the Calgary Stampede."

"I don't know that I've had that pleasure, but I'm sure we'll have time to speak over the coming days." His gaze was back on her face, and she suddenly wondered if there was a streak of dirt on it, or leftover lunch.

Luke had noticed the intense scrutiny as well, and he laid a hand protectively on her shoulder. "Is there something else you needed, sir?"

Timothy Carlyn seem to blink in surprise then smiled. A hint of a distraction remained as he shook his head. "No, no. Just thought I would be polite and introduce myself. I'll see you tonight."

"Looking forward to it," Luke said, even as his arm slid farther around Kelli, possessive and protective at the same time.

The older man tucked his hands behind his back and looked up into the sky as he wandered off, a slow whistle drifting back.

Inside, Kelli was still vibrating, and when Luke groaned and slowly sat down again, she whirled—

"Careful," Luke warned, hand held out protectively.

"Shit. I'm so sorry." She glanced toward the exit, but Mr. Carlyn had disappeared from sight. "What was that all about?"

"I'm not sure, but if he looks at you like that again, I'm giving him a firm talking to."

That eerie sensation at the back of her neck slid off worrying and back into pleasure. "Eccentric trillionaires who run world-class breeding stables in Kentucky are probably used to staring at whomever they want. Ignore him. Thank you for my kiss."

His eyes flashed hot before he cringed, lips twisting into a sarcastic smile. "It shouldn't have happened."

Oh no he didn't. "Don't you start that," she ordered. "It's not as if I twisted your arm and forced you to kiss me, so let's just carry on the way we started."

"I get it. I hear you," Luke insisted. He opened his knees, making a face as he moved, but then he caught her by the hand and tugged her to stand between his legs. When he caressed a finger over her cheek, Kelli wanted to nuzzle against him.

June bugs were jumping in her belly.

"I don't want to hurt you," Luke said. "You're somebody special, Kelli. I'm not going to fall into bed with you just to scratch an itch. No matter how much you say you'd be okay with it."

"It's what I want," she pointed out.

"So you say, but this isn't you and me acting in isolation. There are a whole lot of people at Silver Stone who'd be willing to tie me up and let the goats eat me if I treat you badly."

She'd already thought about this excuse. "We're adults, and last time I checked, neither of us live our lives by committee. For the duration of our time here, I truly am good with us having a red-hot fling."

He was shaking his head. Still touching her, but with sadness on his face. "I'm not going to lie and say I didn't enjoy kissing you. I think it was pretty clear I think you're an attractive woman, but going forward, we're not going to do anything. Not anything else, I mean."

Kelli shrugged. If it was true, she'd accept it, but in the meantime, teasing was in order. "You just keep telling yourself that if it makes you feel better."

A laugh escaped him, and he patted her cheek firmly as if he were dismissing one of the horses. "Come on. We should go unpack and figure out what we're doing this afternoon and evening."

"We're going to impress people, that much we know," Kelli said as she backed up to give him room to stand beside her. She gave him a break and glanced away as he cautiously rearranged himself—guys' nuts must be a pain and a half.

But she was relentless as they stepped toward the hotel. She slipped her fingers into his, raising a brow pointedly when he would've jerked his hand away.

And then damn if he didn't adjust his grip, flipping their hands over to a more comfortable position. His firm clasp held her just right as they paced back to the gorgeous monstrosity that was their home for the next five days and nights.

~

LUKE STONE HAD FALLEN down a rabbit hole and there was no escape.

As they reentered the hotel, Kelli was all eyes again, staring in wonder rather than watching where she put her feet. Luke was glad he had a grip on her. It made it easier to tug her across the floor toward the glass-fronted elevators that led to the tower suites.

She continued to crane her neck, looking everywhere, whispering quietly as she spotted decorating touches that made her grin.

He fixated on the mirror in front of them, staring at her as if it was the first time he'd truly seen the woman.

Kelli was small compared to him and yet a bundle of energy as she swung around, flashing a smile before she fell into jaw-dropped awe at a carving on display on the sideboard table. A couple of strands of hair had fallen loose from her braid, trailing past her cheeks.

In the moments before the elevator doors opened, Luke let

his gaze drop and openly take in the swell of her breasts, the dip where her waist cut in, and the flare of her hips—not very much there because she was so petite everywhere except up top.

Her image slid into nothingness as the doors gaped, and she tugged him after her, pressing the floor number.

Kissing her had been a revelation.

His over-the-top reaction might partly stem from being officially solo since the end of summer. It had been July since he'd actually had sex, what with the way the relationship had worked out between him and Penny, but he didn't think this was just his body craving a woman after a long dry spell.

Kelli was sweet and spicy at the same time. Like the discussion he and Josiah had regarding chicken wings, and the damnedest thing was that Luke was a split second from opening his mouth and sharing his thoughts because he knew that Kelli would get a kick out of the comparison.

He was so screwed. He liked her. He always had, but there'd been that barrier that said *hands off and leave her alone*. Kelli had thoroughly shredded that to ribbons with her blunt request and offer.

Only she hadn't thought this through. No more than he had making his boneheaded move and getting them into this circumstance in the first place.

She said she'd had the hots for me forever.

The elevator let them off on the top floor. Luke wasn't sure if he could stop himself from marching down the hall like a rooster.

They stopped outside the elaborately carved wooden door leading into their rooms for the next week. Kelli grinned at him. "This is going to be fun."

"Entertaining, no matter what," he drawled.

He placed his wristband to the keyless lock and it buzzed lightly, opening for them. He pushed the door open, holding it so Kelli could enter ahead of him.

The enormous space was elaborate and yet comfortable at the

same time. The room was a wide triangular shape with floor-to-ceiling windows opposite them that faced the Rocky Mountains. Outside the hotel, snow-covered peaks flared skyward close enough he could almost touch them, but inside was all about warmth and luxury.

A gas fireplace stood freestyle as the centerpiece of the room. Tucked up against the wall with the massive windows on either side of it, the tall black stovepipe reached into the lofted ceiling. Three couches were arranged in a semicircle facing the view, and there were thick soft carpets underfoot and beautiful tapestries on the walls.

Kelli's fingers slipped back into his, but this time it didn't seem as if she was trying to make a point. More like she was grounding herself. "Holy moly."

"Yeah, this is not going to suck." Luke squeezed her fingers then twisted to take in the rest of the room. He slipped off his coat and hung it on one of the open wrought-iron hooks lining one wall. There was space for their boots underneath, although he caught Kelli wrinkling her nose as she arranged her well-polished but worn footwear next to Diane's shining knee-high leather boots.

Then she shrugged, distracting him with a bright smile. "Come on. I want to see our room."

She turned on her heel, and he trucked after her.

"How do you know where you're going?" he teased. "There are two identical doors in either corner of this place."

Kelli pointed across the distance as she turned the doorknob and leaned her hip against the heavy weight. "That one has a sock on it."

Luke snorted as he spotted what she was talking about. Sure enough, Jack had placed a plain white sock over the doorknob leading to their room.

A further clue—behind their door, neat blue-and-white luggage was lined up at the foot of a king-size bed.

Kelli was already moving toward the far wall and the door there. "Tell me there's a bathtub in here with a view…" She cracked open the door then peeked over her shoulder at him, grinning from ear to ear. "I apologize now, but I might never come out."

He leaned over her shoulder. "Jeez, could they use a little more chrome and tile?"

"You need to make a shower like this in your house." Kelli pulled him farther forward, pointing at a glass-fronted monstrosity with three round showerheads directly overhead. "It's going to be like standing in a downpour."

Her excitement was high enough to distract him from everything else he needed to worry about. "Let's check the schedule and see when we need to be somewhere, then you can have free rein in here."

She suddenly straightened, glancing at him with a sly smile. "I don't mind sharing," she offered.

"I'm going to unpack." It was safer to ignore her invitations than to keep turning them down.

Sure enough, Kelli was hard on his heels a moment later, still grinning, but she'd dropped the topic. "Which bag is mine?"

"Not sure." He undid the zipper on the first one, flipping the hard case open.

Slamming it shut a second later.

He pushed it to one side and pointed to the other bag. "That one is yours."

Kelli folded her arms over her chest, amusement on her face. "Shy about letting me see your underwear?"

"Go unpack," he ordered.

Without another word Luke picked up his bag and carried it into the bathroom, locking the door behind him to make sure she didn't trail after him.

There was enough room to lay the suitcase on the counter, and he opened it carefully. Suits, shoes, slacks—all of that was folded and tucked neatly inside, but nothing explained the box of condoms nestled on top of the rest, safely held in place under the elastic straps.

He hauled out his phone and hit the number for his sister-in-law.

"Hello. Lisa Coleman speaking."

Luke figured she'd answer Tamara's phone. Good thing, because Lisa was the one he wanted to yell at. This had to be her fault. No way would Tamara pull a stunt like this, and none of his brothers would've either. "What the hell, Lisa?"

The woman had the audacity to laugh. "So. Did you have a good drive?"

"Yes. We got here safe, and we've checked in, and everything is going fine. Now answer the damn question. What the hell were you thinking?"

"You didn't like my packing job?" She clicked her tongue. "Relax. I didn't mean anything by it other than you are away with a certain young lady who has become important to me in a very short time. And if by some chance one thing leads to another, I didn't want you either making a stupid mistake and stopping because you didn't have supplies with you, or worse, making a stupid mistake and not stopping. Now you're covered, if you'll excuse the pun."

Luke eyed the box. Large size, bonus pack. He held his tongue about that part, still not happy with her. "I don't appreciate you poking your nose into my business."

"If you don't need them, whatever. Otherwise, consider it an early birthday present. I have to go. The girls will be home any minute. Have fun." She hung up, and the line went dead before he had a chance to growl his frustration.

He took the box and shoved it in the bottom drawer under the sink, covering it with a facecloth. Hopefully Kelli wouldn't look in that drawer, or if she did, best-case scenario, she might think it was part of the standard supplies offered by the hotel.

Luke dropped his shaving kit and bathroom stuff on the counter, picked up the suitcase and headed into the bedroom.

Kelli had headphones in and was dancing as she unpacked, hips swinging as she tucked clothes into the set of drawers on the far side of the room.

He did the same, slipping past her to the closet to hang up the suit and jackets Josiah had lent him. Doing everything with narrow focus in an attempt to ignore the enormous bed in the middle of the room, which was damn hard considering it was so big.

Something to be thankful for, he supposed. More room to stay away from Kelli in a California king. Not that she'd take up a ton of room in the first place.

He loaded the rest of his shirts and underwear into the dresser on his side of the bed—

God, he had a side of the bed.

He stopped with a jolt when something shimmery and pink slid from between his hands to hang over his arm. "Dammit, Lisa."

He must've said it too loudly because Kelli stopped her dancing, pulling one earbud free as she stepped to the side. "So that's where that went."

She caught hold of his hand then slid the bra strap over his wrist and onto her own arm. "Pretty, isn't it?"

The only reason he didn't stick his fingers in his ears was because he had frozen at the sight of the bra—and didn't that prove he was nothing but a teenage boy, immobilized by a woman's underwear?

"I guess."

She lifted her eyes to meet his, and that vulnerable woman who'd been making comments about not being "feminine" was back. "Can I tell you a secret?"

He waited, wordlessly.

Kelli smoothed her knuckles over the soft fabric of the cup.

Her attention drifted onto the material as she spoke softly. "I told my friends I'd never had anything fancy like this. I kind of thought women who wore stuff like this were crazy to waste the money. But you know what? I tried a set on the other day, and I think I'm hooked. It was so comfortable."

This was not happening. He was not really standing there next to Kelli James listening to her talk about unmentionables as she stroked its satiny finish.

But it was happening. It was far too easy for his brain to do the next step which was picture the swells of her breasts behind that soft fabric. And the hands stroking the material were his, and the cursed part was he had a really good imagination.

The next part that killed him? If he wanted to, he could totally admire the real thing. Kelli would be more than willing to model if he asked.

She glanced back up, and that rush of protectiveness he'd felt standing in the ice garden flared again. She might be driving him wild, but she was doing it by taking a risk. There was worry in her eyes, and damn if he didn't want to wipe away her fears.

But he was damned if he took what she was offering—

The long-time friendship between them won, forcing him to offer reassuring words. "There's nothing wrong with liking pretty things."

Her smile brightened the room, and something inside his gut flipped. They had so much history between them, and he really did care about her, but when it came right down to it, a new door had opened between them, and now it was time to decide whether to take a step through or not.

He still wasn't certain what he would do when it came to her green-light challenge, but one thing he was certain of.

Wanting to see her wearing a happy expression like she'd just flashed could get addictive.

9

As Kelli changed into the most comfortable of her dress-casual outfits, she scolded herself.

She'd hesitated instead of simply stripping down and dressing in front of him. While she'd dilly-dallied, Luke had grabbed what he needed and retreated into the bathroom.

Chicken.

By the time Luke returned, she was ready as well. He must have stuck his head under the tap or something, because his hair was a shade darker with lingering wetness, and he finger combed it into place as he checked the mirror on the dresser hutch.

"You missed a spot." Kelli crooked her finger to get him to draw closer.

To her shock he moved as ordered, and she stroked a hand around the back of his head, patting the errant strands that had been standing upright.

It was too tempting to resist. She did it a second time, playing with a curl at the base of his neck before withdrawing her hand.

Luke stared back as his breathing deepened slightly. His eyes—mesmerizing.

He stood abruptly and cleared his throat. "We should see if our hosts are ready to go mingle."

Kelli nodded and trucked ahead of him back into the living room. It took a moment for her to find her balance. The view out the window was nearly as mesmerizing as his eyes. Nearly, but not quite.

Still, she found herself pacing across the room to the window to stare into the majestic wilderness.

The view was amazing. Old-growth pine trees reached nearly as tall as the fourth-floor windows where she stood. Snow balanced on their limbs from the afternoon storm creating a picture-perfect Christmas card with a faint dusting of green and silver where the feature lighting from the hotel shone through the fluffy layers.

Luke stepped beside her. "It's a miracle every time I get to see nature in all her glory like this."

"It's even better because we don't have to go search for missing cattle," Kelli murmured. "Warm, *hmm*."

"Trust me, I'm appreciating that as well." With a laugh, he draped an arm around her shoulders in a "good ol' boy's" way.

She took total advantage and buried in tighter, wrapping herself against his side. Luke stiffened, and she debated backing off, when he sighed, relaxing and twisting toward her.

His familiar features were still for a moment, and then he smiled. Not the wide optimistic grin she loved, but the one he made when he was happy because something special had happened. Like the arrival of a foal, or the time she'd dragged him across the fields to show him the first crocuses of spring she'd discovered, poking their heads up way too early one February.

He slipped his fingers under her chin. "You are one big complication, Kelli James. But I guess I like complicated."

Luke tipped her head and leaned toward her, the faintest brush of his lips over hers sending her senses reeling.

Something had changed. Between unpacking and stepping out here in front of the window, something inside Luke seemed to have softened. She didn't want to think too hard about what it might mean other than he was kissing her.

Gentle but insistent. Nothing but his fingers under her chin, his mouth against hers, but their entire bodies could have been naked and pressed together for how turned on she was.

He licked her top lip, and she gasped. The next second he'd taken advantage of the opportunity, teasing his tongue against hers. Drawing back before she could fully engage. Making her wild as he pressed his teeth into her lower lip for the briefest second.

Something tugged deep in her core, but she forced her hands to stay at her sides instead of reaching for him for fear that adding to the touch might destroy the whole dream.

A distinctive *click* sounded as the door to the other suite opened. Luke pulled back far enough that when her lashes fluttered open he was inches away, that secretive smile still in place.

"You ready for this?" he asked.

She'd been ready years ago. Heck, three seconds ago she would have climbed him like a tree, and waiting any longer—

Oh, wait. He wasn't talking about sex.

Their roomies were chatting as they entered the room, and there wasn't really time to answer Luke's question now that Kelli had figured out what he was actually talking about.

Still, she took advantage of how close they stood to slip her hands around his waist, keeping their bodies together as she turned to smile at Diane's greeting.

"Now, don't you two look cozy," Diane offered, sliding onto the couch and patting the space next to her. "If I can drag her way from you, Luke, I'd like to borrow your woman."

"We're supposed to be heading downstairs, sugar," Jack warned.

Diane gave a dramatic sigh, but she winked at Kelli. "The man is right. Come on, girlfriend. Let's pull on our dancing shoes and go see what mischief we can make."

Kelli glanced at Luke, not quite sure what was going on. All the agenda had said was the name of a room, and she wasn't sure she wanted to be separated from him, for more than one reason.

He nodded briefly, tugging her in tight for a hug. "Jack and I are coming with you girls," he promised.

She could've sworn he pressed a kiss to the top of her head before he let her go. What was certain was he patted her on the butt as she stepped away. She did a double take back at him and set him grinning.

Jack laughed. "This is going to be fun," he said, clasping Luke firmly on the shoulder before the two men grabbed shoes and light jackets and passed them around. "I'm not sure who's more trouble, yours or mine."

"Two are always better than one," Kelli pointed out, "especially when it comes to making trouble."

"Amen, girlfriend." Diana raised a fist in the air. Kelli bumped their knuckles together.

Easy talk and comfortable laughter hung around them as they made their way to the second floor where the room was rented for the evening.

This was the best part of having met someone already. There was a whole crush of brand-new people in the room. The hotel had done their best to turn the place into a welcoming environment, but it was busy. Not a thousand people busy, but still clusters of strangers, and Kelli shifted closer to Luke's side before she realized what she'd done.

It was amazingly comfortable to feel his hand slide to her lower back, centering her and rooting her. "You got this," he said, bending until his lips were right beside her ear.

She tilted her head to respond which put her mouth a fraction of an inch away from his. "Piece of cake, baby."

A huff of amusement escaped him, air brushing her cheek, and it took a great deal of control to stop from simply closing the gap between them.

The way he was looking at her told her she wasn't the only one with that thought, and suddenly the tangle inside unraveled just a little.

It didn't really matter how many strangers she was about to have to impress. Luke Stone was watching her with eyes that said this entire roller coaster ride of second-guessing their sexual tension might not be headed toward derailment.

"Kelli, there's someone over here you need to meet." Diane had her by the hand, tugging her away from Luke without a by-her-leave, yet that was fine.

Kelli wiggled her fingers at an obviously amused pair of men.

"Take care of her for me," Luke called after them.

"It's okay. I've got bail money set aside," Jack announced, their laughter fading in the distance as Diane dragged her away.

The whirlwind began. For the next four hours Kelli was enticed from one set of people to the next. Diane introduced her at times, Luke shuffling back into the mix to stand beside her and bring her into conversation with the people he already knew from his years travelling to deliver sales or while supervising stud services.

It was exciting to be in a place with so many people who honestly loved the industry. Before long, Kelli found any lingering anxiety she had over chatting with the big-wigs had vanished like dandelion fluff in a strong wind. She felt swept away to places unknown as she settled in a chair opposite a woman with hair that was teased to the heavens, her Texas drawl making Kelli smile.

Her friends from Heart Falls Girls' Night Out would have rolled their eyes if they could see her now, because the evening had turned into a little bit of Kelli-heaven. Talking horses nonstop and hearing what was going on in a world that was far beyond her reach—perfect.

Not even the sensation that she was being watched closely by more than just Luke was enough to send her tumbling from her euphoria. The watchers weren't scary. They were just...

Curious about her? Wondering about Luke's new partner?

Timothy Carlyn was one. The older man had that distinguished look about him, with the grey hair and neatly trimmed beard and moustache; he could've been a poster boy for *horseracing billionaire of the month.*

His attention wasn't really creepy, but he definitely stared at her more often than seemed right.

Sweet, caring, *bossy* Diane was keeping an eye on her too, which made Kelli feel all kinds of happy and curious. After being pulled into a few conversations by her new bestie, it had become clear from the way others reacted that Ms. Jakarta was someone *big* in the industry. Kelli itched to break out her phone and do a Google search, but she decided it would be far too rude.

So instead, Kelli buckled down and schmoozed.

The room held little clusters of seating arrangements and small tables where people could grab a drink and a bite to eat. They would chat for a while then move into a new setting with new people.

The setup was simple and, as it turned out, immensely enjoyable for Kelli because she had two wonderful things going on.

Bragging about Silver Stone was easy. She loved the place, loved everything about it. Add in the fact that Luke couldn't seem to keep his eyes off her—

Concentrate, Kelli warned herself, dragging her gaze away from where she'd gotten stuck staring at him. She focused deliberately on the Texas woman in front of her.

Sadie Petrie paused to take a sip of her tea, a knowing smile curling her lips as her gaze darted between Kelli and Luke. "It's nice to see two young people so obviously in love."

Kelli wasn't about to point out the difference between love and awakening lust.

The heat scalding her cheeks must've been enough of an answer to satisfy Mrs. Petrie because the woman laughed, patting Kelli's fingers. "I won't tease. Come. Let's grab your young man, and the two of you can sit with me during dinner. I'll introduce you to my husband."

Nice people, Kelli decided. Diane and Jack and the Petries, and many more. She'd been wrong to assume just because they had money in their pockets that the entire group were going to be terrible or stuffy.

Then again, she'd made that assumption based on the only truly rich person she'd had much contact with. And *Penny's* past behavior meant Kelli couldn't really be blamed for having jumped to some conclusions.

Through the rest of the evening, both dinner and the time afterward where, to her great surprise, everyone broke into groups and the cards came out for some family-friendly games, the sensation of Luke's gaze upon her grew stronger. As if he were actually touching her.

She thought she was doing a good job at the gala, but as much fun and as important as the entire event was she couldn't help but hope a little of the magic spilled over to the rest of their evening.

What would happen when they left and went up to their room?

~

LUKE WASN'T sure what he was doing anymore.

The gala—fantastic. That part he had zero doubts about. As

he suspected, Kelli was in her element as soon as she'd forgotten to be nervous. Watching her work her magic as she chatted excitedly about anything and everything related to their horses, well, after a while he hadn't bothered doing anything more than run interference to make sure she didn't get monopolized for too long. People seemed to want to take her home and adopt her as a pet.

There were a few couples to avoid, but Diane had also taken Kelli under her wing, which meant there were two of them running interference. It was awesome.

Speaking of Diane—Luke's jaw had nearly hit the floor when he'd realized exactly who they'd fallen in with. The Jarkatas were partners in, or outright owned, a half a dozen of the top breeding stables in the south.

Including, it turned out, Jack's family's operation.

He'd stared at his friend in shock when Jack had finally informed him of all the tangled details.

Jack raised a brow, amusement covering his face. "You honestly didn't know?" he asked.

Luke shook his head. "Last time we talked you were foreman for your family's stables. You said you were dating someone—but you didn't say who, or that it was serious. You moved fast."

"Diane's parents bought out my parents without mentioning a thing to either of us until it was a done deal. Thank God I'd already told Diane I loved her before the final paperwork went through."

Luke could see how that could have caused problems. "When's the wedding?"

Jack shrugged. "I've asked her, but she's said even though she loves me too, she's not ready yet. And while I'd love to get my ring on her finger, whatever makes her happy is what I'm going with."

He slapped Jack on the back as they were drawn into another conversation.

Luke's gaze had drifted across to where Kelli sat beside Diane, the two of them laughing wildly as the youngest woman in the room, the seventeen-year-old granddaughter and heir apparent to one of the most successful dynasties represented at the event, laid her cards on the table in front of them with a squeal before shooting her arms upward.

No, the evening hadn't been what he'd expected. It had been better.

And now, hours later, as Luke opened the door to the suite and Kelli slipped inside in front of him, a new set of *better than expected* hopes dared to rise.

When she'd hit him with her...

He wasn't even sure what to call it. *Proposition?* Suggestion?

Radical new way of thinking?

He hadn't been ready for it. But after the evening and time to see her in a new light, things were changing. He'd reminded himself over and over that this was not Kelli, the ranch hand who eavesdropped and teased and worked at his side because she was an employee.

She was *Kelli.* The woman who'd seen him hurt and dirty and exhausted. The one who done her damnedest at times, he'd finally realized, to make him smile on the days when he hadn't had much to smile about.

She was a woman who, now that he got to think of her as a woman, cleaned up damn nice.

Jack and Diane were nowhere to be seen. They'd left the gathering after mentioning time zones and jetlag. At least another half an hour had passed before Luke could haul Kelli away from the far too vigorous game of whist she'd been playing against three silver-haired gentlemen.

He glanced at his watch. It wasn't late enough to call it a night. Not even with the drive that day and all the rest of the activity.

To tell the truth, he was scared to head into the bedroom yet because he wasn't sure how he was going to face the night.

Once again Kelli came to his rescue. She kicked off her boots then sauntered across the room to the still-burning gas fireplace. She dropped to her knees in front of it and let out a happy sigh.

He followed suit, getting comfy before crossing the floor to join her.

Luke stopped by her side and glanced down to discover she'd crossed her legs and was sitting in the familiar twisted-limb position he used to catch his foster sister relaxing in. "I'd join you, but I don't think my pants bend that way."

A smile twisted her lips. "Take them off."

Tempting, but no. "I don't think *I* bend that way."

Instead he settled beside her, leaning against the couch conveniently at his back.

Outside, snow continued to fall. Big white fluffy flakes drifted gently downward, a wonderland. The hotel's feature spotlights shone in different directions. Inside, the fire had turned the room warm and cozy.

"The heat is nice, but gas fireplaces don't sound right or smell right," Kelli complained softly, easing her neck from side to side.

She had closed her eyes, so it was safe to watch her. To let his gaze drift over the long line of her neck reflected in the firelight glow. To admire the sweep of her breasts under her shimmering yellow blouse.

He eased forward far enough to give into temptation and drag a finger down her sleeve to once again enjoy the soft texture. "I was going to tell you earlier how much I like that top."

"It's Rose's. You should see how good it looks against her dark skin."

He snorted. Deflection, again. "It looks good on *you*."

"Thanks."

They sat in silence. Luke was tempted to slide forward until he sat right behind her. Close enough he could rub his cheek against hers. Maybe press his lips to the spot under her ear that, when he'd touched it earlier that day, had made her quiver in his arms.

Close enough that he could reach around and undo the buttons on that blouse, one by one, until the fabric slid apart and more of her skin was exposed to the dancing light from the orange and red flames.

He wasn't sure anymore what was stopping him, other than they were in a semipublic room, a problem that could be fixed with a quick change of location.

Her eyes drifted open, and she twisted toward him. "Tell me about Penny."

Okay, there was an instant libido killer. He raised a brow. "Now? I thought you told me not to mention her name."

"We were in the middle of a fight, and it wasn't an appropriate time. But over the course of the evening enough people mentioned her name that I realized I probably should know a bit more."

"I don't think most men talk details about their ex-fiancée with their current fiancée," Luke drawled, folding his arms behind his head. "If anyone was asking you about her, they were out of line."

"Duly noted, and yet me being me, I am curious." She untangled her legs and wrapped her arms around her knees. "Why were you with her? I mean, I watched Caleb fall in love. There's plenty of good reasons why Tamara kicked his feet out from under him. And I get why Walker's with Ivy. But I never understood why you were with Penny."

"That's why we're not together anymore, I guess," Luke confessed. For some reason it was easier than he'd expected to keep going. "You know parts of this. We met at the Stampede. She was actually getting harassed by some dude. I stepped in and pretended I was her boyfriend to get him to lay off."

Kelli rolled her eyes. "Dear God, don't tell me this fake relationship thing is a habit with you."

"Twice in over thirty years. I don't think that's a habit."

But she was smiling. "Go on."

He stared into the fire. "She was all excited about Silver Stone and the things she said she was learning from me, but when I think back, it might've been more that she wanted to be excited about something. It made her seem more serious so her father would agree she should be brought in on their family business. I was convenient, and after a while, so was she."

The lights on the plastic piece of log rotated again, a pattern that was too easy to predict. Fake, not full of life and unexpected, the way a true fire would dance.

Kind of like his relationship with Penny had been, if he was honest.

"Being with her—associated with her family—wasn't a bad thing for Silver Stone," he confessed.

A soft curse drifted from Kelli. "*That's* why it went on for so long. That's the part I couldn't figure out."

He dragged his gaze up to hers. "So, you see, it's not as if she was the only one who made a mistake. She's not a terrible person, but in the end, we weren't right for each other. I wish her well."

She watched him intently before dropping her chin firmly. "You're a good man, Luke Stone."

"I make mistakes, same as anyone. Some more spectacular than others," he said wryly, drawing a smile from her.

She rubbed her palms against her thighs then unraveled herself to vertical, looking down at him. "I'm gonna grab a quick shower then crawl into bed. Good night."

Luke stared after her, watching her heart-shaped ass sway as she strode across the room and disappeared behind the bedroom door. He stayed where he was, desperately trying not to think about her getting naked under the water. To not imagine the heated streams rolling down her skin, or her hands moving over her breasts, between her legs...

He closed his eyes and fought with himself. Staying there as time ticked past to give her time to get wrapped up and safely under the covers, because there was one thing he'd just realized with complete and utter surety. Didn't matter that she'd called him a good man not even thirty minutes ago.

The things he wanted to do to Kelli James were utterly wicked.

10

The room was dark when the door finally cracked open and Luke slipped in. Kelli lay curled up on her side of the bed, eyes closed so she wasn't tempted to gawk.

The bathroom door opened and closed, water ran, and enough time passed that under any other circumstances she would have fallen asleep.

This wasn't a normal night. On a normal evening, she wasn't waiting for Luke to join her in bed.

His footsteps were almost soundless as he paced across the carpeted floor toward her, and when he sat, the mattress was big and firm enough to barely shift position.

He lay back, head on his pillow, adjusted the quilt, and then lay motionless.

Fairly anticlimactic after all of her hopeful expectations.

Only the longer she lay there trying to relax, and the longer *he* lay there pretending to sleep—because there was no way anyone could possibly stay that motionless unless it was deliberate or they'd been hit on the head—the more amused she got.

She opened her eyes.

Enough light stole in the open curtain to see he was staring at the ceiling.

"I'm tempted to shout 'Boo,'" she confessed softly, "but you might hurt something breaking out of that rigid position you've got yourself encased in."

His lips twitched, and he rolled, brown eyes shifting as his gaze drifted over her face. "Very considerate you restrained yourself then."

They stared at each other until Kelli noticed that their breathing had become synchronized. The repetitions were slow and even, strangely enough, considering how frantically her heart pounded.

She reached across the distance between them, caressing her fingers over his cheek. The rough stubble on his chin scratched against her palm briefly before she slid her fingers into the curls at the back of his neck.

His face tightened. Not in anger, but as if he were hurting. She didn't bother to ask what was wrong because it was pretty obvious what was going on. The same pleasure and pain rippled through her system.

If she were smarter, she would know the perfect words to say.

If she were braver, she wouldn't bother with words at all. She'd simply roll on top of him and let the next thing happen.

Luke caught her wrist in his fingers, and she thought everything was going to end right then. Instead, he tugged her hand closer. Opening her fingers and pressing a kiss to her palm.

Her heart shot to an even higher cadence as he twisted her hand to reach the inside of her wrist. Pressing his lips there as well. No way could she hide how fast her pulse was racing now. Not as he put his tongue to her skin and slowly worked his way up the inside of her forearm to her elbow. Lips and teeth stealing along as if he was afraid she would bolt.

Run away? *No*. Fall apart, possibly, completely unmade by the swirling need rushing through her.

Luke tugged at the sheets, tossing them back as he slid closer, and the next moment he was braced over her, lips teasing her shoulder and upward, brushing the ticklish spot at the base of her neck.

"Oh my God," she whispered.

There was too much to think about. Too much to experience. She chose to focus on the way his mouth sent shockwaves through her system, kisses inching up her neck to below her ear.

His body covered hers, his torso naked as she discovered when her hands lifted of their own accord. Hot skin stretched over taut muscles, and she let herself explore the way she'd longed to do for so damn long.

She dragged her fingertips up his back, her nails barely long enough to scratch his skin, but it was oh-so-satisfying when a tortured groan escaped his lips, his mouth jerking away from where he'd been teasing her earlobe.

Her legs were trapped between his, and he held his groin above her. Considering her track record from earlier in the day, she wasn't about to move her knees anywhere too close.

And then she didn't have to make any decisions because he'd made them for her. Adjusting his weight slightly, dropping a knee between her thighs and pushing them apart so he could settle between them.

Luke pulled back far enough to stare into her face as he lowered his body against hers.

"Kelli?" he asked.

She lifted her hands, wrapped them around the back of his head and brought their mouths together. Kissing him fiercely, taking the heat that he returned.

She lifted her legs and wrapped them around him with a groan as he flexed against her core. The thick length of his erection lay against her, and her head was spinning already just from the *idea* of this contact.

She didn't know if she should be cursing or thankful that

she'd wore pyjamas to bed. He wore something as well, which meant there were two layers between them at the bottom, just her tank top between their torsos.

Nothing between their lips. Nothing between their tongues except a wild dance of sexual need and urgency.

He leaned on one elbow. Still kissing her, still teasing his tongue against hers, while his other hand dropped to her waist. A sharp tug separated her tank top from her pyjama bottoms, then he slid his hand under the elastic, his fingers drifting over her belly and upward.

She needed air. She needed—

"God, Kelli. You feel so good under me. The things you do to me..."

His hand had reached her breast, and without hesitation he cupped her firmly. A low rumble rose from his chest and his body shook slightly.

"Ditto," was all she got out before he moved again. Shoving her shirt upward to expose her breast.

After moving so slowly, it was a shock to have him change pace, because a second later he had both her breasts bared, his hands cupped around them as he stared in admiration.

Just enough light stole across the covers to give her a perfect image to tuck away into her memory bank: Luke Stone—mooning over her boobs.

He shook his head slightly. "It's sinful you've had these covered up and hidden away for so long."

Kelli laughed. "Don't think I'm about to start doing chores naked. Straw is scratchy, and dust would get everywhere."

He flashed a smile as his gaze met hers. "Honestly? I don't want you naked around the barn. I don't want anyone else seeing these because, *damn*..."

He knelt over her, strong thighs supporting him and keeping him from crushing her as he lifted both palms to caress her sensitive skin. Her nipples tightened against him, the rough calluses on his hands perfect, just like she'd always imagined.

His teasing touch intensified as he caught the tips between his fingers and rolled gently.

"Oh God, *yes*. Like that." She arched her back, pleasure driving through her.

He hummed in appreciation. "Sensitive?"

"Sometimes. Right now—" She stopped because it was impossible to speak when he had his mouth on her. He sucked her nipple into his mouth, hard and then soft, flicking the tip of his tongue against the sensitized peak.

But when he left her to slide farther down her body, kissing his way to her navel, Kelli forgot to breathe.

He chuckled, the sound out of place and yet perfect.

Kelli wiggled up on her elbows and stared.

Luke Stone, between her legs. There was a sight to behold. "What are you laughing about?"

He tugged at the waistband of her favourite pyjama pants, the red with black lines well-worn and soft from repetitive washings. "Why am I not surprised?"

"Don't mock my Spidey-suit," she said as seriously as she could, considering Luke Stone was between her legs and all.

"I'm not mocking them," he said, raising a brow as he tucked a finger under the elastic edge and slowly tugged them downward. "I think they're perfect for you. It explains a lot."

He abandoned his task with the fabric tangled around her shins, but he'd moved on to a better job, so Kelli figured it wasn't the time to distract him. Not when he was sliding a thick finger through her curls and between her legs. Rubbing his fingertip over her clit, then deeper. Back up, and deeper again.

Luke took a controlled breath as he continued to stroke her, high pleasure tingling and rising with his every motion. When he spoke, his voice had gone lower and harsher, as if he'd swallowed a load of gravel. "If I'm going to go to hell, I may as well get you to heaven first."

He put his mouth over her, catching hold of her clit. At the same time, he rotated his hand and slid two fingers ruthlessly into her sex.

"Yes," Kelli moaned. He picked up the pace, both his mouth and his fingers driving her higher. She wasn't that far from the cliff to begin with, but with each determined thrust he teased all the places inside that needed filling. Using tongue and fingers to torment her, the two combined together as if he'd put a balloon to the top of a helium-tank nozzle and opened the valve all the way.

Between one breath and the next, she swept from anticipation into climax, slamming her heels to the mattress and jamming her hips against him.

Only now she realized her fingers were tangled in his hair as she tugged him from her too sensitive clit. "Oh my God, that was perfect."

He tilted his head back to look up at her, wiping the back of his hand across his wet mouth to reveal a wide smile. "Glad you think so. I had fun."

She caught his shoulders and tried to pull him up higher, back over her body.

"I have condoms—" she began, but the rest of the sentence was buried under the onslaught of his mouth as he kissed her vigorously.

She wrapped her arms and legs around him, trying to roll so she could take the evening to a logical conclusion.

Instead, he slowed them down. He pinned her in place with his body even as he softened the kiss. Teasing now, a touch, then away. Another touch, until it was clear that in spite of the firm erection pressed against her, he didn't plan to progress to sex.

No idea why, but she figured in this too, he was a grownup.

She relaxed under him. Not as if she were giving up or mad or falling asleep. More like she was letting him take the lead.

Continue to take the lead since the last minutes had been all about him being in charge.

But she did press her palms against his cheeks, putting as much tenderness into her kiss as possible until he adjusted position, reaching down to help put her clothes back in place before returning to rest at her side.

~

HAVING her pressed against him was pretty damn perfect. Yes, he still had a hard-on, but while his body wanted to continue, his brain had reached its limit.

Separating the Kelli he'd known for eight years from this brand-new woman wasn't something he could do in under the space of twelve hours.

The fact he'd given in to the temptation to touch her had more to do with the fact she deserved something special for being a big enough person to deal with his stupidity in a mature and positive manner.

Orgasms for acting like an adult. He laughed softly as he rearranged them, tucking her against his body as he spooned against her back.

She adjusted his arm under her head until it was where she wanted it, which just made him chuckle again.

"You're way too comfortable shoving me around," he teased.

"I'm too fussy to compromise when it comes to being comfortable." She took a deep breath and let it out slowly, wiggling in tighter. Her soft ass cradled his cock temptingly, but it was clear she wasn't trying to push tonight's agenda further. She truly was getting comfortable.

Kelli caressed a hand along his forearm to where his hand rested against her belly. It had been tempting to slip under her shirt, but as she stroked up and down the lines of his fingers, he leaned in to press his nose against her neck and inhaled deeply. He didn't need more.

Slow, easy breaths followed. Kelli slipped off to sleep.

Luke lay there for a long time, thinking.

His mind played through a mess of memories. Kelli wandering around the ranch, up on horseback, driving a tractor while hauling a combine.

Was that part of the problem? That she'd always been there?

Maybe that was part of the reason why this felt so right. Kelli had been a part of his life for a good long time. What's more, she'd been a friend. Someone he trusted. She knew how to make him smile, and she knew exactly how to get his temper rolling, and yet she always seemed so unflappable.

She was just—Kelli.

A little snore escaped her, which he found absolutely adorable. And then she wiggled enough that he eased off, giving her space to change position.

She rolled instantly, arms and legs shooting out. One arm slapped his face, a foot caught him sharply on the shin. He twisted instinctively, far too late to have been any good if she had accidentally aimed at his nuts again.

"You are one hell of a dangerous woman," he murmured, staring at her face. He stroked the hair back from her forehead and watched her until sleep snuck up on him.

She woke him twice in the night with her flailing arms and kicking legs. The second time it happened he was too tired to be amused anymore, gathering her *oblivious to the world* body against him and pinning her in place.

She might be little, but one errant kick would turn her green light to full red on his side of the equation.

Luke woke to an empty bed, the bathroom door still moving as he peered around the room in search of his missing bed partner.

"Kelli?"

Her head poked out the doorway a second later, eyes twinkling as she crooked a finger and motioned for him to join her. "Hurry up."

He hesitated too long because she rolled her eyes then marched out to whip back the top sheet and grab his hand. "Don't worry, I'm not about to ravish you in the shower or anything. You've got to see this."

This time he followed, curiosity winning out. She guided him to the deep soaker tub that sat in the corner of the bathroom, stepping into the empty basin so she could sit on the far side and point toward the mountains. "Look."

It was a little strange, stepping into the empty tub. He leaned over her, and happiness bubbled up from inside as her laughter rang out.

The massive snowfall had been put to good use already this morning. Someone had built a field full of snowmen, with typical branches for arms and carrots for noses. Here and there were hats and scarves.

A herd of deer were foraging on the edge of the tree line. A couple of the does had fawns with them, yearlings by now, but still with a heightened sense of curiosity. Two of the young ones had wandered in amongst the snowmen, sniffing and scratching at the snow near the base of the rounded balls.

One fawn took a great liking to a scarf around a snow woman's neck, grabbing hold of the end and giving it a tentative nibble. The deer tugged too hard, and the scarf tightened, knocking against the snow woman's neck and decapitating the poor creature.

The loosened head rolled toward the deer, and chaos ensued.

Tails were lifted, flashes of white warning rang out. Deer jumped back, knocking into other snowmen. Within seconds the herd had trampled the snowy field, and most of the snowman army lay in ruins.

Kelli was laughing so hard she couldn't breathe. She turned to toward him, catching his arm and dragging him with her into the bottom of the tub where she gasped for air between peals of laughter.

He felt pretty lightheaded himself.

How had he missed seeing this? How had he missed seeing Kelli?

11

By the time they reached the afternoon, Kelli was in dire need of a break. It wasn't that anything had gone wrong, but between the buffet breakfast, a morning filled with more meet-and-greet, and a lunchtime movie event where they ate burgers and watched *Hidalgo*, she was done.

She sat patiently though as replays of the previous year's Kentucky Derby started, plotting her escape, when a soft voice sounded in her ear.

"Ready to sneak away?"

She discovered Diane at her side, the beautiful black woman lifting a finger to her lips then motioning for Kelli to join her.

If she couldn't have her first choice, which was stealing upstairs to have a nap with Luke, stealing away with Diane sounded like a solid second.

Considering she didn't know where Luke was, she was very willing to upgrade Diane to first place.

Besides, she had to admit the truth—the possibilities of napping if she had found the man were slim.

Thankfully the noise and chaos in the meeting room allowed

them to slip away unseen. Diane linked her arm companionably through Kelli's as they strolled to the main foyer.

"You having fun?" Kelli asked, before realizing the question might be a little too juvenile.

One delicate brow rose in a perfect arch. "What's not to love about being immersed in all things equine?"

Okay, Diane might be richer than God, but damn, Kelli liked her. "My point exactly, but there are times my friends seem to think something else exists."

Diane pulled to a stop, placed a finger against her lips and looked deep in thought. Then she shook her head, curls bouncing enthusiastically. "No. Can't think of a single thing."

They were both still laughing as they headed back upstairs, kicking off their boots and getting comfy.

"Jack sent me a text earlier. He picked up some snacks and left them for us in the minifridge." Diane dropped bags of potato chips, dip and chocolate bars on the coffee table before stretching out on a couch. "Come to think of it, I lied earlier. There is more to enjoy in this world than horses."

Kelli nabbed a KitKat off the table, sinking her teeth into the chocolate with a happy moan. "Food."

"The four food groups," Diane elaborated. "Chips, bacon, chocolate, and more chocolate."

"He's a good man, your Jack," Kelli said, raising a loaded chip in the air in a toast before munching enthusiastically.

Her new friend's eyes lit up. "There's another thing to add to the list of enjoyable pastimes. Men. I like your Luke."

Kelli liked the sound of him being called *hers*, even if it was just for a short while. "He's a good one," she said honestly.

Diane eyed her closely. "I'm curious, but if it isn't something you want to talk about, feel free to tell me to mind my own business."

That sounded ominous. "What's your question?"

"You must've met Penny Talisman, considering you've worked around Silver Stone for a long time."

"That's not a secret. Of course, I've met her."

"Is it going to be awkward when you see her in the future? I mean, our world is not really that big," Diane pointed out.

"Still don't see why it would be a problem," Kelli said honestly even as it she gave it a little more thought.

She and Penny were never going to be besties, but knowing that Luke wasn't holding a grudge meant Kelli couldn't cling to much more than jealousy that the other woman had gotten a taste of the man she still lacked.

Jealousy was a silly emotion, though. It was in the past. Penny had no future with Luke—

Kelli lifted her gaze to Diane's. "I don't think she knew what she had."

The door swung open behind them, but Diane was nodding slowly, something that looked an awful lot like approval in her expression before she turned to blow a kiss at her man.

"Thought we'd find you beautiful ladies here," Jack teased.

Luke entered the room on Jack's heels, grinning as he made his way to the couch where Kelli was sprawled. He collapsed beside her hard enough she bounced, taking advantage of her momentary distraction to steal her bag of chips.

"Hey, that's my bag of junk food," Kelli complained.

"No time to argue." Luke folded the top of the bag down and dropped it on the table. "Put on your swimsuit, we're hitting the pool."

"But we were relaxing," Diane complained. "And having girl talk,"

Jack pulled her in for a kiss. "Which means you were talking about us. That's like a magic spell. You summoned us to your side, and now you're stuck with us."

"Oh," Kelli said, wiggling a finger at Diane knowingly. "It's like one of those curses. You know, recite the wrong lines and get stuck in limbo forever. Or recite *Bloody Mary* three times—"

Luke tipped her into his arms, ignoring her shout as he rose and tossed her over his shoulder before marching toward their bedroom. "Meet you back here in five minutes, Jack," he offered.

A squeal rang from behind them, and then Diane's laughter. "Caveman," she complained.

"Og's woman needs swimsuit," Jack growled. "Ten minutes, Luke. I'll try not to get distracted."

Kelli planted her hands against Luke's back and pushed upward far enough to see Diane was being carried across the floor. She was cradled in her boyfriend's arms, the two of them kissing as Jack blindly shuffled forward.

The last thing Kelli saw before the view cut off was him knocking into a wall. Diane's laughter echoed loudly.

Then Kelli was flying through the air, bouncing on the bed. A second later she was pinned in place by a strong, masculine body, Luke's lips on hers.

Oh *yes*.

Sadly, the kiss was brief. Quick, but dirty enough to leave her gasping as he rolled and left her alone and abandoned.

She curled to a sitting position to watch as he dug into his dresser drawer and pulled out a pair of board shorts.

Ten minutes would pass quickly.

Kelli grabbed the swimsuit Ivy had not just lent but outright gifted her with, claiming it was too beautiful to send back to the shop. Someone had messed up big time because the outfit was three sizes too small for Ivy, making it a nearly perfect fit for Kelli.

It was also a far cry from the one piece she usually wore when she went swimming in Big Sky Lake or down at Heart Falls.

There was no time to be shy, or coy, so she turned her back on Luke and stripped to nothing, pulling on the boy short part of the swim suit then wiggling her way into the bikini top.

She bent over to adjust her boobs into the bra cups like Tansy had taught her, and a loud groan rang from behind her.

Kelli snapped upright, glancing over her shoulder to discover Luke staring at her butt, one hand pressed firmly to the front of his swim trunks.

"Your ass is a thing of beauty," he growled. The words came out low and gravelly. She turned to face him, and his gaze shot up to her breasts. He swore again softly as he slid his hand up and down the length of his erection. "Bury me now, because I'm about to fucking die."

It was hard to speak. Her mouth had gone dry just watching him. What were the chances Jack and Diane would actually be ready on time?

Or maybe the real question was, why did people think punctuality was such an important concept, anyway?

She crawled on the bed, moving toward him like a cat. "Do you want to set a timer?"

"Kelli," Luke warned, but he didn't move away.

Didn't take his eyes off her, although he didn't seem able to decide whether he wanted to look at her top or bottom.

"We're doing this. You want my mouth or hand?" she asked, the words coming out breathless and low.

Luke swore again before he lifted his hand far enough to jam it under the waist band of his shorts. He adjusted his grip, fingers now obviously wrapped around his cock. Jacking himself up and down rapidly.

Kelli crawled closer. "Luke?"

"Touch me." The words came out a guttural plea, and she levered up on her knees so she could lower the elastic waistband far enough to see him working.

He kept stroking his length, the purplish cock head peeking from his fist like an erotic jack-in-the-box. Kelli laid her fingers on his rigid abdominal muscles that formed a grid pattern, his every muscle tight as he stared at her.

She etched the edges of his six-pack, down to his hip then along the line between leg and groin. The rapid pumping continued, and he groaned again as she touched the delicate skin under his cock, stroking his tight sac.

And then he was coming, stroking forward, eyes closed as his upper body arched. He brought his other hand up to cover the head of his cock, catching the come spurting free.

Kelli was like a kid in a candy store—she didn't know where to look.

No, she did. Because as fascinating as it was to see the beauty of his body, it was the expression on his face that made her smile. Pain turned to pleasure. Satisfaction...and yet unmet craving.

His dark eyes met hers and she shivered in anticipation.

This was just the beginning.

THEY'D BEEN in the swimming pool for over thirty minutes, and Kelli hadn't stopped grinning.

Luke stretched his arms along the edge of the hot tub where he and Jack had retreated, but his gaze stayed fixed on the dark-haired pixie who seemed determined to blow his mind at every turn.

Who knew she'd been hiding a bombshell under those layers of denim?

He supposed he had to congratulate himself for having kept his brain far away from anything dirty when it came to her over the past years. But the change meant that he was now really enjoying exploring this new mental territory. Kelli climbed out of the pool to escape a laughing group of preteens, and he let his eyes drift over her with pleasure.

Trim, and yet curvy enough that when he'd had her under him in bed it'd been far too difficult to stop. Far too pleasurable to continue.

Maybe he *was* as smart as he'd always imagined, because it was twenty-four hours ago when she dropped her bomb on him, and now that he'd gotten over being shocked, he was more than ready to fulfill her request.

That sense that something was very right continued to rise.

"I was going to ask for a few more details regarding you and Kelli, but I can cross half the items off my list." Jack's voice held a volume of amusement.

Luke dragged his gaze off Kelli's breasts reluctantly. They were like a late Christmas present, all wrapped up in a cherry-red bow.

Jack grinned harder, and Luke prepared to be taunted.

"What?" he demanded.

"I don't need to ask what you see in her, besides the obvious."

Jack's appreciative glance sent a bristle along Luke's spine. "Put your eyes back in your head. You've got your own woman."

"Who I love and adore, but that doesn't mean I can't appreciate your good luck. And I was talking about more than the packaging." Jack twisted toward him his expression going a little more serious." "I haven't seen her in the field, but it sounds as if she knows her stuff."

"Kelli is the best," Luke affirmed.

"When's the wedding?" Jack asked. "Because if you don't mind me saying so, I think you'd be smart to lock that up as soon as you can."

It'd been too easy to turn back to the pool and watch her with the kids as she and Diane played keep-away with them. The heat in his belly rose from a blatant physical attraction. Something that hadn't registered until now.

Kelli was great with kids. She adored his nieces and was wonderful with their friends, even when it came to helping with birthday parties and the like.

An image flashed into his brain of her holding a kid, and it didn't freak him out. Maybe it was that whole *she's already mostly family* business, but this was another part of their relationship that seemed right.

"Earth to Luke, come in."

Damn, he was staring at her again.

He turned back to Jack and tried to remember the last question, but he lost it. "What did you ask me?"

His friend patted him on the shoulder. "You are so gone."

The comment should've sent Luke into a panic, and yet it still felt right. "We need some time. The change in our relationship is new, and while it's going well, we have a lot of things to figure out."

None of that answer was a lie, and the discovery gave Luke hope. He might be able to turn this situation from disaster, to positive, to perfect without a lot of effort.

Jack raised a brow. "A bit of advice. She's now on the radar of more than a dozen ranches, and while only some of them have eligible competitors who'd be interested in fighting you for a spot in her bed, all of them want to see what she can do with their stock."

It was a fair warning, but not one that Luke wanted to spend any time on. Not when a sense of urgency was rising to let her know he'd not only seen the change in the traffic signals, he was ready to hit the highway at full speed.

"On that note, I think we need to gather our women." Luke stood, water sliding away. Jack joined him and the two of them closed the distance to the main pool.

Kelli was out of the water, chasing after a ball that had rolled onto the deck and under a chair. She was on her hands and knees as he strode up, nodding politely to the woman sitting on the chair who wore street clothes and a snow jacket.

"Excuse me."

He scooped Kelli around the waist, lifting her in the air as she shrieked in surprise.

"What—? *Luke?!*"

He knocked the ball from her hands toward Jack, enjoying the warmth of her body against his as he strode for the water. “Were you expecting someone else?”

She wrapped her arms around his shoulders, clutching tightly. Eyes wide as she stared into his face. “Maybe. I ordered a battery-operated inflatable boyfriend from Amazon.”

A burst of laughter escaped. “I’m better. Life-sized *and* I don’t deflate that easily.”

Whatever she was about to answer in retaliation was lost under her squeal as he threw them forward. They crashed into the deep end of the pool. He pushed off the bottom and brought them to the surface, turning her in his arms as he headed shallow enough he could stand.

Water dripped down her cheeks, one of her braids lying over both their shoulders.

She held on tight as she stared. “You’ll make my team lose,” she warned.

“We can’t have that,” he responded even as he slid his hands to her hips, and lower. He cupped her ass briefly, dragging their bodies together just to torment himself.

“Luke,” she murmured, motioning with her head over her shoulder. “Kids. Behave.”

“I know,” he promised, but he didn’t let go. Just twisted her in his arms and held on tight, an arm hooked around her belly to keep her in contact. He put a hand in the air and waved at Diane. “Here. Throw here.”

Diane stood in the shallow end, gauging the distance between her and the group of a dozen kids closing in fast.

“Go long,” she shouted before smacking the beach ball with a fist.

Kelli shot her arms into the air as Luke lifted her, giving her the extra height she needed to take control of the wayward toy.

She crowed as she caught it, flashing him a delighted smile before panic set in. “Oops. They’re after us now.”

The next fifteen minutes were a rush of energy and chaos. Children shouted, water splashed, laughter rang. The teams were mostly fluid, with anyone holding the ball fair game.

The only thing consistent was Luke stayed within touching distance because even a step farther from Kelli would have been too far.

Lifting her, hands on waist or hips. Lowering her against his body and letting her soft skin brush his. Twisting past her and secretly copping a feel—he made sure not to do that one too often because it was dangerous. He didn't need to get more turned on than he already was.

By the time the moms who had been chatting clapped their hands and informed the kids it was time to get ready for supper, Luke was hard as a spike and ready to do something about it.

Kelli was momentarily surrounded by a pack of preteen girls who all had to get in a hug before they climbed out of the water and left with their moms.

Jack and Diane had retreated to the hot tub. Kelli turned, lowering her chin slightly as heat flashed in her eyes. "I should make you walk out of the pool right now as punishment for getting me all hot and bothered."

He closed the distance between them again, holding her against his body. "You want me to walk with this handicap?"

Sneaky woman. She slid her hand around his neck, shaking her head slightly. "Whose fault is it you're suffering? I thought we did something about *that* before we came downstairs."

Luke glanced around, but everyone else had abandoned the pool and the growing chill. Jack and Diane remained in the hot pool, but they were busy kissing. He caught hold of Kelli's free hand and slid it down his body so her palm pressed his hard length. "I told you I'm better than any inflatable boyfriend."

She snickered. "Is this like one of those trick birthday candles that you can never blow out? Get your never-ending, selfreinflating erection here. No matter how many times you deal with it, there's always a new one right behind."

The feel of her hand on him was driving him wild, but they weren't doing this again. Not when there were so many other better options.

"We need to go," he told her.

Even to him, his voice sounded scary. Borderline dangerous and definitely needy.

She pushed back, and he let her go, following slowly. Marching up the stairs at the end of the pool and ignoring his erection that was fully visible and tenting his shorts.

He pulled on his robe, watching Kelli do the same. He interrupted when she would've hauled the belt around her, crossing the fabric over her body himself. Brushing his fingers over the swells of her breasts as he pretended to adjust the fuzzy fabric.

He tightened the ties of her belt as he stared into her face. Her cheeks were flushed as if she'd spent hours in the hot tub, and when she licked her lips, he was done.

If they made it back to their bedroom, it was going to be a fucking miracle.

12

She was lightheaded as Luke caught her fingers in his and led her off the pool deck. In the distance bells were ringing, the delicate rumble of elevators and behind-the-scenes noises, all cool and peaceful.

Inside, she was fire and ice.

The blood rushing past her eardrums was the loudest sound. They stood side-by-side in front of the elevator, the lit-up numbers slowly descending to where they waited on the ground floor. Luke clutched her hand in his, brushing his thumb over her knuckles again and again.

She was afraid to look at him. Afraid to meet his gaze in the mirror in case it was the final straw that broke her control.

All the touching had built the pressure inside until, forget the talk about inflatable boyfriends, *she* was a balloon puffed up to half a notch before bursting. All it would take was one too-blunt suggestion and she would jump him. Right here, right now.

She jammed her free hand into the pocket of the robe, drawing in a gasp as her fingers closed around a square that crinkled under her touch.

"Oh my God," she whispered.

"What?" His voice—gravel and lust and steely self-control.

The elevator door opened, and he dragged her in, using his wristband to access the button for their floor.

Instead of answering she looked up, checking the corners of the elevator.

A trace of amusement broke in. "I'm pretty sure they have security cameras in here."

She twisted toward him. "Then I suppose I shouldn't start a scandal by using this."

She inched her hand upward far enough to expose the corner of the condom.

He closed his eyes and let out a long, slow breath, broad shoulders flexing, fingers clenched tight at his side. "Don't tempt me."

"I'm not doing anything," she claimed.

Luke stepped against her, scooping her against his body. "You're you. That's enough to tempt a saint."

Screw decorum. Kelli wrapped herself around him, thrusting her fingers into his hair to drag their lips together.

Or that was her plan. He met her more than halfway, kissing her hungrily. His fingers squeezed her ass tightly. His tongue battled with hers, driving her so wild with lust she didn't notice the elevator doors opening.

They had to have opened, though, because suddenly they were in the hallway, and she was being pressed against the nearest wall, the thick length of Luke's erection grinding against her clit through the thin layers of their swimsuits. Her breasts crushed against him, and it was good, but it wasn't nearly enough.

It was all him. *Luke* kissing her, consuming her. Making her head spin. Pulling back far enough to carry her a little farther down the wall before he'd lose control, pivot on the spot, and seal her against the closest vertical surface.

The third time he did it, there was finally wood at her back instead of drywall. Kelli stretched her arm blindly downward, desperately twisting her wristband in front of the security lock as his teeth sank into her neck.

A beep sounded, and he shoved at the door handle. The doorframe shifted at her back then he was two steps into the room and she couldn't wait any longer.

She pushed frantically at his robe, shoving the material aside even as he was doing the same to her.

Fabric fell to the floor, his hands going for her bikini top. She caught the top of his board shorts and dragged them down his thighs. His cock sprang free, and she reached—

"*Damn.*" Kelli whirled back, grabbing her robe at the same moment Luke caught the top of her bikini shorts and stripped them off.

He picked her up again. She had just enough time to grab the condom from her robe pocket before he stumbled the final distance to their bedroom.

So many possibilities beckoned now that they had a bed and all the privacy they wanted, but the urgency remained. "Right now," Kelli demanded, holding up the condom.

Temptation flashed in his eyes, but he shook his head. "I need to get you ready—"

Damn the man. The instant he loosened his grip she wiggled free, catching her balance before wrapping her fingers around his girth.

Luke groaned as she dragged her hand upward. "*Kelli.*"

He had a hand on her breast, squeezing tightly before deliberately easing off.

"Now," she snapped. "Dammit, Luke. Fuck me already."

As if a dam had burst, he moved. Crowding her against the wall, pinning her hips in place, he cupped her breasts and put his mouth over her. Sucking and biting as he worked his teeth along her skin and up her neck.

Multitasking somehow because when he lifted her a second

later, dragging her left leg over his hip and opening her wide, he already had the condom on.

He rocked his erection between her folds, moisture spreading against her clit as her labia opened. Wrapping around him, getting him wet.

His tongue drove into her mouth with the same rhythm. Mimicking sex, driving her higher.

Luke pulled back far enough to look into her eyes as he lifted her slightly higher. The thick head of his cock slipped a little deeper. Poised now at her opening.

"Yes," she hissed.

Slow, slow and then, as his face tightened, he rocked his hips forward and buried himself deep. Filling her completely with one thrust.

Oh my God, it felt good. Kelli dug her fingers into his shoulders and panted, waiting for her body to stop buzzing, but that wasn't happening anytime soon. Not with him touching her, teasing her.

Dragging his hands over her thighs and ass as if he couldn't stop.

She was just about to tell him to get *going* when he read her mind, slipping an arm under her knee and widening her thighs to the point if she wasn't flexible, it wouldn't have worked.

A smartass comment rose to her tongue, but before she could get it out, he was fucking her. Pulling back slow enough that every thick inch rubbed hypersensitive nerves.

Plunging forward in a way that knocked his shaft against her clit before connecting his firm abdomen on hers. Each move crushed her breasts against him and gave her nowhere to retreat.

Pull back, *thrust*. Back, then forward again. Harder now, the sound of his breathing harsh in her ears as he leaned his head on the wall beside her. Fingers dug into her butt cheeks as he controlled the motion, relentlessly driving deep. Again, and again, as tension spiraled out of control.

The faint scent of chlorine clung to their skin, but it was all Luke in her nostrils. The taste of him in her mouth. The feel of him draped over her, and on her, and in her.

Connected and so very deliciously dirty as he sped up. Harsh, short motions meant to send her over the edge. He adjusted position to put her weight on one arm. When he brought his free hand up to his mouth and licked his fingers, Kelli held her breath.

He slid his hand over her belly and made contact with her clit, rubbing hard as he pounded deep.

She rocked back, arching as pleasure descended in a rush. Her sex squeezed tight around him and she moaned his name.

Luke swore, leaning into her. His thrusts grew erratic, out-of-sync, as he threw back his head and came.

The two of them jerked and jolted as if they'd pressed up against an electric fence. Twitching. Shaking. Panting.

The room spun for a long time, and until the world went solid, she just stayed there, satisfaction rolling through her system.

Wow.

Finally, Kelli loosened her grip, releasing her fingers one at a time from where she'd dug into his shoulders.

Luke twisted his head until he could press his lips to her cheek. She turned toward him, and they reconnected. Gentler touches now, and another unsteady inhale as they attempted to get their breathing under control.

He was still inside her.

Just the thought of that was huge, and as Kelli let her fingers drift over the side of his face, staring into his eyes, she felt a little fragile.

It'd been more perfect than she'd expected. With how many years she'd had to work on this fantasy, he'd had a lot to live up to.

She traced a finger over his lips, staring at them. "We might want to go clean up the living room," she whispered. "Before Jack and Diane get back."

"Good idea. I'll get right on that as soon as my legs decide to work again." He nipped at her fingertips, a soft smile curling his lips. "Was that fun?"

She hummed as if giving it thought. "I think so, but to be absolutely sure, we'd better try again."

"Of course. Practice makes perfect." He pulled out slowly, ignoring her noise of complaint. And as he carried her to the shower and put her down with a look of promised heat, Kelli realized she didn't have much to complain about.

"Again?" she asked.

His sexy grin answered that question.

~

IT WAS TEMPTING to forget the entire reason they were there and just stay in bed with Kelli. Only the fact that she would be too sore to walk if he kept this up made Luke resist from going back for a third time in rapid succession.

The shower had been a great chance to explore and play until they'd driven each other so wild he was thankful he only had to march across to the vanity to grab a condom.

Although he was *not* telling Lisa her gift had come in handy.

He brought Kelli back to their bed and dried her off, her amused expression clear that she was humouring him.

"Grin all you want, I'm not embarrassed." He tossed the towel away, stretching beside her so he could continue to run his hands over her skin.

"You're a lot more touchy-feely than I expected, that's all."

He swooped the back of his knuckles over her breasts, circling her nipples. Smiling as they peaked. "What makes you say that?"

"None of you Stone boys are big huggers," she pointed out.

"Except maybe Dustin, and I think he tries to hide it because he doesn't want any of you giving him grief."

"Maybe it has something to do with the fact we're constantly touching stuff doing chores." He frowned as he spotted faint bruises on her forearms. "You did end up hurt."

Kelli wiggled up on her elbows. "Took you until now to notice?"

Luke shrugged, leaning in to kiss her skin delicately. "I wasn't looking at your arms earlier. There were a few more distracting parts."

Like her breasts, which were right there, inches from his lips...

Before he could give in to temptation, he pushed up and kissed the tip of her nose. "Get dressed."

She sighed. "Okay. Suiting up."

They were dealing with the breadcrumb trail of clothing they'd left from the front door to their bedroom, the evidence nearly hidden away, when Kelli's phone rang.

She glanced down with a frown. "Unknown number." She answered it, her eyes widening instantly. "Yes, ma'am. I'm free right now. Where would you like to meet?"

Kelli flashed a thumbs-up right as Luke's phone went off, and he reached to check his messages.

Walker.

In the background, Kelli was still on the phone. "I can be down in about five minutes," she offered. "Okay, I'll see you then."

She hung up, mouth open in a silent scream.

Luke lifted a brow. "I take it you're abandoning me?"

"For a bit. Oh my God, Luke. Mrs. Petrie wants to chat. Said she needs to know more about Silver Stone, and did I like my tea sweet or not?"

Kelli bounced with excitement. He pulled her against him

and squeezed tightly before tipping her head. Locking gazes. "Said you were a rock star."

"I don't think rock stars have this much fun," she offered, leaning upon her tiptoes and kissing him enthusiastically before slipping from his arms and shoving her feet into her boots. A second later she had a jacket on and was headed out the door. "If you see Diane before me, tell her we'll talk later. Oh, and text me if you need me."

"Same," he reminded her.

She was off before he could say anything else. No time to share how much fun he'd had, or how perfect the last few hours had been.

Maybe it was a good thing because his brain was really pushing forward too fast, the way this new status quo felt so very right. Damn, Kelli was the best thing that had happened to him, and finally becoming aware of it—

Instead of texting his brother back, Luke put through a call in the hopes Walker was somewhere with reception.

"Hey. I didn't want to interrupt you in case you were in the middle of a deal," Walker said. "You keeping busy?"

Momentary guilt set in, because for the last couple of hours Luke hadn't been doing anything to progress the financial interests of Silver Stone.

Then again, he couldn't be socializing the entire time. "Just taking a break. It's not like attending the rodeo or a press event. We're talking about horses, and Silver Stone, but it's definitely more about getting to know people."

Walker made a noncommittal noise. "Not to put the pressure on or anything, but any of those people seemed interested in tossing cash our direction?"

"Kelli just headed out to an invite with the grande dame from Trafalgar stables." Luke grinned as he spoke. "Kelli's charming the birds out of the trees, Walker. So damn cool to watch her."

His brother didn't answer for a moment, and when he did he sounded amused. "I take it you're happy you asked her along?"

Shit. Had he misjudged the situation? "Yeah, she's doing wonders, but I'm sorry. I should've asked if you wanted to come."

"Oh, hell no. I wasn't giving you grief for leaving me out. I'm *glad* you didn't thrust me into the limelight again. I've done my share of that. I was just wondering how things were going between you and Kelli."

It was on the tip of Luke's tongue to confess everything, but that was a potential disaster since he still didn't really know what was going on, or what would be happening when he got home.

When *they* got home.

Yeah, the fact he and Kelli had hit the sheets wasn't something to toss out in a phone call. He'd prefer to be home to deal with any problems in person. *If* there were problems.

There might not be, if their fling was over.

I'm not ready for it to be over...

Lord, he didn't know what was going on. Keeping his mouth shut was the smartest idea.

"We're great. Having a blast." He thought that through a little harder and hurried to add, "Actually, we're slaving night and day. You know, it's been totally exhausting. I might need to have a bit of a holiday when I get home."

Walker chuckled. "Ass."

"Bro. You should've seen the size of the steak I was forced to eat last night."

"Because Silver Stone's honour depended on it?"

"Pretty much." His phone buzzed. "Got another call. Chat later."

"Break a leg."

Luke switched lines, eyes widening as he spotted the name on the call display. Arabian Treasures. That was Timothy Carlyn's spread.

The man got straight to the point. "You have time for a coffee?"

"Of course. Where would you like to meet?"

Timothy gave him directions. Luke hung up with the sense of fairytale magic stealing over him. For scoring them an invitation to this event, Bertram was not getting a bottle of the good stuff, he was getting a case.

Luke double-checked in the mirror before heading to his meeting, hurrying to the main floor and keeping an eye out for Kelli. Not that she needed checking up on, but it would give him a kick to see her hobnobbing with Mrs. Petrie again.

Timothy Carlyn rose to his feet and shook Luke's hand, but his gaze drifted. "I hoped Kelli would be with you."

Something a little dark and dangerous slid into his gut before Luke could choke it off. "She's with the ladies. Is that a problem?"

Carlyn gestured to the edge of the room. Comfortable overstuffed leather seats were arranged on either side of a low table that held a coffee pot and a tray of goodies. "Not at all. I just wanted you to know she's always welcome. I don't believe in keeping women shuttered off when we talk business."

As an excuse, his explanation made some sense, but it was also strange considering they weren't really here to talk business. Unless they were—

Luke gave up trying to second-guess.

Carlyn was the ultimate professional, bringing the conversation around to a discussion of recent Silver Stone bloodlines that were showing great strength. Luke fell into data and breeding plans, and things were going smoothly until Carlyn turned the topic.

Back on Kelli.

"So it's just a recent thing, your engagement?"

Luke's spine stiffened. "Very."

Grey eyes examined him before the man glanced out the

window, coffee held in mid-air. "Weren't you engaged to Miss Talisman for a number of years?"

A blunt question after everyone else had inched around this topic. Still, it wasn't something Luke needed to hide. "We were, but we called it off in August. It was mutual, and we're still friends."

"And now you're with Kelli." Timothy put his cup down. "Relax, son. I'm not accusing you of anything. I find it interesting that Kelli's been at Silver Stone for a long time, and you're just now discovering what a good match you are."

"Sometimes it's hard to see things that are right before our eyes," Luke admitted with complete honesty.

Something in his tone must have made that clear because Carlyn nodded slowly. "You know anything about Kelli's family? She reminds me of someone."

That was a shot in the dark. Luke opened his mouth then closed it.

Damn. He didn't know *anything* about Kelli's family. No way was he was going to confess that, though.

He scrambled for something else to say. "Not sure where there might be a connection. Who does she remind you of? Maybe we can figure out if there's a reason."

Timothy suddenly straightened, fidgeting with his coat. "Oh, it was just a random thought. Nothing to worry about. I'll think about it a bit more. See if I can't figure it out on my own."

The other man stood abruptly, catching Luke unawares.

He had to scramble to his feet as Timothy offered a farewell handshake. "Sorry, have to run. Forgot I was expecting a call."

"No problem," Luke assured him.

But Timothy Carlyn was already gone, the square cut of his shoulders ramrod straight as he rapidly marched away.

Luke watched him go, thoroughly confused, and now thoroughly curious.

Why had he never asked Kelli about her family before?

13

By the time Saturday came to a close, it was late. Jack and Diane were curled up by the fire, which meant she and Luke had retreated to their bedroom.

They sat on the bed, and she finally got to tell Luke all the things she'd chatted about with Sadie Petrie. Luke was quiet as she shared, but he nodded at all the right places.

Then he turned out the lights and made love to her, teasing and touching until she squirmed with desire. Sexual satisfaction stole in and wrapped her up as tightly as the grip he used to hold her against his body.

The next two days passed quickly, and Kelli should have felt exhausted. Truth was, between the excitement and the sex, she was running on sheer adrenaline.

It's not as if she hadn't worked around the clock before, but she didn't want to miss a thing.

Monday she and Luke joined the Petries for dinner. Joseph Petrie apologized for monopolizing them, but Kelli didn't mind. Sadie was a hoot, and neither of the couple blinked an eye when she ordered a steak the size of Luke's then stole a few slices off his plate to boot.

They were back up in the room when Diane announced all four of them were going dancing for the evening. Kelli was tempted to leap at Luke with a squeal of delight.

Instead she patted his cheek mischievously. "Told you we needed our jeans."

Jack laughed. Diane pulled him from the room, but none of them wasted any time before regrouping and heading downstairs.

"This isn't a part of the hotel that's been booked off for the gala and our all-inclusive setup," Jack warned them. "It's the regular hotel pub, but it sounds as if they draw a good crowd."

"So it's not an open bar." Kelli shrugged. "Not a problem. I don't want to drink, I want to dance."

The place was strangely packed for a resort hidden in the mountains. When she said something about it to Luke, he shrugged.

His arm was draped around her shoulders as they made their way into the crowded room. "There are a lot of staff working places like the Palisade. I imagine when they get time to kick up their heels, it's nice to not have to travel far."

She glanced around, eyeing the couples already on the floor. Checking out which guys looked as if they could keep the beat.

Utter shock struck when Luke pulled her forward with him, and for a second she just stood there, staring at him in confusion.

He laughed as he slipped their fingers together, using the hand on her hip to pull her against his body. "Were you really looking for a dance partner?"

"Old habits die hard," she offered as an excuse. "Maybe we can't dance," Kelli teased.

The heat in Luke's eyes deepened. "Darlin', we've been dancing. We'll do just fine."

He whirled her, and he was right. There was no awkwardness, no uneasy steps. It was as if they were made for each other. Kelli relaxed into his arms and let him take control.

They'd gone around for a half-dozen songs before he motioned to the side. "Break time."

"I need some water," she agreed, "and a pit stop."

He pointed toward the ladies' room. She went up on her toes and kissed his cheek before heading off. A quick glance over her shoulder showed he was staring at her ass, a smile stretching across his face. Kelli wiggled her hips a little harder as she sashayed away.

Top of the world, that's where she was. Absolutely top of the world.

She stepped into the bathroom, whistling happily then jerking to a stop as a woman snapped back from her position in front of the mirror.

Warning signals went off in Kelli's head. She moved slowly, ignoring the bathroom stalls as if the only reason she was in the room was to check her makeup—which was a bit of a stretch considering she wasn't wearing much more than lip balm.

Her charade must have been convincing enough because the other woman didn't bolt.

Kelli played a little with her hair, tucking a few lose strands behind her ears before oh-so-casually glancing in the mirror to check out her neighbour. The woman had been cleaning up tears. Possibly applying extra makeup to a bruise.

This was bullshit. While she had to say something, Kelli knew to move warily. "Sometimes it's easier to ask a stranger for help than your friends."

The woman blinked, startling like one of the deer in the snow field earlier in the week. "What?"

Kelli turned slowly, lifting a finger toward her own face. "Sometimes accidents happen, and I get that. But sometimes we need a helping hand." She took a deep breath and tried to make eye contact. Leaning over to make herself look as small and unintimidating as possible. "You need a hand, honey?"

The woman hesitated as she looked Kelli over. Her mouth opened and closed.

Then finally, the smallest dip of her chin. "I could use a ride home."

Kelli's mind raced. A ride was definitely doable. If she had to pay for a taxi, so be it. "Is that going to be enough to keep you safe?"

Another thoughtful nod. "I've got roommates. They won't let anything else happen. I just met him a few weeks ago, and he was really nice until today."

"They're all really nice until they aren't. The assholes, that is." Kelli moved in closer. "There are good ones out there. Hey, I'm Kelli."

"Gina."

"Is he out in the bar waiting for you?"

Gina nodded.

"How much longer do you think he'll wait before he comes looking for you?"

The woman shrugged. "He's drinking. No idea."

Okay. This might go easier than she thought. "Can you stay here while I get some help?"

The woman's eyes widened. "Don't call the cops."

Sometimes that was the right thing to do, but Kelli was more worried about getting Gina out of there in one piece. "I won't, but I have to get my fiancée. He's one of the good ones I told you about. We'll get you home."

Gina hesitated, or at least she did until she glanced in the mirror. She grimaced. "Don't know why you're willing to help me, but I'm not about to turn you down."

Kelli nodded quickly. "Stay here. Hide in a stall if you want. I'll come back and say my name when we're ready. I'll be as quick as I can."

She rushed back to the dance floor, looking around frantically for Luke. He and their friends were standing to one side, and she slipped up to him, heart pounding.

Luke slid an arm around her, his smile fading. "What's wrong?"

"I need your help."

~

AN HOUR later they were on their way home, and Luke was wrestling with the strangest emotions.

Jack and Diane had helped get the woman out of the bar without her date spotting her, then Kelli had sat in the middle seat of Luke's truck, her arm around Gina, as he drove the three of them to Gina's place in Canmore.

They'd both insisted on making sure Gina's roommates were home before leaving. There'd been a flurry of hugs from all the grateful women after they'd escorted Gina up the front steps of her townhouse.

Minutes after getting back in the truck, Kelli sent a quick text off to Diane to let her know everything had gone well, then read the reply out loud.

"She says 'Thank God. Drive safe, and we'll see you in the morning. We're calling it a night.'" Kelli curled against Luke's side, fingers wrapped around his biceps as she leaned her head against him. "Not the ending to the evening I expected."

Maybe that was why such a struggle was going on inside his head. Luke was proud of Kelli for having helped someone and kind of choked up that this time she'd been honest enough to come and get him.

But a big part of him was scared shitless that stepping into dangerous situations was so high on her radar. She was like a magnet for trouble that could get her seriously hurt someday.

He caught her fingers in his and lifted them to his mouth, pressing a kiss to her knuckles. "You did a good thing."

"If the jerk who hit her doesn't come back. If she's strong enough to tell him to leave her alone." Kelli took a deep breath and let it out slowly. They sat in the darkness, the headlights shining on the road as it twisted back into Kananaskis Country.

This wasn't a conversation he wanted to have while he needed to concentrate on the road. So he pressed a quick kiss to her temple and laid his arm around her shoulders, holding her against him as they sat in silence.

Comfortable, and yet not. They didn't need noise to fill the space, not with the years they'd spent working together. But there were so many questions Luke wanted to ask. Things he wanted to understand better than he ever had before.

He kept her tucked against his side as they made their way back up to the penthouse suite. Jack had left the fire place going, and warmth hovered on the air.

Luke stroked a finger down her cheek. "Want a drink?"

She reached for him, tugging him toward the floor. "I need to relax."

He helped her settle on the soft carpet in front of the flames but evaded her hands. "I can help with that. Back in a second."

By the time he returned from the bathroom she was staring into the fire, a sad look in her eyes.

He slid across from her, pulling off her socks and watching as her brows rose toward her hairline.

"What are you doing?"

He lifted the bottle of body lotion he'd taken from the bathroom counter. "Foot rub?"

"Oh, God. Yes, please." She reached over her head and grabbed a pillow off the couch. She jammed it behind her back so she could slouch more comfortably.

Her eyes closed as he pressed his thumb along her arch. Over and over in smooth glides, he massaged her heels and toes, and they sat in silence except for the fake crackle of the fireplace.

What to ask? Because this was going to be an uncomfortable conversation no matter what.

She broke the silence. "I'm glad you were there to help me. I mean, to help Gina."

"Me too, but it worries me," he admitted softly. "I know there are a lot of bad situations out there, Kelli, and I'm glad we could help Gina. But if I hadn't been around, you still would've helped her. Yes?"

She twisted to meet his eyes. "Yes."

"Even if it meant you might get hurt?"

"If I won't help because I'm too afraid, what if nobody else steps in? What then, Luke?"

There was no answer to that, because she was right.

But so was he for being scared shitless that this was going to end poorly someday. "You've gotten seriously hurt before, haven't you? Last summer."

She barely hesitated before nodding. "When you flipped out so hard about me having some bruises. I got in the middle, and he wasn't very happy."

"I still want to know who that was," he growled. "But since you won't tell me *who*, will you tell me why?"

She curled up and put her hands into his, speaking with utter conviction. "Because it's the right thing to do."

He shook his head. "That's not good enough. I mean, I agree it is something that needs to be done, but why are you fighting this battle?"

She went motionless, which was eerie when it came to Kelli. Her fingers tangled around his as if she were centering herself with his touch. "My mom."

It was Luke's turn to hold his breath. Waiting until she was ready.

She licked her lips nervously before she gave a small nod, as if she'd gathered her courage. "I don't talk about her much." He made a noise, and she sighed in exasperation. "Okay, fine. I've *never* talked about her. I don't think she was very brave, or very smart when it comes down to it. And yet I don't know the whole story, so who am I to judge?"

"Was she with someone abusive?" he asked quietly. *My God.* He slipped his fingers under her chin and lifted until her gaze met his. "Did someone hurt *you*?"

"I left before anyone could smack me around. And I wanted her to leave too, but she refused." Kelli looked concerned. "You're not going to freak out, are you? Or go off the deep end?"

"Is there a reason you think I'll do either of those things?"

She wrinkled her nose. "Before I tell you anything else shocking, I'll finish answering your first question. I think that's why it bugs me so much I feel like I have to do something. Fifteen-year-old me couldn't save my mom, but maybe I can save someone else."

Too damn brave and too damn strong for her own good. "I have no problem with you saving the world as long as you let me help you. You need to stay safe, Kelli. Promise me."

She nodded.

And then something else sank in.

"Fifteen?" Luke looked her over. "Explain."

"I left. He wasn't my dad. The guy mom was living with brought home fake ID for me. He said it was so I could grab beer and smokes for him and his buddies, but I didn't trust him. And I didn't trust the way his friends who were hanging around were eyeing me—I doubt they had my best interests at heart, if you know what I mean."

"So you left."

"It seemed the safest option." For the first time since she started talking, Kelli looked guilty. "I kind of emptied all their wallets and took the money in the freezer when I left. It wasn't that much, but it was enough with what I'd already saved to get me to Silver Stone."

Wait. Luke's brain skittered off-line again. "You were *fifteen* when you showed up at Silver Stone? You're bullshitting me."

Her lips twitched. "God, I remember that day so clearly. You guys were branding calves. Total chaos because some of the hands from Uncle Frank's who were supposed to show up, didn't. It was perfect because all I had to do was get up on a ride and start working. Before we were done, Ashton was ready to adopt me."

Luke was flabbergasted. "Okay, now that you've completely thrown me for a loop with all of this, help me with the math. How old are you?"

"Twenty-three. Nearly twenty-four," she pointed out. "Which is only three years younger than you thought I was, so don't make a fuss about the age difference between us. If that's what you were going to do, don't bother."

"Does anybody else know this?" he asked.

She shook her head then nodded once, reluctantly. "Tansy does. Nobody else, because they didn't need to, and I'm not even sure why I'm telling you except—" She took a deep breath then adjusted position to crawl over him. Straddling his hips so she sat in his lap cuddled up close. Her palms cupped his cheeks. "It seems right to tell you."

"I can't believe I never asked about your family."

"I didn't volunteer," she pointed out.

That didn't ease the guilt, or the stupidity of his non-actions.

"Mom left home just after graduating from high school. She said her parents were a drag. Always bossing her around and not approving of her friends or the guys she liked." Kelli snorted, hard. "Considering what I know about my dad—which is that he left when she got pregnant—and the shitheads she was with later, her parents were probably not wrong."

"So you've never met your grandparents?"

"Nope. I don't think they know I exist. Mom had dual citizenship, and I know her folks lived in the US. She only told me a few things about them, usually when she was drunk or out of it."

Kelli had slipped her fingers into his hair and was stroking him gently. Over and over like a touchstone.

"I'm sorry." He said it softly, but he felt it to his very toes. She'd deserved more.

She shook her head. "How I grew up and the fact I left when I did is not really a sad thing. It's not like when you lost your parents. My mom made choices. They were wrong ones, but she was still in control. Your mom and dad didn't choose what happened to them."

"I don't think we have to rate how sad the tragedies in our lives are for them to be devastating," Luke pointed out. "But I'm glad you told me. I'm honoured that you trust me, and I won't share it around. I promise."

She leaned in and kissed him, lips soft and delicate against his. And while it would've been easy to take that and turn up the heat, it didn't seem right.

They certainly had the chemistry, and if they'd kept fooling around it would have been natural and logical. But he didn't push, keeping the kiss gentle, and after a few moments Kelli broke the contact between their mouths and leaned in, hugging him tightly.

He stroked her, undoing her braids and pulling his fingers through her hair until it lay over her back in a soft curtain. Tender touches that connected them as intimately as being inside her body.

They sat there, holding each other, until Kelli was on the verge of falling asleep in his arms. He brought her to the bedroom and tucked her into her Spiderman pyjamas before crawling into bed and wrapping himself around her.

Whatever mistakes he'd made in his past, it felt as if he'd turned the corner. He still wasn't sure how Kelli had ended up at Silver Stone of all places. That would be a story for another time, but fate had brought her there, and now after so many years, fate had brought her into his arms.

Where she belonged—

—and wasn't that thought enough to rock him off his logical, orderly, simple feet?

Yet it only made sense. Having her beside him felt perfect.

Maybe it was wild to be thinking this way when she'd only suggested a fling, but what was growing between them was far deeper than a fling. This was *right*.

He wasn't going to turn away a gift straight from the hands of fate.

14

The next couple of days passed in a blur. There were pockets of activity tucked between quiet moments chatting with all the gala attendees. Kelli was fascinated and entertained and exhilarated and exhausted.

The last one was because of the sex. Oh my God, the *sex*.

Luke had woken her up both nights. Said it was her fault because she'd kicked out and woken him first, and him using his fingers to drive her to a fever pitch was his way of getting even.

Middle-of-the-night sex was the kind of justice she had zero problems with.

The morning sex had been pretty spectacular as well. She liked waking up warm and cozy in bed with him, his arousal thickening against her as she wiggled in tight.

He'd teased and tormented until she trembled, and then tucked her under him and took her against the mattress hard, driving into her until she was ready to scream. She'd had to bury her face against his chest to stop from waking the entire hotel—yeah, she was going to miss this when it was over.

The sweet little moments of affection outside of the bedroom, though, were the ones that set her heart going like a freight train. The way he'd tug her against his side, or would casually catch her fingers in his as they spoke with other attendees...

Kelli warned herself to enjoy every minute but not to read anything into it other than two people who, while definitely compatible, simply shared a common goal. They'd moved well beyond their initial problem of Luke's overstepping propriety. She didn't think anyone suspected his *significant other* mistake. She forced herself to feel very happy about that for Silver Stone's sake.

Heading back to reality was going to suck.

There were other things to be happy about for Silver Stone. She'd been able to chat about how fantastic the operation was with everyone by that point. Probably ad nauseam, if she was honest.

The final full day arrived, and she and Diane went to breakfast alone, the guys having taken off to go cross-country skiing or some such nonsense.

They shared their meal with the owners of another smaller stable who'd been invited to the gala. The young couple were hoping to take their family operation to the next level. They were in the process of shifting their family to the next level as well, as the woman was a good six months pregnant and her husband was in charge of the two-year-old who'd been strapped tightly in a high chair to keep him in place.

Kelli grinned as the young family left, and she reached across the table for her third and what should be her final breakfast doughnut. Diane poured more coffee into her cup and sat back, gazing over the brim thoughtfully as she sipped.

Her new friend seemed intent on focusing anywhere in particular rather than on Kelli's face.

"Is something wrong? Am I wearing my breakfast?" she asked.

Diane offered a quick headshake. "I was thinking how sad it is we have to go back to reality tomorrow."

Now there was a sobering thought. Her idyllic fantasy getaway was drawing to an end. Still—

"There are things to look forward to back home, as well. I'm eager to try that technique you suggested on Chili Pepper."

"I'll have to get Jack to bring me up to Silver Stone so I can see you working with her myself."

Wouldn't that be exciting? "You guys are always welcome."

—horror slammed into Kelli as she realized her mistake.

It was the same one she'd given Luke hell for, in a way, which meant she should have seen it coming. It was her own damn fault for agreeing to the deception in the first place.

Jack and Diane would come to visit Silver Stone, which was wonderful and fantastic. And considering what Kelli now knew about the things that Diane planned for the future, it could mean wonderful things for the ranch.

But it also meant they'd expect to see her and Luke *together*.

The idea churned everything inside and shredded Kelli's happiness to ribbons.

She scrambled for something to say that didn't involve blurting out the truth, because, although that's what she wanted to share, she couldn't. Not without talking to Luke first.

So she held her tongue. But her doughnut didn't taste nearly as sweet. It had turned to sawdust on her tongue, and it was nearly impossible to swallow around the knot in her throat.

Her new friend—the sweet woman Kelli had been deceiving, now that she comprehended her folly—leaned forward, concern in Diane's eyes.

Kelli tightened her grip on her cup. Had she accidentally said something without meaning to?

"Tonight's the big party," Diane began slowly. "And I happened to find out something I think you should know."

The sickening sensation in Kelli's gut was a firm reminder why she stuck with telling the truth. Her imagination was working overtime coming up with horrifying revelations.

Once again, her face must've given her away because Diane clicked her tongue reassuringly. "Oh, honey. I didn't mean to scare you. It's nothing terrible, but I wanted to warn you ahead of time that the Talismans will be at the event. My father mentioned it to me because there's a business item I'm supposed to ask Sean Talisman about, and it's the only opportunity this week."

Relief rushed in. "So, Penny will be there—"

"I assume so."

Damn, this was the best news, relatively speaking, considering all the other disasters Kelli had been imagining. "It's really not a problem."

"So you said before, and I believe you," Diane said quickly. "It's just that I know if it were *me* heading to an event where *Jack's* ex-fiancée was about to make an appearance—not that he has one, but you know what I'm saying—I'd want to know."

Kelli nodded. "Being forewarned she'll be there saves me from a few awkward moments. Thanks for telling me, but really, everything's fine."

Diane pulled apart her doughnut, tucking a tidbit in her mouth as she eyed Kelli closely. "You've got a dress?"

"One that will knock your socks off," Kelli said proudly. "My girlfriends hooked me up, because like we talked about before, I'm more of a jeans-and-flannel girl."

"Clothes don't make a woman or a man." Although, Diane was tapping her fingers on the table as she said it, and a mischievous smile was spreading. "But fine feathers are nice, and there's nothing like the right knock-em-dead outfit to make a woman feel like a million dollars." She checked her watch. "The schedule is light today, what with the formal dance this evening. I'm going to call the spa and sneak us in this afternoon for some pampering."

Kelli hesitated.

"My treat," Diane added. She lifted a hand as Kelli tried to protest. "You'd be doing me a favour. We'll get to spend more time together, and frankly, even though you're too nice to want to rub it in with Penny, I'm a little baser. I've seen the way Luke looks at you on an average day. I want to watch her face when she sees how he responds to you all done up."

Damn, Luke needed to win an acting award or something if he was pulling off the "hooked on her" thing that hard.

Kelli didn't say anything about that part, though. She was working up to accept the offer, not because of Penny per se, but because of that frothy gown, and how much her girlfriends had gone out of their way to help her.

Hanna's brimming cup of happiness in finding Brad—maybe some of that magic had spilled over, because getting to be with Luke this past week was a memory Kelli would always cherish.

She offered Diane a nod. "I'd love to be Cinderella to your fairy godmother, but I'll warn you now, I'm not very keen on makeup."

The other woman slid out from the table. She waited for Kelli to join her before wrapping an arm around Kelli's waist and guiding her from the room. "You let me worry about that. Fairy godmothers have a way with magic."

The guys had returned, and the four of them spent the rest of the morning and lunch together before Diane whisked Kelli off to be buffed and polished. Her nails were done, and her hair was trimmed. When she protested the fancy up-do Diane ordered, her friend stopped dead, planting her hands on her hips to better give her the evil eye.

"You are *not* wearing your hair in braids," Diane told her firmly. "They are perfect for you and ninety-nine percent of the tasks you do. And if I looked cute in braids, I would use them too, but not tonight. Tonight I'm going to let them tame my curls, so you are getting fancied up as well."

"I like your hair," Kelli told her honestly.

Diane tugged one of the long spirals, and they both smiled as it bounced back.

"It's alive and full of energy. It suits you. I'm just not the fancy type," Kelli insisted.

Diane's eyes lit up, but she stayed bossy. "Give me your phone."

Kelli wasn't sure what was going on, but she pulled it out and opened it up.

Diane typed rapidly. Kelli assumed it was in search for a hairstyle to suggest, although why she wasn't using her own phone—

A moment later, the familiar sound of a text message pinged.

Diane read the screen then passed the phone back with a gleam of satisfaction in her eyes. "See? We agree."

Messenger was open and there was a text to *and* from Tansy.

Diane had written first: *hey. This is Diane, and I'm with Kelli. She says you're one of her BFFs, so help me out and tell her she can't wear braids to the formal dance.*

Tansy: *Hi, Diane. <3 for taking care of my girl.*

Tansy: *Hey, Kelli? Don't be an ass, listen to Diane. You'll make Hanna cry if you don't do that dress justice. Also—pictures or it never happened.*

Which is why an hour later Kelli was working hard to keep a smile on her face because Diane had gone all-out in charge and then had the guts to refuse to let Kelli watch whatever it was the hairdresser was doing to her.

The gleam in Diane's eye got brighter and brighter as Kelli struggled to not fidget like a two-year-old.

"That's perfect," Diane finally told the hairdresser. "I'll take her upstairs so I can do her makeup."

The chair turned back to the mirror, and Kelli spotted her reflection for the first time. She swore softly. "Is that really me?"

Diane stepped behind the chair, her hair pulled back in a sleek bun with a gorgeous brightly coloured half-turban wrapped around it. "Our guys are not going to know what hit them."

Kelli, lifting her hand to the ringlets hanging on either side of her temples. It wasn't something she was going to fuss with every day, but it was good to know that she cleaned up nice. "It looks good. Thank you, Diane."

Her friend held up a finger, her phone in her hand. "Hey, darlin'. We're done with our primping, but we need to get our makeup and dresses on. You boys dressed up yet?"

Diane had set her phone to speaker, and Jack's deep tones carried clearly on the air. "Nearly ready. You want me to get him out of here?"

"You read my mind, lovely man. We'll meet you at the ball."

A hearty chuckle carried over the line. "What're you up to, woman?"

"Good trouble," Diane promised. "Now, skedaddle."

He blew her a kiss then hung up.

Diane flashed her a grin. "Come on, Cinderella. We have a little more work to do before storming the castle."

~

THE WEEK HAD BEEN AMAZING, but as it came to a close, Luke was tempted to ignore the final event and curl up in front of the fireplace with Kelli.

The only reason he hadn't was because she actually seemed excited by the idea of the fancy ball, and by this point he was getting more entertainment out of watching her than the sheer pleasure of their indulgent getaway.

He ignored the glasses of wine on the table and grabbed a longneck instead, twisting to observe the growing crowd. "It's going to be a shock to the system heading home," he admitted to Jack.

"Don't kid yourself," Jack replied. "You're just as eager as I am to get back to find out what's been going on while we've been gone. There's something about being in the field that does a man good."

"Amen to that."

They clinked bottles, grinning at each other.

Music played softly in the background, and a few people were already on the dance floor. There was another thing to look forward to, Luke reminded himself. Dancing offered a reason to have Kelli in his arms, and he was grateful.

Getting horizontal with her was amazing. Having her against him, or close by and just talking had turned out to be nearly as sweet.

"We're thinking about having you come south in May." Jack dropped the bomb like it was nothing. Luke wiped beer from the side of his mouth as he tried to stay calm. "Want you to take a look at what we've got that might work with any of the bloodlines you're developing."

Luke caught Jack by the hand and shook it gratefully. "We'd be delighted."

"No guarantees yet." Jack seemed reluctant to point that out. "But you and Kelli have impressed the hell out of Diane. She's not an easy sell."

"She's a good businesswoman. No expectations, but we'd sure appreciate the chance to work closer with you."

"Luke?"

The familiar female voice had the bubbles of excitement in his belly fading far too quickly.

Jack's eyes widened slightly in the second before Luke pivoted to find Penny Talisman standing before him.

Her parents were farther behind her, pacing into the room. Sean nodded briefly as he met Luke's gaze. Then he ignored him, sliding forward to shake hands with Timothy Carlyn.

Luke pulled himself together and focused on the woman in front of him. "Penny. How've you been?"

She shrugged, smoothing back her long blonde hair and tucking it behind her ear. Everything exactly in place. "Keeping busy, same as usual. My father has me dealing with the European market. The contacts I made this last summer are turning out to be very profitable."

"Good for you."

She looked uncomfortable, reaching around him to introduce herself to Jack.

Luke probably should've done that. But then again, he didn't really feel like it. He didn't feel like doing her any favours, or making the effort to be rude, or...anything. He was pretty much not registering on the emotional scale when it came to her. Which was interesting.

He glanced at his watch and wondered exactly when the girls were going to show up. He debated sending Kelli a text to warn her Penny was there, but before he could act, a slim man in a very expensive suit marched up to join them.

Luke didn't recognize the stranger, but when the man stopped next to Penny and grabbed her hand, Luke raised a brow.

It *wasn't* jealousy. All he felt for Penny was a lingering business interest because of their ranches' continuing interaction.

Still, Penny's cheeks flushed. She pulled herself together to introduce the man. "Dimitri Zabou. From Italy."

"And now from here," he said with a whisper of an accent, lifting Penny's hand to his mouth and kissing her knuckles as he stared into her eyes. "Penny and I are engaged."

Oh, *really*? Luke was doing some math and coming up with intriguing information.

Dimitri excused himself. "Your father promised to introduce me to someone. Come join us as soon as you can, *Cara Mia*."

Jack wandered off after offering Luke a particularly

meaningful glance. Penny wavered, unsteady on her elegant heels in a way he'd never seen in all their years together.

He glanced toward the door, wondering again where the hell Kelli was. "Congratulations. I wish you and Dimitri well."

Happily, he meant it. It was good to feel no lingering animosity toward her.

Penny slid sideways to get his attention. "This might sound stupid, but I wanted to say thank you. Thank you for helping us come to our senses and calling off our engagement."

He shrugged. "You're welcome."

She rushed on, fidgeting on the spot as if she were eager to leave but determined to have her say. "I'm glad you're with Kelli. I'm glad to know you have someone who makes you happy. Because I know I wasn't it. And the situation might look bad, but I really am in love with Dimitri. Our relationship is different than what you and I had. Maybe that's why it's so good to see you've found the same thing. With Kelli."

"You can tell that from just five minutes and a couple lines of conversation?" He didn't mean the comment to come out so blunt, but so be it.

Her lips twisted into a smile. Something far more genuine than he remembered seeing over all their years together. "I could tell from the first minute. You're a lot happier than I've ever seen you, Luke. And I'm glad. I wish you the best."

Penny laid her fingers on top of his arm and stepped closer, leaning in to kiss his cheek. She could've vanished, because at that moment, the doors opened and Kelli walked in.

Lights shimmered off her cream-coloured dress. Like usual, her hair was pulled back from her face, but this time instead of the long length lying over her shoulder in a braid, some magic held it high on her head like a crown.

Their gazes met, and he couldn't look away. It wasn't only that she was beautiful, though she was. So much happiness shone in her eyes, his kneecaps turned to jelly as he walked forward to join her.

She moved slowly, sliding across the floor as if she were sneaking up on a newborn foal. Her hips swayed under the dress, fabric sparkling as she moved. The neckline swooped downward, lying in a half circle that exposed the top swells of her breasts. Demure and yet sexy as sin.

They met in the middle of the room, and he caught her fingers in his. "I'd kiss you, but I don't want to mess you up."

Kelli grinned. "I like it when you mess me up, but yeah, considering how long it took Diane to put on my lipstick, maybe you should hold back for a minute."

It would take a lot more willpower than she might realize. "You look incredible."

She twirled on the spot, the skirt flaring from her thighs, her cream-coloured cowboy boots the only somewhat-familiar part of her outfit.

"It feels weird, and yet really, really good." She turned back and smoothed a hand up his lapels. "And wow. Shiny man."

He pulled out his phone and slid an arm around her. "Smile," he prompted.

She laughed and leaned against him as he took a selfie.

"Hold still," someone else ordered, lifting a huge camera to indicate what was going on. "I'm taking official shots for the gala."

Luke put his phone away, and they posed for a bit before the man handed them a card. Luke slipped it into his pocket before guiding Kelli to the dance floor.

Holding her against his body as they slid into a slow dance was near perfection.

"Did I see Penny?" Kelli asked.

He couldn't take his eyes off her lips. "I guess."

She laughed, the sound seeming to roll all the way up from her toes before bursting over both of them like bright sunshine. "Good answer."

"Not that I want to spend a lot of time talking about her, but FYI, she's engaged to someone she met this past summer."

Kelli's eyes widened then anger rolled across her face.

"Shush. Don't look so indignant. She and I are over and done. I just thought I should let you know."

"She's really lucky you're not the vindictive type," Kelli said.

"She's lucky you believe me when I say it's okay, because I'm sure you would have made her life hell in my defense, wouldn't you, my wild woman?"

Kelli growled, but her smile was back as she covertly rocked against him in a way that had to be designed to blow his mind and shred his self-control.

They danced, trading off as others came in to steal her from him. He took his turn with the other women, the wives and daughters, but through it all he couldn't keep his gaze off Kelli.

He'd started their week unthinkingly, but somewhere in there, the magic had happened. The blinkers had been taken off, and he'd finally figured out what was there all along.

Kelli truly was perfect for *him*, not just for Silver Stone.

As the dance continued, cameras clicked. Conversations drifted from general to more specific, invitations were hinted at, and Luke knew it was a turning point for his entire life.

15

Kelli had never really thought in detail about what happened to Cinderella that night after she'd left the ball.

Oh, she knew about the escaping-down-the-stairs business and losing the shoe. Even though fairytales hadn't been a huge part of her repertoire growing up, she'd read enough to Caleb's girls. While Disney played it down, Kelli was fairly certain that the hours right after the ball had involved a ton of tears and regret that the beautiful adventure was over.

Those emotions were in her future as well, but as Luke led her into their bedroom she pushed aside the impending sadness and focused on here and now.

She'd been a princess tonight. Something she'd never expected or longed for, but damn, once in her life, the evening had been truly magical.

Tomorrow was back to reality, but tonight she would cling to the make-believe world and let Luke pull her into his arms again in the privacy of the darkened room.

He hummed, one of Walker's songs, if Kelli recognized it properly, as the two of them danced in their bare feet on the soft carpet in front of the window. Light spilled over them, sparkles reflecting every now and then off the dress.

His hands held her so firmly. She rested her head against his chest and sighed happily. "I had a wonderful time. Thank you so much for bringing me."

He chuckled. "We both fit in well. I knew you would."

"I don't know if this really is me," Kelli teased, changing position so she could slide her hands around his neck, swaying against his body. "I'm a ranch hand, not a debutante."

"You're *Kelli*. You're strong, you're beautiful, and I can't fucking wait to be inside you again."

A zing shot through her entire system. "Okay."

The magic of the evening continued, and Kelli grabbed on to it with both hands as firmly as she held his shoulders.

Luke kissed her, and her mind fled. Nothing anchored her to the ground except his hands roving over her, curving under her butt before he slid one hand up the bare skin of her back and into her hair.

His lips teased the corner of her mouth before drifting across her cheek to her earlobe. "Thank God I get to muss you up now. I couldn't decide all evening if I wanted to strip you out of that dress, or just lift the skirt and fuck you right then and there."

A shudder struck, and another, as he sucked her earlobe into his mouth and all the oxygen in the room vanished. "That might have been awkward in the middle of the dance floor."

He hummed, turning her to face the window. The darkness outside turned the glass into a mirror, reflecting their image back as he continued to rock their hips together. The thick length of his erection teased against her.

"Let's pretend," he whispered. "Say you want me."

She lifted a hand, using the image before her to help drape it around his neck. The feel of him against her back, a wall of desire.

Part of the truth spilled out. "Desperately."

What she held back was the *always and forever* parts of the confession, because no way was she messing up something so appallingly beautiful as tonight.

He kissed her neck. His hands settled firmly on her hips for a second before he gathered the fabric with his fingers, inching her skirt higher as he watched over her shoulder and slowly revealed more of her legs.

Bit by bit until his fingertips brushed across her thighs, and a strange gasping noise escaped her lips.

A happy hum rumbled at her back. "So fucking sexy."

Oh lordy.

His hand slid between her legs and cupped her sex, and the noise of approval got louder. "You're wet, Kelli. I can feel it through your panties."

He pressed a finger against the fabric and teased between her folds. White lightning struck as he made deliberate contact with her clit.

Luke slid one of her shoulder straps off the dress, and the fabric folded in on itself far enough to leave her breast exposed. "God damn. If I'd known you were mostly naked under this, we would've left the room hours ago."

"Anticipation is part of the fun," she teased, wiggling her hips a little harder as she reached back to press a hand over his cock. Squeezing the thick length in her hand.

He pushed aside the gusset of her panties and slid a finger inside. Teasing in and out, just enough sensation to get her body craving more.

Two fingers, now, a little deeper. Kelli widened her stance, clutching his wrist as he worked.

His left hand slid across her chest, palm cradling her naked breast. Lifting and squeezing, hands moving in unison until she wanted desperately to strip everything away and use the enormous bed beside them.

He wouldn't let her retreat. He pushed two fingers deep then stood motionless, locking her in place as she wiggled. "I need you," he warned. "Need to put my cock in you." His fingers pulled out then thrust in again. "Deep inside so you can squeeze the hell out of me."

She pushed against him. "*Yes.*"

His hands vanished, and she whimpered like a puppy abandoned alone in the barn.

But he was moving, reaching between them to unzip and pull his cock free. Covering his shaft with a condom and catching hold of her again as he anchored her against his body with his left hand.

He pulled up the skirt in the back and pushed aside her underwear, and then his cock was at her sex and he was sliding in even as he stared at her face in the reflection before them.

Oh *God*, it felt good.

It felt impossible, his thick length so much more imposing from this angle. He held her high enough her toes barely touched the ground as he bent his knees and thrust the rest of the way in.

"*Luke.*" The word shot from her as she clutched his wrist. He left her unable to do anything except experience. Feel.

Revel in the pleasure he was forcing on her body.

The reflection was dirty enough to make her wild without even trying. But as he pumped into her, so hard that her breasts bounced, his fingers slid over her until he made contact again with her clit.

"Look at us," he ordered. "God damn, look at *you*. You're perfection, pushing back as if you can't get enough of my cock. Like an angel who's been teasing until the devil has come out to fuck you hard."

She moaned, the precipice right there in front of her, between his relentless strokes and the dirty talk.

"Harder," she demanded. "Do it."

Luke lost it. With a roar, he twisted on the spot and planted her belly down on the bed. Her legs hung toward the floor, her body pressed to the mattress. He put his hand in the middle of her back, pinned her in place and let his hips fly. Faster now, spearing deep, his thickness spreading her, tugging the lips of her sex on every drive.

The mattress bounced, and his fingers clutched her hips hard enough to keep her right where she needed to be as an orgasm rolled in and swept her away.

"*Luke...*"

He slammed against her, body covering her like a stallion over a mare as he put his mouth against her neck and damn near bit down.

Aftershocks continued to roll as he came. His cock jerked within her. The fabric of his pants rubbed her naked thighs. Their bodies rocked, breathing erratic. For long minutes after they were done the mattress kept shaking.

He released part of his weight, trapping her, as if he were imprinting himself on her.

Meanwhile, Kelli was storing up every possible memory. At some point magical moments always came to an end, but until the final second she wasn't letting any of it go unappreciated.

"That was damn dirty, and very much appreciated," she whispered.

Luke chuckled, lifting far enough to press a kiss to the back of her neck before rolling away and disengaging. "You look thoroughly debauched for a debutante."

She was too boneless to move. "If that's a job perk, I might have to look into future opportunities more thoroughly."

He trailed his fingers up her thigh, teasing her wet sex. "I'm willing to practice my debauching," he told her. "Just to make sure you have the right skill set. But I'm pretty sure you'll be a superstar no matter what you do."

She forced herself away from his enticing fingers. Rolling on her side she pulled her legs under her. He sat on the edge of the bed and stared, seemingly uncaring that he was completely dressed except for his cock hanging out the open zipper of his dress pants.

And as impressive as that part of him was, his cock was no longer what she was looking at anyway. It was his face—his *eyes* and the contented expression there. Those were things she wanted to memorize. Those were the things she would to miss.

He caught her fingers in his and lifted them to his mouth. "Shower with me?"

Another thing Cinderella would have never turned down. "Start the water, I'll be there in a minute."

He leaned over the bed and pressed a quick kiss to her lips, standing and walking away, his perfect ass shifting under his trousers.

Kelli lay in the moonlight, her heart pounding, while euphoria still blazed through her system. In the midst of that perfection, she searched for the next path she needed to follow. The one that would allow her to retreat, to find safety and a solid place to stand.

The magic had lasted longer than one night, but it was beginning to fade. Soon enough it would be back to Silver Stone and the ordinary, everyday magic they made there.

And Kelli was fine with that. Really, she was. She was glad she'd got to experience for a brief while something far beyond the dreams of a runaway.

She stood and peered at her reflection one last time. A princess? A debutante? The woman before her lifted a hand to her tumbled hair and smiled softly. As Kelli slipped out of the borrowed dress, she said goodbye to the borrowed persona in the mirror.

It was okay. Kelli James, head ranch hand at Silver Stone, was an all-right woman, with a kick-ass set of skills and a whole lot of friends.

The only thing she wouldn't have was Luke Stone.

Not after tonight.

THE BREAKFAST ROOM was full of people. Some hurrying in to grab a final cup of coffee before rushing to the airport. Some moving slower—those who hadn't as much distance to travel, or later flights.

Everyone took an opportunity to say farewell and double-check contact information.

Jack slapped his hand on Luke's shoulder a couple times before squeezing tightly, his bright smile one hundred percent sincere. "You'll hear from me before too long," the man promised, "but I'm pretty sure the girls will be the ones to tell us when and where we'll meet next."

Luke caught him by the hand and gave it an extra squeeze. "Appreciate that, man. And thanks for the shared suite, and for taking such good care of Kelli. Both you and Diane."

"Hey, she's easy to be around. As are you." Jack motioned with his head. "Diane, honey. We need to move."

Diane gave Kelli a big hug then shook her finger in Kelli's face.

Kelli smiled, but she looked a little sad. She was once again clad head to toe in denim, her braids back in place, boots on her feet.

He was so busy staring he nearly fell over when Diane wrapped her arms around him and gave him an enthusiastic hug.

"We'll be in touch," she promised. Then she lowered her voice. "My girl's got something on her mind, but she won't tell me what. Take care of her, okay?"

"That was the plan," he promised.

There was a rush, and then the foyer quieted. He turned to Kelli, who had just finished saying goodbye to Mrs. Petrie, and now stood before the massive fireplace in the waiting area, staring into the flames.

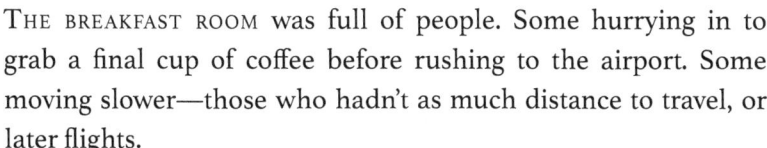

Luke tugged on one of Kelli's braids to get her attention. "We should hit the road too," he told her. "It's clear now, but you never know when that pressure system is going to move in."

Kelli nodded. "I'm ready."

She climbed into a cab, dropping into the passenger seat and putting her travel bag on the seat between them. When she hauled out some paperwork and began going through it, he chuckled then left her to it.

It had been a long week, and he hadn't given her much space to herself.

Luke turned on some music and relaxed, enjoying the easy drive back to the ranch. He worked through a few mental checklists, but even as he did, contentment stole in. Their time at the gala had been a complete success.

His mistake had turned out to be pretty much the best thing he'd ever done.

Tomorrow. Tomorrow they'd sit down and make a joint list of everyone they should follow up with via an email or phone call, but for the next twelve hours he would get them home, have a hot shower then fall into bed. Somewhere in there they would offer the family a hopeful news update, but definitely a shower and bed were first priorities.

Maybe he'd drive straight to his house. They'd have to grab Kelli's things out of her bunk room, but it didn't have to be done right away. No reason why he couldn't throw all their dirty stuff in the laundry at his place.

He looked forward to seeing her in one of his shirts, wandering around his house. Although there was a certain charm to her Spiderman pyjamas.

When they hit the outskirts of Heart Falls, Kelli folded up the work in her lap and packed it away, glancing at him. "Stop at the dry cleaners, please. I should drop off Hanna's dress."

He was a breath away from offering to buy her a duplicate, but something about her face warned him she was too tired for teasing. "Good idea. I'll drop off the things Josiah lent me."

A few minutes later they were back on the road and nearly home.

Kelli twisted toward him with a little of her old enthusiasm back. "Thank you for everything. I really think it went well. Everyone thought Silver Stone sounded fantastic, and I bet the orders are going to start coming in."

He reached around the bag on the seat between them and caught her fingers, rubbing his thumb over her knuckles. "Everyone thought *you* were fantastic. Told you they'd love you."

She made a rude noise. "Yeah, well, it turned out better than I expected, but it's not the kind of setting I want to be in on a regular basis." He was just about to ask if there was anything she absolutely needed from her room when she pointed at the house. "Everyone's here. Did something happen?"

He let go of her hand, suddenly concerned. There were a whole lot of trucks parked outside the house. "Oh my God, what if something's wrong with Tamara?"

They were only a minute away from the house, but Kelli was already texting.

Tension rose as he pulled into the open space beside Walker's truck, releasing as she breathed a sigh of relief. "Tamara's fine. *God*, but I'm going to kill her, though."

"What's going on?"

Kelli pushed open her door, still reading her phone. "She says it's a family meeting. They've been waiting for you."

Fear was replaced with annoyance. "Would have been nice if they could have sent me a heads-up this morning," he grumbled.

He headed toward the back door, pausing after two steps when he realized Kelli wasn't with him. He pivoted to find her marching resolutely down the snowy road, suitcase in hand.

"Hey. Where're you going?"

She stopped, her shoulders visibly stiff even from this distance. "To unpack."

Something was definitely wrong. "You need to come."

Her face tightened. "Luke, it's a *family* meeting. Go. They're waiting for you."

Something snapped. He stomped across the snow to her side and grabbed hold of the suitcase, jerking it from her hand. "What the hell is wrong?"

"Nothing's wrong. I told you, I need to get unpacked, have a shower and get to work."

"Really?"

Kelli looked confused. "Does that sound off?"

"Very fucking off."

Before he could read her the riot act or grab her by the shoulder to shake some sense into her, his name rang out.

They both twirled toward the house where Caleb stood on the back porch. "Hey. Sorry I didn't give you more warning, but it's the only time we could get everybody together. Get up here, we need to talk."

It wasn't as if Luke could complain. Not after having been gone for a week, but talk about shitty timing.

He stuck his hand in the air to acknowledge he'd heard. "Be right there."

"You too, Kelli," Caleb added.

This command made Kelli wilt like a bouquet of daisies left too long in the hot sun. "You sure?" she asked.

Caleb had already turned and headed into the house. Kelli let out a heavy sigh before pushing past Luke and marching toward the house.

He followed after her, holding his tongue. But inside he was wrestling to make sense of the past five minutes.

What the hell had gone wrong?

16

It was the farthest thing from a clean getaway that could have happened.

Kelli walked through the mudroom door, stopping far enough to one side of the entrance to allow Luke to step in as well. Then she realized that was a mistake, because instead of taking off his stuff and heading to join the rest of the family, he stayed beside her, glaring as if he wanted to pick up the conversation she'd been attempting to avoid outside.

She turned her back and slid off her boots, making tracks to a spot closer to Tamara. She stole a cookie off the island as she passed, taking a bite and hoping the calorie rush would give her the energy to get through this chaos.

It was *supposed* to have been simple. She was supposed to have been able to walk away.

Tamara looked her over and nodded briskly. "The holiday did you good."

Kelli opened her mouth then closed it. She glanced at Luke who had just stood after pulling off his boots. He appeared to be one second away from bursting into rain like a storm cloud.

Definitely not the direction she needed to face. She forced a smile and nodded briskly. "I think it was a success. But what's going on?"

Caleb stood, stepping in front of the fireplace. He took his time glancing over the family gathered, which along with Luke included Tamara, Walker and Ivy, and Dustin, who was perched on the back of the couch.

Ashton was there as well, which made Kelli feel a little better instead of being the only non-Stone person in the room.

Luke came and stood beside Kelli, but he folded his arms instead of touching her. She stared at Caleb, working hard to keep from bouncing on her toes.

"I'm glad things went well, and we want to hear all about it, but Tamara and I were talking and realized we need to get things out on the table sooner than later. You all know we've been fighting to get the red off our ledger. It wouldn't take much, but the truth is, it won't take much to send us the other direction, either."

"Is it really that dire?" Ivy asked, her fingers tangled in Walker's where they sat at the very edge of the room.

"Possibly. Like I said, it could go either way. The thing is, some of the measures we can take start us down new paths, and some of those need to happen as early as this spring." Caleb shuffled to the right, reaching down to accept the hand Tamara had extended him. As if he was drawing strength from the contact.

He turned back to his family. "I know we all love Silver Stone, but we need to do what's responsible for the whole family. For all of us, and that means at the end we're all happy with the new direction, if possible."

"Can't live your life by committee," Ashton said bluntly. "And you can rarely make a whole group of people happy when you're changing things up."

"Agreed," Walker said. "But let's lay out what our options are, and we'll take it from there."

Caleb nodded. "Just so you know, Tamara and I talked to Ginny. She shared a few ideas, but she knows what's going on."

"Is she planning on coming back early and getting the CSA gardens running?" Dustin asked. "Because, if we're short on money, I don't mind working double time to make sure we get that going."

Caleb nodded. "Ginny offered, but she's in the middle of an incredible opportunity. If she cancels out of her journeyman experience now, she'll never get another chance. I don't want that for her."

"But what if it means she's got somewhere to come home to," Dustin insisted.

Tamara held up a hand to assure him. "It's on the list, Dustin. Trust me, we're thinking of everything."

Dustin folded his arms across his chest. His expression was far more stubborn than Kelli remembered seeing. It had to be hard, at that point between being a boy and a man, to face the possibility of losing the only home he'd ever known.

"We'll give you the details later," Luke said, "But I feel our income is going to rise after the week in Kananaskis."

"Any orders right now?" Walker asked.

Kelli and Luke exchanged glances but had to shake their heads. "Maybe soon."

"It's on the list," Tamara promised.

Why did that sound as feeble and patronizing as it had when she'd said the same thing to Dustin?

"We have family in the south. If we end up selling Silver Stone, we'll have enough money to buy in with Uncle Frank." Caleb glared as Dustin made a rude noise. "Be civil, or I'll kick your ass out of this room and give you the summary at the end the way we give the little girls."

Dustin looked slightly ashamed at Caleb's reprimand, but it didn't stop him from making a comment. "I'm not going to live with that man."

"Duly noted," Caleb said.

"We might be able to head north," Tamara offered. "With the Coleman family amalgamating, it's possible we might be able to do some sort of buy-in. We wouldn't own land, but we'd still be able to ranch."

Walker was nodding slowly, but he and Ivy had exchanged a glance. "If we end up having to sell Silver Stone, I'll figure out something else to do. Ivy and I will be staying here in Heart Falls to be close with her family."

Dustin swore.

All heads snapped toward him as he rolled off the back of the couch to his feet. Fists smacked against his hips, and he glared around the room as if not sure who to take his frustrations out on. "So that's it. That's the only thing you can think of? Sell the ranch, move away. That's *bullshit*," he snapped.

Caleb opened his mouth, but Ashton's response was far more immediate and direct. The foreman reached out and caught Dustin by the ear, tugging him to one side as if the young man didn't have three inches on him. "You talk like that one more time in front of the ladies, and I don't care that you do think you're an adult. I will wash your mouth out with soap *and* make you clean stalls for a month."

Dustin slammed his mouth shut, his lips compressed into a thin line, but he nodded briefly, and Ashton let go.

Dustin took a cautious step away even as he looked slightly ashamed to meet Tamara's eyes. "We can't sell," he said, his voice thick as if he was fighting tears. "We've *got* to stay together as a family. I promised. Silver Stone is the only connection I have to Mom and Dad."

He took off, darting down the hallway. A moment later the front door opened then slammed closed, and the room fell silent.

Tamara let out a sigh. "He's right. Leaving Silver Stone would mean leaving a lot of memories."

"Good and bad ones, if we're being honest," Luke said. "But I agree with Dustin that we need to do everything we can to try and stay."

More ideas were brought up. Caleb shared an update on where the oil and gas research was at—basically still in limbo, as the unobtrusive testing methods they'd chosen hadn't yielded anything positive yet.

They could sell off some land. They could rent out land. There were options, but none of them were about ranching or making the operation stronger.

"Kelli, you haven't said anything," Tamara pointed out.

Kelli blinked. "Why're you asking me? I'm not family."

An exasperated sound shot from Luke, and he put his hand on her shoulder and tugged her toward him. "You've been here for over eight years. You are so family. And besides, you and I—"

She cut him off, knocking his hand off her shoulder before he could say something he'd later regret. "I might live here, but it doesn't make me *family*."

The look of disbelief in his eyes was brutal. "Answer the damn question."

"Watch your language, Luke Stone, or Ashton's going to be over here pulling *your* ear," she snapped back. She twisted toward Tamara. "I think Luke's right that we're about to have good things happen with the horses. Not just from the contacts we made in Kananaskis Country, but honestly, I think by the time this racing season is over, we're going to have more stallions earning their weight in stud fees."

"Anything else?"

"I guess you could sell off more land around Heart Falls," she suggested. "Even though that would break my heart, it's probably the most valuable non-commercial land you own."

"Sell it for what?" Ivy asked, frowning slightly.

"Houses. Big-ass acreages—or smaller ones. You're close enough to Calgary you could be a bedroom community, or a nice quiet retreat for people in the arts."

Tamara nodded slowly. "People who work remotely don't mind living a little bit farther out. I'll write it down. It's not something I thought of because it's not my first choice, but we should consider everything."

Conversation continued, but the first chance Kelli found, she stepped from the room, stealing away as if she were headed to the washroom. She nabbed her boots as she went, sneaking down the hallway Dustin had stomped off.

She closed the front door carefully to keep it from slamming and paused on the front stairs only long enough to slip her feet into her boots. She grabbed her suitcase from where Luke had placed it back in his truck then crossed the yard to her room.

In the distance, Dustin was leaving the barn. He mounted his horse and headed toward the hills. She figured she knew what he felt like. That sense of being out of control wasn't a pleasant one.

Her room was cold and empty, as if all the happiness of the past week had been boxed up and shoved very, very far away. She'd had that brief moment of perfection, but it was over and now she had to do the next thing.

She dumped her suitcase in the corner, grabbed her things and headed to the shower room. After putting up her spa sign to warn people off, she stripped and stepped under the water.

And if she happened to be a little teary-eyed right about then, no one was ever going to know. The water running down her face was just from the tap.

That was her story, and she was sticking to it.

~

TORN between what he knew was an important meeting that deserved his full attention, and the dire need to chase down Kelli —Luke shifted on the spot like a restless kid.

He'd only realized Kelli was gone when he'd glanced toward the door and discovered her boots were missing. Caleb asked a question, and Luke's urge to leave was reined in for another ten minutes.

Until his restlessness got too pronounced.

"What the hell is wrong with you?" Walker leaned in close and spoke softly. "Did you catch fleas while you were out of town? Stop fidgeting."

"I just—" Damn. What was he supposed to say? Blurting out the truth was fraught with danger.

Walker slid forward slightly, frowning as he looked around and rapidly put two and two together. "Where's Kelli?"

"I don't know." Which pissed Luke off way more than it should.

His brother glared harder.

"Why are you asking me?" Luke demanded, forcing his volume down when Tamara frowned in his direction. Ashton and Caleb continued to go over the notes the foreman had written up, so Luke hissed an angry retort at Walker. "Maybe Kelli had something else to do, did you think of that?"

"You two having a private meeting?" Caleb interrupted. "Because you know, this is only our livelihood we're trying to save."

Dammit.

Luke dragged a hand through his hair. "Sorry," he ground out.

Tamara eyed the room, craning her neck as she looked around him. "Where's Kelli?"

"She was here a minute ago." Ashton looked up from his papers and turned to Luke. "Where'd she go?"

That was the last straw. Luke all but snarled an answer. "How the hell am I supposed to know? The damn woman seems to have lost her fucking mind in the past two hours. I'm obviously the last person you should ask since I can't even figure out what I did to make her turn tail and run when..."

He suddenly realized he was not only babbling, he was

bitching about things he most definitely shouldn't be discussing in public. In front of his family.

In front of the man who Kelli said had basically adopted her. Pseudo-parental figures tended to be protective, and his brothers no less so—

Lisa Coleman beat them all, and she hadn't even been in the room the last time he'd looked.

The woman was up in his face, twisting the front of his shirt tightly in her fist. "Luke Stone, did you do something to upset Kelli?"

"No," he retorted, catching hold of her wrist and wiggling free "I mean, maybe. I mean, hell, if I know."

"Luke, what's going on?" Tamara demanded. "I thought things went well at the gala."

"Or did things go *really* well at the gala?" Lisa asked, brow raised.

Luke ignored both of them and focused on his oldest brother. He met Caleb's gaze. "Sorry, but I have to go. Not because this isn't important, but because something is up with Kelli, and I have to find out what."

"Because you and her...?" The question in Caleb's eyes wasn't going away.

"Yes, me and her," Luke snapped, edging for the door because, screw this, he wasn't waiting any longer. "Anyone who has a problem with that can take it up with me later."

Then damn if Caleb didn't roll his eyes. He hauled out his wallet and passed a twenty to Lisa before returning his gaze to Luke's. "Well? What are you doing still here? Go find out what you did wrong."

Luke spun on his heel, cursing softly as he headed for the door. "Because it's got to be my fault, of course."

"Come on, bro, you know this one. The truth is it's *always* our fault," Walker said cheerfully. "Ivy and I have to head out. We'll catch up with you later so you can tell us what you did," he called out before the door swung shut behind Luke.

Luke loved his family. Every interfering, annoying, far-too-observant part of it. And while they had a huge issue with the ranch to figure out, he had a puzzle of his own to solve first.

Kelli had left her room unlocked, her suitcase abandoned. Her favourite boots were dumped in a messy heap, and her riding coat still hung on the hooks, so he doubted she'd headed to the barns.

Luke grabbed the one item he thought he might need from her room, then stomped around the building. His suspicions were confirmed when he spotted the *Kelli's Spa* sign.

His mental debate lasted less than three seconds. Luke used the master key in his pocket, relocking the door behind him.

Water ran at full blast, echoing from the back shower room. The clothes Kelli had been wearing hung on the changing-area wall. He tossed his jacket aside, ignoring everything else as he marched across the tiled floor and through the entrance.

Kelli stood under the water, back to him, head tipped down. Her hair hung in dark brown ribbons over her shoulders, water pouring over her naked body. She had one hand pressed to the wall as if it was helping hold her up.

He uncoiled the rope he'd taken from her room, looped it in his hand and gave a low swing to set it in motion. Another loop, another, and then he set it free.

The hemp rope flew toward her and over her head. Once it dropped past her shoulders, he tugged carefully.

The instant the rope hit her skin, Kelli whirled. Her eyes popped open. "What—?"

He pulled, stepping forward rapidly, sliding his hand up the rope to lock the loop in position and prevent her escape. "Don't try to get away or I swear I will take you to the ground and hogtie you."

She glared as she covered her breasts with her hands. "Get the hell out of here. I put up the privacy sign."

"That sign is for ranch-hand Kelli. It doesn't work on *just Luke*, or *just Kelli*, and it sure the hell doesn't work now that we're goddamn lovers. So"—Luke caught her against his body, ignoring the water streaming down and soaking everything including his boots—"you can finish your shower after we've had our conversation."

"What conversation?" Fire flashed in her eyes, her temper matching his own.

"The one I was *trying* to have when you fucking took off. Maybe it was bad timing for the family to call a meeting, but that doesn't explain why you were walking away from me."

"Because we're home," she growled. "We can be done now."

Luke jerked in surprise, squeezing her involuntarily. "You *want* to be done? You want what we've got to be over?"

Doubt—and hope?—crossed her expression. "We said it was short term. We said that us being a couple was just for the duration of the gala."

"You said it, maybe. I don't remember that part. I'm pretty damn sure that I didn't agree on a time frame."

"You didn't say no."

"If you're talking about when you laid down the law on the way to the gala, I couldn't get a word in edgewise," he roared.

"Because you were being an idiot." Her volume was as high as his, but a hint of a smile twisted the corners of her lips.

"And you're being one now," he retorted. "So we're even, and I forgive you, like you forgave me. But this. Is. Not. Over."

Then he kissed her. He hauled her against his body, letting the fire raging in his gut flow up and out and over them both.

Instantly soaked as he stepped farther under the spray, Luke adjusted her in his arms. Kelli wrapped her legs around him and clung like she was never going to let go.

Then they were moving together, her hands jerking his shirt

open, buttons flying out to bounce across the tiles. Luke loosened off the rope enough to let it slip past her hips and out of the way when he lowered her to her feet for long enough to strip off the rest of his clothes.

Kelli helped drag his jeans down, jerking a condom from his back pocket. Ripping it open and covering his aching cock, her hands were firm and yet delicate. His pants were caught around his ankles, locked in place by his boots. He shuffled four feet forward to the tiled seat in the corner and sat, dragging her after him.

She crawled on the ledge, straddling his thighs. When she would have gone immediately to move over him, Luke took charge. He lifted her to her feet until she stood directly over him, then pressed his mouth to her sex so he could drive her wild.

The way she made him feel—dirty and needy and very much alive.

"*Luke.*" His name was a moan of pleasure and a request for more, so he answered. He increased the tempo of his tongue, slipping a hand up her thigh until he could tease her pussy while he tormented her clit.

His other hand he used to anchor her against him. Fingers pressed hard to her ass. The softness of her skin, the flexing of her muscles, the taste of her against his tongue—

She quivered, and he all but roared as he dropped her down, lifted his cock and lined them up.

Kelli caught his shoulders under her hands and slid into position as if settling on a favourite horse. She adjusted her hips slightly, and his cock sank deep. She sighed contentedly as if ready to go for a long, hard ride.

He could oblige. He could so fucking oblige.

They moved together. Luke thrusting upward, pulling her hips in a rapid rhythm; Kelli leaning in to make sure her breasts rubbed the bare skin of his chest at every opportunity.

He took her mouth again, teasing his tongue past her teeth

and fucking her hard as she tangled her fingers in his hair and squeezed her hands into fists. She was squeezing him inside her as well, and the tingle in his balls raced up his spine and headed for detonation.

They came at the same moment. Kelli ground her hips onto him, letting out a series of noises that made him grin even as they tipped him over the edge. Shooting into the condom, aching goodness raced through his shaft and set his entire system rocking.

Aftershocks bumped him, her body quivering over and over until a chuckle escaped him. She whimpered a little, the sound turning into laughter as she kissed him again, stroked a hand down his face, and pulled back to stare into his eyes.

He took a deep breath. "We're not over," he informed her.

"So I take it."

"And you're not allowed to march off and not tell me what's wrong." May as well try to get all the rules in place he possibly could at one time.

"You're not allowed to make assumptions," Kelli retorted.

Luke fought to get his boots off without letting her out of his arms, kicking them away and ridding himself of his jeans so he could slide back on the bench and cradle her more comfortably. "Look who's talking."

She made a wry face. "Okay, we both screwed up."

"But we made it right," he pointed out. "Are we okay, again?"

Kelli nodded, stroking a hand up his chest and past his head. Her naked breasts bounced in front of his face in a terribly distracting manner.

"Your family must think—" Her eyes widened then met his again in panic. "Luke, you got out here awfully fast. What did you tell your family?"

"That we're a *we*," he admitted, ready to duck if she swung at him. "Not much more—I had a woman to track down before I went into details."

For one horrible moment he thought she would protest, but instead she shrugged slowly, shoulders lifting the slightest bit as she raised her hands to the wall again.

Her breasts danced in a *very* distracting manner.

"Do you think—?"

"My family loves you," Luke pointed out before allowing her to voice her worries. "If anyone is in trouble, it's me."

"Well, I'm okay with that," she admitted. "Because you still need to be punished. If for nothing else than for interrupting me just now."

Then before he could demand she agree to move into his house, or anything else that he wanted to make one hundred percent sure of, she twisted an arm and leaned back...

Icy cold water shot from overhead, drenching him instantly as he roared in surprise.

Kelli scrambled off him, but there was no use in her trying to escape. He scooped her up and held her in his arms. "That wasn't very nice. Now it's your turn for a little cooling off."

She clung to him, shrieking as he dropped them both under the freezing water. As the water heated and any lingering anger washed away, laughter rose.

He wasn't sure what the answer was to a lot of the future, but this part he knew.

Him, Kelli...an empty shower house.

Round two, coming up.

17

Kelli did her best to keep from smirking, but she was pretty sure her amusement was clear as they marched back to her room. Her body was tender in all the right places from Luke's enthusiastic emphasis of their relationship status.

But more entertaining? Luke was dressed in mostly wet clothes, naked from the waist up under his jacket because the shirt he'd worn to the shower house was beyond repair.

With him hard on her heels she paused, hand on the door of her room, to give him a warning glance. "We are *not* starting anything in here."

"Nope," he agreed. "We're grabbing some of your stuff so we can head over to my place."

She'd never considered herself the type to get butterflies, but something was definitely flitting about in her gut as she took in his serious expression. "You really think that's a good idea?"

Luke folded his arms over his chest, biceps pressing against his lined jean jacket. "I thought we got all this nonsense straightened out in the shower house."

"My question has nothing to do with you and me being together," she insisted. "But if we're going to—"

Good grief, what was she supposed to call this? It had been simple enough while they were at the gala to consider it a fling, but now that it was something more?

Oh my God, it was something more...

Another round of insects took wing in her belly.

Luke opened her door, placed a hand low on her back and guided them inside. "No reason to freeze while we figure out what's got your knickers in a knot."

"It's just that I can live *here* like I always have," Kelli started, backing away from him as his brows rose toward his hairline. "We're just starting to..."

Nope. Still had no idea what to call this.

A soft hum escaped him. "Oh, I get it."

Luke slid his hand to the back of her neck, knocking the towel she'd wrapped around her hair off as he wrapped his fingers around her. He tipped her head to examine her face more closely.

"You're right. If we'd started dating even a month ago, I can see you wanting to 'live' in your room and come visit my place sometimes." He closed the distance between them, brushing his lips across hers before inching closer to her ear. "But, sugar plum, now that I've had you in my bed for nearly a week straight, there's no damn way I'm letting you sleep anywhere except right next to me."

"Bossy bastard," Kelli complained.

He snagged her against him, all warm and hard and perfect. "Just the way you like."

Damn if he wasn't right. Except, something—

A heavy knock rang against her door, and she snorted before regaining control.

"I think that's for you," she said, not hiding her amusement.

Luke frowned, but he let her go, backing away and heading to the door. He glanced out the window first, then swore softly as he gave Kelli a warning look. "It's Ashton."

She tilted her head. "I saw him headed this way right before you hustled me inside."

"You're a mean one, Kelli James," Luke growled.

He pulled the door open.

Ashton stood there with a face full of thunder. But he didn't swing at Luke, which Kelli considered a positive start.

The foreman glanced at Kelli, looking her up and down with a careful eye before turning back to the man who, for all intents and purposes, should be considered his boss.

Only Ashton had been around since the days of Luke's parents, and he was more than just a hired hand. And at that moment, he didn't look one bit pleased.

"I need to talk with you," he growled, going face to face with Luke. Ashton eased back his shoulders as if preparing to take a swing if necessary.

That was one thing Kelli wasn't worried about. Luke wasn't a hothead. He wouldn't go off half-cocked, but she sure hoped he'd be moderately polite. Ashton *was* her boss too, after all.

Then damn if Luke didn't make as if he was going to meekly follow directions.

Kelli sighed dramatically, grabbing Luke by the arm to restrain him until she could step in front.

She gave him a dirty look as she passed. "You know how to argue. You've done enough of it with me over the last week. Heck, over the last hour. So I don't know why you're all willing to go off without a peep this time."

Luke's lips twitched.

She focused her attention on Ashton. "And unless I'm jumping to a conclusion and you're here because you need to talk private ranch business with Luke, then maybe you should be talking to me *and* Luke. If you plan to butt into my business, that is."

Ashton raised a single brow. "Fine. We'll do this here." He fixed his eyes on Luke, disapproval visible in every inch of his sturdy body. "You think you've been respectful and proper to a woman who's under my protection? Or should I rightly wallop you from one end of Silver Stone to the other because you've been a stupid cuss, and acted without thinking about the consequences?"

Luke squeezed Kelli's shoulder before sliding her slightly to the side. "I was thoughtless and stupid beyond measure before Kelli and I headed to the gala. But I can honestly say she kicked me hard enough to knock my head out of my ass. Besides, that mistake helped me realize something I should have figured out a long time ago."

Ashton was still frowning, with narrowed eyes and rigid body, but he waited without offering to kill Luke, so...

So far, so good.

Luke slipped his hand around Kelli's waist and tugged her against his side. "I'm not going to say you can ask Kelli's permission to bury my body in the back forty, because you don't need my permission or hers to do what you think is right. But I think she's forgiven me for being stupid"—he shrugged—"and beyond that, this isn't your business."

Okay, that wasn't where Kelli thought this conversation would go.

Neither had Ashton, obviously, his eyes going wide.

"I respect the hell out of you, Ashton," Luke continued softly. "I appreciate that you were there for us after Dad died, more than you can know. But I respect Kelli too. She doesn't need your permission, or your protection, unless she asks for it. Heck, I wish she would take you as backup if she decides to go off on one of her harebrained rescue schemes without me. But about me and her being together?" He shook his head. "Not your concern unless she says it is."

Ashton met Kelli's eyes. "Well, girl?"

She adjusted her stance and leaned more firmly against Luke. It felt strange as hell to do that in front of Ashton, but maybe the practice during the gala had been enough to give her the confidence. "I don't need to borrow the backhoe. Not this week, at least."

Beside her, Luke made a small sound of amusement. Ashton nodded, still eyeing Luke as if he were a leftover piece of manure in an otherwise clean stall. "Let me know if you change your mind."

He adjusted his hat and turned on his heel, closing the door firmly behind him.

As good as it had felt to hear Luke put her in the driver's seat, it was having the first barrier crossed—of people knowing about them—that caused a rush of relief.

She sagged against Luke.

"That was awkward," she pivoted against him, draping her arms around his neck. "And it was wonderful. Once you decided to not screw up, that was awesome."

He rubbed their noses together. "I'm afraid habit predicts I will continue to screw up in bursts, but I'll try to make course corrections as quickly as possible."

"Appreciate that."

He stared down, his lips twisting. "You ready to grab some stuff? Because I'm serious about you coming up to my house."

She wasn't going to lie. Getting the chance to still be in his bed—not a thing a girl wanted to turn down.

"I'll come up, but I'm keeping this room," she informed him.

He didn't argue. Just waited as she put a few more things into a bag then he picked up her suitcase and walked out with her.

It was fast, and yet after being coworkers and friends for so many years, like Luke had said, getting to steal time together in a more physical way was the next logical progression.

Just like facing Ashton was only the first in a long line of challenges.

Luke had some work to do, so she ended up eating supper with the other hands. She faced their questions about the gala, but kept her mouth shut for now about her and Luke. Partly because it wasn't what they were curious about, and partly because—

Just because.

After she was done, Kelli made her way to the ranch house, knocking at the back door tentatively in hopes she could catch Tamara in good enough shape for a visit. It was important that she went and shared what was going on before she got cornered into it. Logical, but...

Logic sucked.

Lisa opened the door, her friendly face breaking into an enormous grin. "Well, now."

"Tamara here?" Kelli asked.

Lisa jerked a thumb over her shoulder. "You want some supper?"

"Already ate in the mess hall. But thanks."

Kelli took off her boots then slid across to the living room. She stopped, holding back her amusement.

Caleb sat in his easy chair, looking none too easy. The younger of his little girls was combing his hair. Emma had pulled most of it into teeny bunches so she could wrap elastics around the ends. The process had left tuffs standing upright asymmetrically all over his head.

Sasha was at his right hand, deploying nail polish. His eyes were closed as if pretending they weren't there would make the torment go away, or at least be over sooner.

Kelli glanced to the right. Tamara was curled up in her usual corner of the couch, laughing silently as tears ran down her cheeks. She had a hand slapped over her mouth to keep the sound from escaping.

"I hope I'm not interrupting anything," Kelli said as deadpan as possible.

Caleb grimaced, keeping his eyes squeezed tight. "If I don't see you that means you're not here. And if you're not here, you can't possibly know what's going on, right?"

"Sounds right to me," Kelli agreed. "The ostrich-head-in-the-sand trick has a long and honourable tradition."

Sasha didn't look up from where she was adding black dots to the red on her father's nails. "Kelli says if you can't fly, be like an ostrich and run like the wind."

"That's a very good Kelli-ism," Tamara assured her daughter, wiping tears away. She offered Kelli a wink then patted the seat next to her. "You. Drop it right here."

She hadn't been planning on a family discussion, so was thankful when a moment later Emma and Sasha hurried over and gave their mom hugs before tugging Caleb from the room.

"Night, Mommy. Night, Kelli," Sasha said.

"Night, Mama. Kelli," Emma echoed, blowing her a kiss before returning to help Sasha drag Caleb away.

Lisa was still in the kitchen, but Tamara spoke softly enough to not be overheard. "All I want to say—promise you'll remember you're a part of this family? No matter what."

Warmth flooded Kelli's heart. "I told Luke that when he was being an ass. So, I think it's a pretty well-established truth."

Tamara grinned. "Good for you."

She closed her eyes and curled her arms around her stomach.

Kelli laid a hand on her knee. "Anything I can do to help?"

"Just nauseous. Again. Or still, whichever way you want to look at it."

Tamara's sister stood beside them, bending down to nudge her shoulder gently. "More fluids."

"You're such a taskmaster," Tamara complained, but she opened her eyes and accepted the cup.

"I learned from the best," Lisa said. "I've got this one sister, and she used to be a nurse. She was the biggest pain when it came to being sick. She always said it was important to do what was right, no matter how much people complained about being bossed around."

"Shut up," Tamara muttered with a smile. "You're not allowed to toss my own lectures back at me."

Lisa offered Kelli a wink. "Good to see you back and looking so chipper. Did you have a good time at the gala?"

My God, was it written on her forehead what she and Luke had been doing? No way was that innocent expression on Lisa's face anything but fake. "What did Luke do after I left the room? Break out photos or a video of everything we got up to?"

Lisa raised a brow. "No, is there footage? Because, *damn*."

Tamara snorted.

Now Kelli didn't know which of them to give the evil eye. "Does this mean it's a very public knowledge that Luke and I are—?"

She still didn't know what to call it.

Fortunately, Tamara didn't seem to have the same trouble finding words. "Dating? Yeah, we kind of all know. Caleb was clueless when the idea came up the other day, so Lisa took advantage of his naiveté to earn a few bucks."

"Good grief, you guys are terrible," Kelli complained. "On top of everything else I was worried about, I thought you'd be at least moderately upset. I've been trying to figure out how much trouble this relationship could cause if things don't work out."

"You're both grownups," Lisa pointed out. "Neither of you are going to do something horrifically stupid like cheat or get spiteful. You seem to honestly like each other." She raised a brow. "It's not a bad way to step into a relationship."

Kelli supposed that was true. "I do like him. A lot," she admitted.

Lisa and Tamara exchanged glances before turning back, both of them smirking. "Honey, tell us something we didn't know."

"Seriously? You did not."

Tamara lifted a brow.

Lisa gave a shrug. "He seems like a really good guy. So enjoy yourself, but know that we've got your back."

"Only if you promise no more bets based on my relationship," Kelli countered. "Because that's just wrong."

A heavy sigh escaped Lisa as if she was oh-so-hard done by. "You're ruining all my fun," she complained.

"No bets," Kelli insisted.

"Okay, fine." The other woman headed to the kitchen, speaking over her shoulder. "Let me grab the tea and cookies. Because there's no time like the present for you to spill the beans about your week at the gala."

"Regarding Silver Stone and the horses, as well as your personal gossip," Tamara said quickly.

"But not necessarily in that order," Lisa quipped.

Kelli caught them up on the gala, sang Diane's praises loudly, and somehow avoided sharing anything too intimate regarding what had happened between her and Luke.

But she blushed. A lot.

When the visit was over and she meandered across the long expanse between the main ranch house and Luke's place, the icy cold air didn't touch her. Kelli was too wrapped up in the warmth of the women's friendship.

The sight of Luke standing in his living room window, watching her approach with a smile on his handsome face, well—

She might not know exactly where this was going, but she planned to hang on with both hands as long as she could.

18

That night was a first for Luke.

It wasn't that his ex-fiancée had never been in his house, but when he thought back, he realized she'd rarely stayed the night. Rarely been around other than for a few hours or because they'd stopped in on the way to an event.

Kelli? She filled his house with more life and energy than any one person should possess.

It was right to have her there, sitting kitty corner to him as they went over the notes from their time at the gala. They put together a list of potential follow-ups for the next day, and the next week, and the next month.

Working together like partners, and maybe that was a big part of what had been missing in his previous relationship. Spending time with Kelli was right, and natural, and easy in all the good ways.

He had a hard time wiping the grin off his face at how good and right and easy it was.

And the sexual chemistry they had going on? Off the fucking charts. Temptation slipped in between one breath and the next, derailing whatever they were doing to shoot the agenda in a completely different direction.

Like when he'd leaned over her shoulder to see what she'd written on her notepad. It was far too easy to drop a little closer and nuzzle against her neck.

Aroused and distracted, he *had* to kiss that one spot. Which led to another kiss, and another until Kelli dropped all pretense of work and turned. The next thing he knew they were headed to his bedroom, paperwork forgotten until the next day.

That night she fell asleep in his arms and he found himself listening to the sound of her breathing, and it was easy to feel like this was coming home. This was right.

She still had shifts to work according to Ashton's schedule, which meant the next day she was the one kissing him sweetly at four a.m., before evading his grasp and sliding from bed.

Kelli held him to his promise and took over training Chili Pepper. Three days later, Luke rested his arms on the rail and watched as she leaned over the saddle, arms hanging on either side of the filly's neck as Kelli drooped like a rag doll.

"I guess that position makes hitting the ground a little easier," he teased.

Kelli's head was turned toward him, and she stuck out her tongue briefly but remained silent, patting Pepper carefully on the withers before tapping with her heels to get the mare moving again.

One of the hands who had been spotting Kelli as she worked stepped up and joined him at the rail. Alex eyed Kelli before looking Luke over with great curiosity.

"So," Alex said.

That was it. Funny how many questions could be put into one word depending on the tone of voice. This one had held both a warning and a *what the fuck*?

"Yes?" Luke had seen the hands looking them over with interest, wondering what exactly was going on. He had no plans of hiding their relationship, but as he'd pointed out to Ashton, this wasn't anyone's business except his and Kelli's.

Alex leaned an elbow on the fence. "I figure because you're still breathing, that Kelli's on board, but just so you know, we're keeping an eye on you. Me, and the rest of the crew."

Luke was tempted to use Kelli's pet phrase and spout off a *good grief*, but he was more entertained than upset.

Besides, there was no use getting indignant. Whether they liked it or not, he and Kelli had the starring positions in the Silver Stone romance of the season.

So he tipped his hat back and looked Alex over, keeping his expression as stonelike as possible. "Good for you."

Alex's lips twitched. "If she decides she wants an upgrade, a dozen or so guys are ready to dig a deep hole." Kelli might not have parents around, but she sure as hell had a ton of family on her side.

Luke offered Alex his hand. "You ever feel a need to dig that hole, I'll come and lie in it willingly."

Alex laughed as he smacked Luke on the shoulder. He glanced into the arena where Kelli was still draped over Pepper's back.

"By the way, what'd you do to her? Fuck her boneless?" Alex asked.

"I heard that," Kelli said with a snap as she slid off Pepper's back, rotating smoothly until she stood beside the horse, lead in hand.

"I hope so. No matter what weird shit you were up to, it shouldn't have involved your ears."

She snickered before forcing a glare. "Be careful about teasing someone who knows the woman *you're* dating," she warned.

"And on that note, if you're done training for the day, I have a chore list as long as my arm to get back to." Alex tipped his hat at Kelli before marching rapidly toward the barn.

Kelli led Pepper to the railing, the horse slipping her head over the top to nuzzle Luke, knocking his hat off with her enthusiastic greeting.

Kelli swooped down to grab it before climbing the fence, reaching up to press the hat onto his head. She perched on the top rail like a little kid, delight in her eyes. "Hey."

He leaned forward, one hand on either side of her body as he brought their lips inches part. "Hey. Interesting training technique, but it looks as if it might work."

"*Might* work? Did you see my ass on the ground like yours was the last time you tried to ride her? I think not." Her expression twisted slightly before she admitted, "Diane gave me a few ideas, and they're really helping."

Luke slid a hand up her back as he adjusted position to ease in closer. "She's a damn good friend. Things will be okay."

He knew Kelli was worried about having lied to Diane and Jack, and he'd done his best to reassure her without making any comments that would freak her out.

Their fake-relationship had already become a reality. He figured they were one step closer to it being even *more*. It was far too soon, though, to push Kelli.

But in his head? Plans and plots were evolving at such high speeds *he* was getting a little frightened. Truth was, them being together made sense. That it had taken him this long to figure it out was a mistake he wasn't about to repeat.

He'd learned from his earlier misstep and wasn't going to assume anything, though. Nope. She needed to be able to buy into this deal one hundred percent, and some other component was still missing. Something itched at the back of his brain that would help make the next stage happen.

Luke just needed to figure out what.

Kelli arrived at Tansy and Rose's place, was ushered in with hugs like usual, and peppered with a set of totally innocuous questions. Her friends showed amazing restraint, asking for details about the gala hotel, what the food had been like, and all the fancy outfits she'd seen the night of the ball.

But there was a limit to their patience.

Now that she was wrapped in a soft throw blanket, a cup of hot chocolate in her hands, two faces peered back at her, wild curiosity on both of them.

"I like that you close the shop on Tuesdays," Kelli said. "This staying up late on Monday nights makes me feel naughty, like I'm breaking curfew."

Tansy and Rose glanced at each other.

"She changed the topic," Rose said. "That was not remotely about the gala, or Luke, or *anything* interesting."

"Someone is trying to avoid sharing any juicy details," Tansy replied blandly.

"I don't know why she's attempting to prevaricate. It's not as if news didn't spread like wildfire the minute someone spotted her and Luke smooching in the barn." Rose faced Kelli. "Alex told me Luke is being all he-man possessive and stuff, too. Grrr, and snarl, and that kind of thing, when the guys are around."

"Oh, now that's just bull." Kelli jerked upright. "Luke is not acting possessive. And we have not been *smooching*. Good grief, what are you guys, twelve?"

"Pretend we are, and you can give us lessons. What exactly happened while you were gone? Because—"

The doorbell rang. Rose shot to her feet.

"Drat. You were late, and my date is right on time." She grabbed her coat and purse from where they lay over the arm of the couch. "I will hear all the good bits at some point, yes?"

"Maybe," Kelli retorted. "If I hear the play by play of what you and Alex get up to."

Rose had been in the middle of swinging the door open, and

he had to have overheard, because the dark-haired man offered the room a wide grin.

"Dancing. That's all I'm going to say." Alex focused on Rose, whistling in appreciation as he hurried to help her with her coat. "You look pretty."

"Thanks." Rose put a hand on his chest, pushing him back into the hallway. "We need to leave now, before Snoopy Thing One and Snoopy Thing Two get their hooks into you."

"Bye, ladies," Alex offered with a chuckle.

"Bye, Alex. Bye, Rose. Don't do anything I wouldn— Never mind," Tansy said dryly. "I forgot who I was talking to."

Rose swooped to grab a boot. Tansy ducked as the chunky object flew past her head.

Kelli laughed softly. As usual, the sisters also tossed each other a quick air kiss and a finger wave before Rose closed the door.

Which left her and Tansy sitting in the suddenly quiet room.

It would have been easy to share some of what had gone down between her and Luke when both Fields sisters were there—the two who lovingly called each other twins even though they were adopted from vastly different backgrounds.

But while the three of them were friends, Kelli and Tansy had things in common at a more intimate level than anyone else. This conversation wasn't going to be just—*holy cow, you're dating Luke*—it would go deeper.

That was scary, no matter how much Kelli wanted it.

Tansy wiggled back in her chair before turning a knowing smile in Kelli's direction. "You want to tell me what's going on?" she asked. "If you say no, I won't poke. You know that. Your secrets are your own. Even after you tell me, I will never share. I am the Fort Knox of Secret Keeperdom."

Which was true. Until this past week and her confession to Luke, Tansy was only person who had heard the full story about Kelli's past—she knew *everything*, including the stealing money and running away. The only thing Kelli hadn't outright shared was her crush on Luke.

Looking back, it appeared she might not have done as good a job of keeping the Luke part as secret as she'd thought. At least not around the female portion of the population.

Thank God *Luke* had never suspected.

Kelli went, as usual, with honest. "I want to tell you about it, only everything is really mixed up and twisted in my brain."

"Talk it out," Tansy suggested. "I can take twisted."

Words poured out of Kelli as if she'd broken through a dam.

"I went into the event thinking we might have a secret, short-term fling, but people there thought we were engaged. Luke had signed us up as a couple. I got mad at him for that, but then I kind of forced him to *make* us a couple anyway, and he didn't get mad at me. And we had the most amazing time, not just the fling part —although, *oh my god*, that was wild—but the people were so nice, and Diane was fantastic. You would love her, and she would love you, but she thinks Luke and I are engaged, but we're not, only"—Kelli took a deep breath—"when we got back, Luke said we *are* dating now and I've moved into his house, which sounds impossible when I say it like that. It can't be real, and yet it is."

Tansy's expression was unreadable, but her eyes were bright, and she nodded sharply before replying. "Twisted is right. And I can see you're in the middle of trying to find all the knots so you can unravel the mess. Figuring it all out. But it really doesn't matter, you know."

Kelli paused. "What doesn't matter?"

"How mixed up the whole situation is. Because the important parts are clear." Tansy leaned forward, her perceptive gaze piercingly bright. "You look happy. Like *super* happy. And you're usually a happy person to begin with, so whatever it is that's going on with Luke is not hurting you."

"I hate that we lied to people. And you have to promise you won't say a word about the engaged thing to anyone. We definitely need to figure out how we're going to explain that away." Kelli felt her bubble of happiness fading. "Like I said, it's twisted and a total mess. How can I be so happy and still feel miserable?"

"Because people are complicated and capable of feeling more than one emotion at a time?" Tansy shrugged. "I mean, really. That annoys the hell out of me."

Usually it would have Kelli, too.

She paused. Thought it through. This time Kelli spoke slower, but with as much honesty as her earlier spew. "I've been pretending that all I wanted was a fling, but that was to protect myself in case I didn't get what I really wanted. But I don't know if what I *think* I want is what I really want, and until I untangle that part, I'm going to stay confused."

"You don't want a fling." Tansy's face stilled in concentration. "You want more. You want to be with Luke for real? You want to be with the St— *Oh*..."

Her friend was far too astute. Kelli let her misery out. "Tamara says I'm like family already. And I *have* had a crush on Luke forever. But how much of me caring for him is because I'm crazy in love with Silver Stone and the Stone family? How much is because I can't fathom living anywhere else? Because they've been my family for so long now? I needed a family so much when I arrived here."

"Of course you did. We all do." Tansy's eyes flashed with indignation. "The woman who was your birth mother was not family. It's not about shared blood. Family is about choice. One hundred percent. You know that."

"Your family is a good example, I know. It's just that..." Kelli paused. "I guess I don't want to screw this up for anyone. Me, him or Silver Stone."

"Oh, honey." Tansy slid across the space between them. She sat on the coffee table and took Kelli's hands in hers. "Do you love him?"

"I don't know if I dare to love him," Kelli admitted. "Because if he doesn't love me back..."

She couldn't finish.

Tansy wasn't going to let it lie. "Because if he doesn't love you back...*what*?"

"I might stay with him anyway because it means I would also be with the Stone family." The words were a whisper. A confession of all her fears. "And while that's not exactly the same as my mom, who stayed with guys who hurt her, it's still not being around for the right reasons."

"Oh boy." Tansy squeezed her fingers tightly before letting go and sitting back. "You did tangle this one up good, girlfriend."

"Doing a job well is something I take pride in." Kelli forced out the joke.

They grinned at each other. Then Tansy rose to her feet. "You know what? You're trying too hard. This relationship is brand new to you, and to Luke, and while it's complicated because you work with him and have a relationship with his family, stop focusing on those bits."

Easier said than done. "And do what?"

"Focus on *him*. On being a couple." Tansy planted her fists on her hips and stared down, lecture mode on her face. "Do you really think you'd have a crush on someone who was an asshole? Because I don't. You're too smart for that."

"My mom stayed with assholes—"

"Hell, no, girl. Don't you go there. The only thing you share with that woman is a bit of DNA. You were smart enough to get out."

"I suppose." Kelli took a deep breath, starting to feel hopeful again.

Tansy pushed her advantage. "You know what's right and what's wrong, which is why you ran away when you did. Give this time. Enjoy yourself and figure out the next steps together. Truth is, you have a lot of family by choice around. You have the Stones, you have me and the Fields—so no matter what happens, you're not alone. But you also deserve to be loved in ways we can't give you, but maybe Luke can."

"I want him to. I think." Kelli wrinkled her nose. "Okay, I'll be patient and focus on us as a couple going forward. I can do that."

"Of course you can. I only have smart people for friends."

Kelli laughed. "We need to find you a boyfriend."

"In time. I'm having fun being single." Tansy nodded firmly. "I mean it, Kelli. I know from experience that real love is more than doing the right thing. Real family, the people who have *real* love inside them—they're the ones who love you in spite of your faults. They want you and keep loving you, even when you screw up. You deserve that, and I hope Luke is the one who can give it to you."

"Me too." Kelli collapsed back on the couch. "Enough. I'm emotionally wiped out. You need to feed me sugary treats and catch me up on all the gossip I missed this past week."

Tansy pulled out the goodies, and Kelli soaked in the happiness of friendship. And at the end of the night when they'd finished the turnovers and chips and talked and eaten to their hearts' content, she headed home with a seed of hope planted.

While she was still worried about troubles that needed to be solved, having a new focus was a good thing. She was doing this. She would try for love in the hopes it would be worth it in the end.

She wished a good Kelli-ism would come to mind. Something that she could recite over and over as a personal mantra, but all she could think of was Diane's advice of how to work with Pepper. To relax and let trust build over time.

Time. Kelli needed to wait.

So, like she had already for many years, she waited.

19

On Saturday, Kelli burst into the barn and raced up to Luke, interrupting his discussion with Caleb. "Sorry, but you've got to see this *right now*."

She shoved a piece of paper into Caleb's hands.

He eyed it suspiciously. "What's this?"

"Stud-fee contract." She slid a finger along the top line as if it was obvious.

Luke wrapped an arm around her waist and leaned over Caleb's shoulder to read the paper.

Caleb whispered softly as he pointed at a number that seemed to have extra zeros behind it. "Is that a typo?"

"Not a typo." Kelli fanned another set of extra papers to show there were a half dozen more just like it. "Look. Look at them all," she said, bouncing with excitement.

"But that's not what we charge for Nemo's fee."

Her grin widened. "You missed the results from the Pegasus World Cup."

"Kelli, we don't have any horses represented," Caleb pointed out, checking his watch. "And the event hasn't even run yet."

"Finished an hour and a half ago. You forgot about the time

zone difference. And we don't know why, but for some reason, one of the four-year-olds entered was a filly out of Nemo. Remember Outside Darling? She came from behind riding wild odds and placed *second*. Tamara and I were watching live on YouTube, and as soon as the results were in, Tamara told Lisa to adjust Nemo's fees. And the website *still* went crazy."

Luke glanced over the pages, swearing softly at the outrageous numbers on each of the contracts. "If these are legal and binding, he's about to earn a shit-ton of money."

"Completely legal," Kelli assured him. "You know that automated system Lisa put into place on the website? Almost all the open stud dates are booked for this coming year *at* that higher fee. These pages are just the people who Silver Stone already preapproved. You still have to approve the new mares, Luke, but stables *really* want Nemo. Stables with lots and lots of money in their pockets." Kelli bounced another couple of times, her gaze darting between his and Caleb's faces. "Does that help? Does that help Silver Stone deal with finances for a little longer?"

Caleb caught hold of her, surprised delight escaping her in a squeal as he spun her in a circle. "It helps," he agreed as he put her back on the ground. "It helps a damn lot."

Then it was Luke's turn to pick her up, but after a quick spin he held her against him, brushing their noses together. "You girls were brilliant." He lowered his voice. "And once again, you did more than your share, considering those names I'd preapproved were breeders we met in Kananaskis Country who you sweet-talked into getting on a short list."

Her face lit up the room. "I want to show Ashton. Can I? I'll take the papers back up to the house when I'm done."

She kissed Luke right there in front of Caleb, squeezing his neck tightly before letting go and taking off at a run.

Luke watched her go, happiness...and something else... stewing inside.

It took a little while before it hit. In fact, it wasn't until two days later that his brain finally offered up the tidbit that had been haunting him. But when it did, he didn't hesitate.

"I finally figured it out," he told Caleb as he tracked him down in Ashton's office later that night. "We need to talk about Nemo."

Ashton glanced up, smile growing. "He's pulling his weight now, isn't he? Good old boy. Glad we stuck it out."

"Me too, but we nearly got rid of him, didn't we?"

Ashton leaned back in his chair. A crease formed between his brows as he thought back. "Come to think of it, you're right. He was pretty surly at one point. Kelli was convinced she could train him to behave and talked us into holding on for another season."

Caleb nodded. "I'd forgotten about that."

So he hadn't been imagining things. Luke took a deep breath. What he was about to propose was a huge change and affected how much Nemo's increased fees helped Silver Stone, but it needed to be done. "I think Kelli should be listed on his ownership papers."

Caleb stopped everything. He turned his perceptive gaze on Luke, examining him carefully. Ashton had gone silent as well.

"That means she gets a cut of every payout," Caleb pointed out. "On one hand, I don't have any problem with that, but...?"

"It's the right thing to do," Luke insisted.

Caleb considered for a long, quiet moment.

Luke knew his brother. He *knew* what was going on in Caleb's head as he weighed the needs of the family and what was proper.

Sooner than expected, his oldest brother shrugged. "We should have done this years ago, but I guess it's better late than never. It's not right for us to keep all the money when we wouldn't have had anything if it hadn't been for her."

Ashton laid a hand on Caleb's shoulder. "Your dad would be proud."

Caleb made a rude noise. "He'd be shaking his head that it took this long for the truth to sink in. Mom would have laughed—she'd have liked Kelli."

"Both of them smart and stubborn—not bad traits in a woman, especially ones who live with us untamed cowboys." Ashton glanced between the brothers. "You need to talk to the rest of the Stones?"

"We should." Caleb checked his watch. "Luke, you call Walker. I'll email Ginny, then track down Dustin for his vote, but I don't see any of them having a problem with it. Even with giving Kelli part of the higher fees, Silver Stone is still really close to turning the corner."

"Let me know when you're ready, and I'll contact our legal guy. He can do it up proper with a contract." Ashton folded his arms, the trace of silver at his temples and the lines on his face the only things showing he was no longer a young man. "I've said it before, and I'll say it again now, Kelli's been an asset to Silver Stone since the day she arrived."

Knowing a little more about the details of that day, and how she'd walked onto the ranch uninvited, Luke let his smile broaden without sharing why.

He and Caleb left Ashton, walking in companionable silence across the snow toward where the packed-down path split in two directions.

They paused as if it had been planned, both of them staring upward. The air was icy cold, stars twinkling in the deep black sky.

Caleb made a noise of approval. "Never gets old. Even when it makes me feel like I'm small as a flea, it's so damn beautiful, I don't really care I'm pretty insignificant in the scheme of things."

"Deep thoughts for a January night," Luke teased.

"It's good to have them once in a while," Caleb acknowledged. He looked Luke directly in the eyes. "I was a little slow on the uptake. You and Kelli being together isn't bad, but it makes things...complicated. Giving her part ownership of Nemo puts a little more power in her hands. She'll have money that doesn't depend on you or her position here at Silver Stone.

It was the answer to so many lingering concerns. Luke exhaled in a rush. "Thank you for understanding."

"Some might say we're being foolish," Caleb pointed out.

"I really care about Kelli." Luke chose his words carefully. "And I'm not saying much more than that because we're still figuring things out, but I don't want her staying on board with Silver Stone because she has nowhere else to go. Hell, I don't want her staying on board with *me* because she has no options."

A low chuckle escaped his brother. "I think you're a far bigger attraction than you're giving yourself credit for."

It was Luke's turn to shrug. "Okay, call it leverage for those times when I screw up. Now she'll have something to beat me over the head with."

"Trust me. You'll do things worth being beat over the head for."

Luke didn't disagree. "Let me tell her?"

Caleb grinned. "Of course. Telling a woman good news is always best done by someone who can truly appreciate the celebration that follows."

Which was pretty much what Luke figured.

"I'll text you as soon as I hear back from Ginny and Dustin," Caleb promised.

Luke squeezed Caleb's shoulder then took off, hoping confirmation came sooner than later so he didn't have to keep this secret from Kelli for too long.

He called Walker as he strode through the darkness to his back door, but as they'd suspected, Walker had no problems with the idea. Another layer of relief flooded in when only moments after Luke hung up his coat, Caleb texted.

Caleb: *Ginny is up for some ungodly reason and already responded. She says, and I quote, "it's about freaking time." I don't know if that's in reference to Nemo's shares, or you and Kelli being together. I haven't heard from Dustin, but I know he considers her family. Go ahead and tell Kelli if you want.*

Luke: *You sure?*

Caleb: *Yes. We've got four out of the five share-holders in agreement. If Dustin's got any worries, I'll talk him through them.*

His brother was right. Didn't make Luke any less grateful to be given the go-ahead.

Luke: *Thanks. For all of it.*

Caleb: *Don't you have something to do? I've had enough typing with my thumbs on this stupid phone.*

Kelli was tangled in a yoga position in front of his fireplace. The sight of her there made him happy with the memory of their time chatting during the gala.

The position made him cringe.

~

KELLI HAD KNOWN he was there the instant he'd stepped a boot on the back stairs. She'd forced her breathing to stay slow and smooth, and by the time he entered the room she was as close to calm as possible.

Her heart rate was always erratic around him—sexy, dangerous man.

"You're going to break something," he warned, his deep voice sweet and tempting like hot chocolate and whipped cream.

"Only if you join me," she teased, unraveling her legs and turning toward him. "Mr. Inflexible."

"I'm very flexible. I change my mind whenever I choose." He

dropped to the floor beside her, stretching out his legs as he leaned back on the couch. He'd pulled off his socks, and his feet were bare.

That shouldn't have seemed so damn sexy, but it did.

She ignored the hum of heat simply looking at him ignited. "You were working late. Ashton making you redo stalls again?"

A burst of laughter escaped him. "God, you know too many secrets. No, there were no double-done chores because I slacked off the first time. I was with Ashton, though. And Caleb."

She nodded knowingly. "Business meeting."

"Yeah, definitely. We were talking about Nemo. And you."

Kelli curled her legs under her, sitting at his side. "Me?"

"How you're good at your job. How you were the one who convinced us to keep him all those years ago."

And then he proceeded to blow her mind.

By the time he was done explaining what the ranch had decided to do in terms of ownership and percentages, her mind was whirling. "I...I don't know what to say."

Luke stroked a hair behind her ear, his gaze fixed on her face. "Not much you have to say. If anything, we're sorry it took this long to figure out you deserved more credit."

"But Silver Stone—"

"Will be fine," he promised. "Nemo is still here, part of the operation. And he's not the only one up and coming. Also, we're waiting to hear back from Jack, and the Petries, and a bunch of other contacts from the gala. You and I both know those are diamonds in the rough just waiting to happen."

"But they haven't happened yet," she warned.

He shrugged. "We're ranchers, Kelli. We know there are no guarantees. You deserve the credit, and that's what this is. Plain and simple. It's only logical."

Kelli was tempted to keep arguing, but the expression on his face and that final comment were enough to dissuade her. "Thank you."

It wasn't enough, but it was all she could say.

Luke grinned. "It's too late to go out and celebrate, but I did have something tucked away for a surprise. Got any room in that bottomless pit you call a stomach?"

Now he was talking. "Does it involve chocolate?"

Luke had made it to his feet, holding down a hand to pull her up as well. "Do I look like the kind of man who would *not* provide you chocolate when it's time for a celebration?"

"Nope, you're too smart to try that nonsense." She followed him into the kitchen and waited as he pulled something from the freezer. He unwrapped a set of small circles and a small pot of dark brown sauce and popped it all in the microwave. She started to drool. "Oh my God, those are Tansy's orgasm bites."

Luke blinked in surprise before he laughed loud and hard. "Jeez, when I bought them they were called doughnut holes with raspberry chocolate dip, but your name is better."

"That's what I told Tansy, but she said the stuffier of her clientele would have kittens if she posted *that* on the menu board."

"Everyone else would buy the stock off her shelves the instant the doors opened."

Five minutes later, he put the piping hot chocolate dip and a stack of doughnut holes and Oreo cookies on a plate, and they sat side by side at the island and demolished a million calories in celebration.

Thirty minutes later, he had her stripped naked under him in bed for the next stage of the celebration.

The evening did not suck for so many reasons.

Kelli stayed on a high for days. She trained Chili Pepper and worked beside Ashton and the guys. Familiar tasks, but somehow the days were shinier because she spent her evenings with Luke enjoying hours of lazy conversation and laughter that inevitably ended in bed.

Tuesday she used her coffee break to climb into the loft after one of the barn cats. She ended up following the creature to the side where a stream of sunlight pooled on the hay bales, forming a perfect bed to lie on her back, stare into the rafters, and daydream about Luke.

Tansy had been right. Giving their relationship time to grow was not a hardship.

It was warm and cozy, and the scents of the barn had lulled her close to sleep before voices brought her to full attention. Caleb's deep rumble and Dustin's younger version echoed off the quiet walls.

She debated calling out to let them know she was there, but the sun on her limbs weighed her down and made her slow to react.

"You okay?" Caleb asked.

Metallic banging rang out—the familiar sound of feed buckets clanging together. Dustin usually carried three in each hand. "Yeah. Just...I want this all to be settled. Everything with Silver Stone and her finances. I hate not knowing what's going on. I hate that I can't do something to fix it."

"You *are* doing something," Caleb assured him. "Every day that you come and work with the family means you're doing something that matters."

Dustin must have dropped the pails to the ground, because a clatter rang out, sharp and piercing. "It doesn't feel like it. Doing chores, moving animals—those are all tasks that get done over and over and don't change a damn thing. I'm not good at anything in particular. Not like you or Walker. Everyone works harder just because they want to impress the big rodeo star. *You* see what needs to be done and who's the best to do it. Luke makes the horses damn near dance for him. Heck, Kelli has contributed more to the family than I have, and she's not even officially part of it yet."

"Stop comparing yourself to others."

It was a sharp reprimand. Sharper than Kelli expected from

Caleb, and sharp enough to shove her shock at being mentioned to the background.

But then Caleb continued the way she expected he would, concern and stubborn humour in every word. "We do not need another Luke, another Walker, or another Caleb in this family. One of each is plenty, thanks. At times, one Luke is *more* than we need."

Dustin snorted softly.

"I'm serious, though. I understand what you're feeling. Those early years after Dad was gone, you would not believe how often I could have put my ass down on the ground and cried like a damn baby because I was screwing up so bad. I couldn't do a thing the way he had—and our father was a damn good man, so it made me feel like a piece of crap to not live up to his standards."

"You've been great," Dustin insisted.

"Silver Stone is in trouble, and I'm in charge. I screwed up somewhere for that to happen," Caleb drawled.

"It's not your fault. You've done everything right. You didn't cause the flooding, or the outbreak from the neighbours that meant we had to cull." Dustin's indignation as he defended his idol was clear. "You've always done your best. You did what you neede—"

He stopped mid word.

A low chuckle rose from Caleb. "There you go. *Now* you understand what I'm talking about. Our best is all we can do, Dustin. Sometimes it works, sometimes it doesn't. The only thing we're in charge of is what we do, day by day. Maybe you're right. Maybe you don't have anything special you're extra good at yet to offer Silver Stone. *Yet*. When I was twenty, I didn't either. Find out what you love and work at it. But in the meantime, do the best job you can at those boring, repetitive tasks that are vital to Silver Stone. Trust me, you're making a difference."

Kelli stared upward, keeping silent as a cat walked across her and settled on her chest.

"I hear you. I really do, but what if—?" He stopped. Lowered his voice. "What if it doesn't work. What if sales drop, or Luke's hopes for the new connections fail? What if Kelli and Luke fight, and she breaks up with him and wants to leave, so she pulls her rights to Nemo and we have to pay her out? What then?"

"Then we deal with it," Caleb said calmly. "But I doubt that will happen. You have a morbid mindset, bro. You should take up writing murders or something."

"She could shut it all down," Dustin warned.

"If she were the type of person who would do that, I'd worry, but she's not. If it were Penny..."

Kelli slammed a hand over her mouth to stifle her gagging noises.

Dustin gagged loud enough for both of them. "Thank God Luke came to his senses. You're right, Kelli is awesome. So far."

Caleb chuckled. "Feel better, now?"

"Yeah." Dustin cleared his throat. "Caleb? Thanks. You really have been the best. I mean that."

Kelli could imagine the scene below her by the sounds that followed. A man hug, with accompanying back pounding. Caleb strode off and Dustin picked up his pails, the clatter of them banging together fading as he marched toward distant pens.

The calico cat using her as a cushion rose and stretched, arching her back before stalking off, tail held high. Kelli watched her go as she considered what she'd learned.

Luke had always taunted that someday she was going to regret eavesdropping, but this conversation had been particularly informative. She hadn't realized the full repercussions of Silver Stone sharing Nemo's rights with her.

A plot and plan rose to mind. Something that would not throw away the good thing she'd been granted, but that would help Silver Stone at the same time. A move that would offer everyone positive proof that Luke wasn't only interested in her because it made sense for them to stay together.

Proof that her love for Silver Stone and her love for Luke were two separate things.

It meant contacting the same lawyer who had drawn up the papers for the ownership split in the first place. She had to do it on the sly, but meanwhile, she was really enjoying the training that had been added to her job list. Luke had asked her to take on another of the new horses, which was amazing.

But Chili Pepper was still her first priority.

Luke had joined her on Wednesday afternoon. Training had gone well, and they were guiding the horse back to her stall when his phone buzzed with a message, and Pepper wiggled anxiously.

Luke gave Kelli a quick kiss then let her climb down. He walked at her side into the barn, checking his phone as they went.

His feet faltered, and Kelli left him standing there as she guided Pepper into her stall.

"Hell, yeah." Luke kept his comment quiet to avoid spooking the horses, but he was excited.

Kelli patted Pepper on the back, closing the stall gate behind her as Luke faced her.

"What's up?" she asked, because from the look on his face, it was something big.

Luke read the message out loud.

Hope this finds you well.

I'd like to come out to Silver Stone sometime next week to discuss an important issue.

Sincerely,
Timothy Carlyn

20

Luke was pretty sure that someone along the line had made a mistake. Hell was not burning hot, desperate and needy, because that sounded an awful lot like what happened when he and Kelli hit the sheets.

Hell was waiting.

Day by day passed, and there was nothing Luke could do to hurry them up and rush forward. There were chores to do, animals to care for. Bills to pay and long conversations filled with concern and worry.

And hope—because that was the one thing noticeable as he crossed off days on the calendar until Timothy Carlyn's visit to Silver Stone arrived.

The man had finally arrived in their yard, ten-gallon hat and all, every inch the southern gentleman. Walker stood beside Luke, shaking Carlyn's hand and accepting words of praise for his bull-riding achievements.

Timothy turned to Luke, smile widening. They shook hands heartily but even as he did, the man was looking past him, as if disappointed. "Where's your lovely fiancée?"

Walker stiffened noticeably, and Luke hurried to answer

before something dangerous got said. "She's out in the fields checking relocation sites for stock if that storm hits that's expected."

Timothy wilted then frowned. "I told you I have no problem talking business with her around."

"I remember that," Luke assured him, "but I'm not in charge of her schedule. I'm not about to second-guess our foreman when he assigns the best person to the job."

Luke wasn't sure if this had been some sort of test, and if Silver Stone had failed without even knowing they were being judged.

But Carlyn nodded firmly. He glanced between Luke and Walker. "This isn't the easiest of conversations to have, but it's an important one. I trust what I tell you will stay in confidence. The parts of it that need to remain private."

It all seemed a lot more cloak and dagger than simply wanting to purchase some of Silver Stone's stock.

"You can speak freely," Luke assured him.

Walker was giving Luke meaningful glances. He had totally caught that fiancée thing and was going to rake Luke over the coals first chance he got.

Then Luke wasn't worried about Walker because Timothy Carlyn had pulled out a photo and was presenting it to them.

"Look familiar?"

"That's Kelli, from the night of the gala," Luke began before his words faded off.

It *wasn't*, because the woman wasn't wearing what Kelli had worn that night. Kelli's dress had thin straps and clean lines, and this was narrow strips and frilly edges, with a corsage on her chest where one strap met her dress.

Carlyn's face had gone rigid. "You see it too."

Walker glanced between the two of them. "That's not Kelli?"

"It's not." Carlyn pulled out a second picture and held the two images side by side. Nearly identical, but now clearly two different women. Their hair was slightly different, and the spark in Kelli's eyes made her look much happier than the other woman.

"I don't understand," Luke said honestly.

"I got the one of Kelli from the official photographer for the event." Carlyn lifted the older picture in the air. "This? This is my daughter on her graduation night."

"Shit." Walker took a step closer to Luke and laid a hand on his shoulder.

It was impossible. Luke looked into Carlyn's eyes and saw the question there. He remembered back to when the man had been fishing for information about Kelli's family. "You think Kelli is related to you?"

"I think there's more than a good possibility," the man admitted. "In fact, I'm pretty sure Kelli is my granddaughter, and I'm ready to do whatever is necessary to get her back into my life. It was bad enough to lose her mother, but if this is real—if what I suspect is true—she's the only family I've got left."

Walker squeezed Luke's shoulder in soundless support.

"I'm not trying to mess anything up for you," Carlyn said. "I just need to know."

"We understand," Walker assured him.

Carlyn spoke briefly, sharing information regarding his daughter, and all of it made sense. Yet as Luke listened, dumbfounded, he was thankful he didn't need to speak as there was no way he could form words.

His head was spinning, and there didn't seem to be any one direction he could aim himself at...

But that kind of confusion wasn't acceptable. It wasn't what Kelli would need from him, so he shook himself alert.

"Call Kelli in," he ordered Walker.

His brother nodded hard. He pulled out his phone and turned his back to make contact with the team in the fields.

Luke faced down Carlyn, not an inch of give in his voice. "I'm going to talk to her first. This is going to be a huge shock, and I need to find out what she wants."

For a brief moment Carlyn looked ready to complain before he folded with a sigh. "You're protecting her, and I won't take exception to that. It's what I'd want for any woman, not only someone related to me."

"You're staying in town?"

Carlyn nodded. "Give me a call when you're ready. I can come back, or you can come out. Whichever you prefer."

"Thank you." Luke accepted the two pictures, slipping them into his breast pocket and accepting a final handshake before Carlyn turned on his heel and headed back to the parking area.

Luke stood staring after the man, brain fumbling.

"I have so many questions, I don't even know where to begin." Walker stepped in front of him, concern written on every inch of his body. "But, first, bro, what the hell? *Fiancée?*"

Guilt rushed in. "I made a mistake, okay? Kelli already called me on it, and while we didn't end up in a perfect situation, in a way, nothing could have been better than me being an idiot in the first place."

"He thinks you're her goddamn *fiancé*," Walker snarled. "And while I think it's great that the two of you have decided to stop dancing around your attraction, zero to marriage is a little over the top, even for you."

Luke shook his head, glancing at his watch. "There was no dancing around involved. I was totally oblivious to the fact she's been under my nose forever."

"Maybe you want to tell yourself that, but it was pretty clear to me some part of you already cared last summer when you lost your shit over her being banged up." Walker sighed heavily, but his body language finally relaxed. "We'll deal with the rest of that later. You've got enough on your plate."

"Is she coming in?" Luke asked.

Walker nodded. "Ashton is sending her back on a quad. If you want to meet her, you can probably waylay her by Heart Falls."

It was a warm enough day they wouldn't freeze their butts off. "Great idea."

Walker laid a hand on his shoulder. "Be gentle," he warned. "I don't think this was on her radar."

"I know that. I'm not going to do anything that hurts her." Luke swore. "Look, our relationship might have started because I acted without thinking, but being with her is the rightest thing that's ever happened to me."

Which made the sensation so much worse as it arrived with a thumping jolt. It seemed everything he had begun to hope for was once again slipping out of reach.

~

KELLI FOUND one of the ranch ATVs parked across the trail, blocking her route.

She pulled to a stop and turned off her own engine, following a set of footprints through the snow to the rocks at the base of the pool of Heart Falls.

Her involuntary annoyance faded when she spotted Luke's tall figure staring over the frozen water.

His arms were folded over his chest, his gaze fixed across the icy surface to the small patch of open water. The trickle from the falls that remained flowing all winter was enough to keep the entire surface too thin to skate on.

It was beautiful and mesmerizing at the same time. The cascading water on the far left had frozen into a curtain made of deep blue to shimmering white.

She waited until she was close enough to speak without shouting. "I was worried there was an emergency when Ashton told me to go home, but I don't think you'd be out here relaxing if something was wrong with the family."

He turned and offered a smile that didn't reach his eyes. "Everyone is fine," he assured her. "But we need to talk."

A million different worrisome troubles raced through her brain. "I'm not going to give myself an ulcer trying to guess, so spit it out."

Luke caught her by the hand and pulled her with him toward the game trail. "You know how you told me you ran away from your mom? That she'd been keeping bad company, and making bad decisions, and you didn't want to be part of it?"

Anything she'd been worried about faded into nothing as he brought up the one thing she had never dreamed possible. "Oh my God. Did my mom show up?"

He squeezed her fingers tightly. "No. And if she did, I'd have been tempted to send her packing without ever letting you know. But something—"

He stopped, settling on top of a fallen log and drawing her between his knees so they were face to face.

Such concern and worry was written there. "You're scaring me and stirring up maternal instincts I didn't know I had. I want to do whatever I can to get you to stop being so sad."

"Seems we're doing the same thing, because I'm trying to protect you," Luke admitted. "I found out some information today that I don't know how you're going to take."

"Does it involve you kicking me out of Silver Stone?"

With how serious he looked, it was surprising to hear a soft chuckle escape. "Since you've already informed me I *can't* kick you out, that's obviously not the issue." He slipped his hand around the back of her, holding her close. "One of the pictures we took at the gala turned out amazing. You look beautiful. You also look nearly identical to another woman someone knows, and he was wondering if it's possible the two of you are related."

She tried to untangle that. "Someone says they know a woman who looks like me? I don't have any sisters, Luke. I'm an only child."

"I said it wrong. You look identical to how someone looked twenty years ago. It's possible they're thinking of your mom. You told me part of her story, but not enough for me to be sure if I should tell this person to leave or not. You said your mom left home and never went back—she complained about strict parents. But did she also have a good reason to leave?"

Oh. Now his worries made sense. "You're trying to figure out if she was getting out of a bad situation, like me?" Kelli thought back to her early days and what she had overheard. She shook her head gently. "She liked to complain that she was hard done by, but even to me as a teenager, it sounded like an excuse. As if she'd hoped life would be easier if she got to be in charge, but instead it wasn't all it was cracked up to be. She was probably too proud to admit she'd made a mistake and go home. But honestly, Luke, while I have a few good memories from growing up, I'm very aware of how *not good* a mother she was, and that was her choice. One hundred percent. I want nothing to do with her."

Luke nodded slowly. "Let me ask you this. If it was possible to meet your grandfather, is *that* something you'd liked to do?"

She leaned into him, fighting to make her tongue work. Wow. Talk about unexpected. "I don't know how to answer that. It's not anything I've ever thought of before."

She found herself wrapped up in two strong arms as Luke pulled her against his body. Using his hand to tug her head against him, he squeezed her tight and held her. Their breathing slowed even as her mind raced.

There was someone out there who might be her family? It was shocking, and yet...

And yet it wasn't as life altering as maybe it should feel. Like she and Tansy had talked about, Kelli already had a family—people she cared about and who obviously cared about her.

She twisted until she could look up at Luke. "What do you think?"

"Uh-uh. I'm not going to make this decision for you." He

looked far too serious, considering this should be a happy moment.

Shouldn't it?

He tucked his fingers under her chin and tipped her head back. Then his lips were on hers in a tender kiss filled with concern and something else that tasted very sweet.

He pulled back, smiling at her. "Want to see the pictures?"

Kelli nodded.

He handed her the first one and her heart skipped a beat before she looked down and saw herself. "I didn't look ridiculous," she admitted. "And, damn, my rack looks great."

A huge laugh escaped him, bursting free at a level more in line with what she expected from him. "Your rack always looks great," he assured her. "Here's the other picture."

It was easy to see why they'd concluded she and this mysterious woman were related. It was like looking into a slightly off-kilter mirror. Just enough changes Kelli could tell it wasn't her face, but that of a doppelgänger.

Then her eyes fell on the locket hanging around the other woman's neck, and everything inside her went still. "Holy moly. It is my mom."

"Seriously?" Luke straightened, twisting the picture toward himself as if trying to see what it made her so certain.

She pointed to the necklace. "Mom wore that all the time. She never took it off until—" A memory crashed in. "It got broken one day when a boyfriend got rough. I remember picking it up off the floor and hiding it until I could give it back."

He stiffened, body tightening in anger at her words.

"That was one of the only times I actually saw her cry. She told me it had been a Christmas gift when she was thirteen."

Luke met her gaze as both sadness and wonder tangled inside her. "So he probably is your grandpa, the man who says he knows this woman."

Kelli nodded.

"Do you want to meet him?"

No. Yes.

"Maybe? I haven't been desperately trying to find the past all these years. I've been trying to have a good life here and now."

He held her close again, his strong arms centering her. "It's up to you. It really is."

Something was still wrong. She pushed against his chest until she could peer at his face. "What's going on? You tend to be more opinionated," she informed him.

Luke stiffened. "It's your life, it's your decision."

"I get that, and it is. But that's never stopped you before from telling me what you think I should do. Why are you stopping now?"

He made a face. "I'm in a tough spot to give you advice, because there's no way this is going to come out without me looking as if I wasn't being mercenary."

Just when she thought she had figured it all out, he lost her again. "Mercenary? Are you planning to auction me back to this long-lost relative?"

The look of horror on his face was mixed with too much worry.

"Oh my God, just tell me who it is," she demanded.

"Timothy Carlyn."

21

Kelli waited outside the motel room door, glancing at the rough condition of the place as she compared it with the over-the-top hotel where they'd first met the man. The motel was most often occupied by road crews looking for a place to lay their heads and not people used to luxury or even comfort.

Mr. Carlyn was obviously serious to be willing to put up with these conditions.

She held a little tighter to Luke's fingers. "You should've told him to meet us at your house."

Luke didn't answer, because the door swung open in front of them, and the somewhat familiar features of the older gentleman she'd met in Kananaskis Country came into view.

Timothy Carlyn stared at her with something in his eyes that looked suspiciously like tears. "Kelli. Thank you for agreeing to meet."

He stepped back and gestured them in.

The room they entered held a small kitchen and living space with a worn couch, an older TV, and a kitchen table with four chairs.

Another man rose to his feet from where he'd been sitting at the table, stepping forward to extend a hand. "Dean McCoy."

Kelli introduced herself, and Luke did the same before Timothy gestured them to the seats.

Luke pulled out a chair, waiting until she settled before adjusting his chair to rest beside hers. Kelli grabbed his fingers like a lifeline.

Mr. Carlyn was still staring, but he shook himself and gestured to Dean. "At Silver Stone you have your...Ashton, I believe? This is my man who helps with all things as necessary. In the field and out of it."

Kelli eyed the newcomer. The second man was giving her the heebie-jeebies, his judgmental assessment a half a notch away from sniffing as if he smelt shit on their shoes. In spite of her nervousness, his attitude got her back up. "I doubt you do much mucking-out of stalls in that suit," she said plainly.

Luke covered up a snort of laughter with a cough.

Dean somehow managed to look even more disapproving, but he answered. "Seems we have different areas of expertise, Ms. James."

The hell?

"That's enough, Dean. I didn't want you here in the first place, but you insisted. Make one more smart comment or rude snipe at either of our guests, and I'll find myself someone new to work with."

Well, then.

Kelli ignored Dean and focused instead on the man who might be her grandfather. The word alone was enough to make an impossible mess in her brain.

"Luke showed me the pictures, and I'm almost certain the second photo is my mom."

"Easy to say without proof—" Dean interrupted himself, coughing sternly before starting again. "Excuse me. It would be important if you have any *proof* that you share it with us."

Mr. Carlyn reached out as if he were going to grab Kelli's hand before he caught himself, instead folding his fingers together on the table. "When Dean isn't being a jackass, he does his best to protect my interests. But since I'm the one who approached you, I think it's completely different than when someone I don't know shows up on my doorstep claiming they're a long-lost relative."

"I don't know that I have anything that would be proof. And I don't know where my mom is now. It's been a lot of years since I last saw her, and I like it that way. When I left, I didn't take anything of hers." The money was not going to be mentioned. Kelli pushed the picture back across the table. "I can tell you inside that locket was a bit of purple glass. It was polished—"

Timothy Carlyn's face went absolutely white.

Luke rose halfway to his feet. "Sir? Are you okay?"

Mr. Carlyn waved him down, pressing his hands to the table and taking a few steadying breaths. "I'm sorry. Please continue."

Kelli glanced at Luke. He nodded. "The glass was polished, not to a shine but rough, like winter frost. It was heart-shaped, and when the locket was closed, the stone was small enough to shift and move. I used to shake the locket sometimes, and Mom would laugh and say that it was her heartbeat."

It was one of the few sweet memories that had remained.

The serious-faced man in the suit swore softly, the stern unforgiving expression on his face changed to one of incredulousness.

Dean turned to Mr. Carlyn. "I would still insist on a DNA test, just for legal purposes, but that's pretty convincing."

"I don't think she said it to try and be convincing," Timothy Carlyn drawled. He reached across the table, and Kelli leaned in to accept a third picture. "My wife. She passed away unexpectedly last year."

Kelli was pretty sure this was what she would look like in

another forty or fifty years. "Wow. It's probably a little self-serving if I say she was beautiful."

"She was beautiful," Mr. Carlyn said.

"You *are* beautiful," Luke announced at the same moment.

Mr. Carlyn reached into his pocket and pulled out something, laying it on the table.

It was a locket. The same as she remembered from her youth, and something tightened in Kelli's throat as she glanced at him for permission to pick it up.

When he indicated it was okay, she slipped the locket into her hand, the smooth metal an echo of a childhood memory. She closed her eyes and held it to her ear, shaking her wrist in a side-to-side motion.

In the palm of her hand, a gentle *knock, knock, knock* sounded —like a heartbeat.

She took a breath, shocked to discover her hands shook as she pulled the locket from her ear, automatically hitting the clasp to undo the two sides. She looked down to discover, not a purple heart, but one that was robin-egg blue, like the Alberta sky on a cloudless summer day.

"It's beautiful."

"It was your grandmother's." There was no doubt in Mr. Carlyn's voice as he said the phrase. "I gave my girls matching necklaces one Christmas. They picked the colour for the stone. Danielle said she wanted purple to match the Virginia Bluebells that came up in early spring. And my Toni wanted blue because she said that was the colour of joy."

Kelli's throat tightened further, but Luke's arms were around her and she was safe in his embrace. "She sounds like a wonderful woman. I'm sorry I never got to meet her."

"I'm sorry too," Mr. Carlyn said. "We had no idea you even existed. When Danielle first ran away, I managed to locate her a couple of times. She told me forcefully to leave her alone. I tried to keep in touch in case she ever changed her mind…" He let out a long, slow breath. "I was sick for a while, and lost track. I never thought she'd come to Canada. I wish I'd tried harder."

The regret in his voice was real, and the emotion just messed Kelli up even further.

She shot to her feet. All the men around the table rushed to join her, but she was pushing back from the table, suddenly desperate to escape.

"I need some time," she said. "I mean, this is very exciting, and I'm very glad to meet you. Even you, I suppose." She indicated Dean before tucking herself tighter against Luke's side. "But I need to go."

"Of course, sweetie." Luke nodded at Timothy Carlyn. "Talk tomorrow?"

"Call when you're ready. I'd love to come out to Silver Stone if that works for you. I *am* interested in what you're doing there, beyond tracking down Kelli."

Luke gave her a quick squeeze as he peeked out the window. "It's snowing heavy. Stay here for a minute, and I'll warm the truck up and clear the windshield."

Luke waited until she nodded her approval, but when he left, Dean disappeared and she ended up alone with her grandfather.

"I'm not going to make any demands." Mr. Carlyn spoke softly. "But I want you to know how much I want you to come home."

Not *Mr. Carlyn*— Her *grandfather*, she supposed, although it was going to take some work to think of him that way.

Kelli stared at him, seeing the truth in his eyes, and the hopefulness. "You don't know me. You don't know anything about me, so why would you say something like that?"

"Because when I look at you I see Toni. I see Danielle before she got rebellious and decided that whatever we said, she would do the exact opposite. I see a young woman full of life and energy and who is simply delightful to be around, and I would love very much to have family back in my home. So think about it, Kelli. It's an option for you. You and Luke, of course. There's a home waiting for you."

Kelli nodded slowly. But she had to tell the truth, and this she *didn't* need to think about even a minute longer. "I already have a home, and I have a family. So I'm not saying no, but I am saying I'm not willing to give up what I've already got."

"Fair enough." He looked a little disappointed but nodded in approval. "You might have been raised a world away from us, but you'd be shocked to know how much you remind me of your grandmother."

The door opened behind her, and Luke was there, escorting her away.

A blur of snowflakes mixed with the blur in her brain. Kelli leaned her head on Luke's shoulder and didn't even try to think. She was numb inside, which seemed odd.

Luke sat quietly beside her, his body a rock of comfort. When they arrived at his house after the slow trip home through the falling snow, she followed him meekly into the mudroom.

Her coat vanished, and her boots, and she ended up on the couch, sitting in his lap before she truly knew what was going on.

"Thank you," she started before having to break off.

"Nothing to thank me for, darling. Now hush. You're all but quivering. Let me hold you."

She snuggled in and didn't fight it. His strong body became a cage of protection around her. Like a wall guarding her from the things that would have hurt her, things that would have challenged her too much at this moment.

"I don't know why I'm acting like such a baby," she complained a few minutes later. "It's a good thing, I guess. Finding family. Only—I didn't expect it. And I didn't really want it—I mean, I wasn't looking for it."

"All of those are good reasons for not being sure which end is up," Luke assured her. He stroked his fingers through her hair. "On the good side of the ledger, Carlyn's a solid man. I've never heard anything negative."

"Me either. I liked him at the gala, although I guess this explains why he was staring at me so much." She breathed deep, curling against Luke harder. "I don't want to think right now," she complained.

A soft chuckle escaped him. "Really? Did you have something else to do that's higher on your list?"

Kelli slid her fingers along the placard of his shirt, circling each button one by one. "Possibly. If you've got some time to kill."

Luke hummed as she popped the top button loose, and then the next. "Time? I have a few minutes."

"That all? Too bad…" She let her fingers drift downward until her fingertips trailed over the button of his jeans. She would have rubbed his cock, but she was sitting against it. Which was obvious, because with each passing moment it grew thicker and harder beneath her hip.

"Maybe a bit more than minutes," Luke growled, tucking his arms under her legs and picking her up. She draped her arms around his neck and nuzzled in tight, kissing him and teasing with her tongue as he carried her to his bedroom.

Luke stripped away her blouse, pushing the fabric from her shoulders and stopping to kiss the skin he'd bared. "I need to see you naked," he told her. "Need you under me, need to feel you surround me."

"Need you too," she whispered back.

She closed her eyes and felt.

With every inch he exposed, Luke took the time to explore with his lips. With his tongue. He kissed and licked and teased and nibbled until every inch of her felt alive and so sensitive she was near to spontaneous combustion.

Something was different. Something trembled at the edge of cracking. Like a too-warm spring day when the sunshine on the ice by the falls would make it creak and moan in the seconds before a fissure would open, and the whole thing would come tumbling down. Shards flying, breaking apart—coming undone. A complete reversal of only moments before.

Only, was it breaking, or renewing? Springtime always meant growth, and as Luke touched her, Kelli felt the change coming in every bit of her.

He'd laid her out, bare to his gaze as he stripped the last of his own clothes away then joined her. Stretching at her side and holding her close as he stroked. A gentle touch that was possessive and perfect.

Fingers dipping between her legs, mouth on her breasts, easing away so he could cover her with his weight and kiss her senseless.

She'd already flown once, Luke sending her soaring into an orgasm before he wrapped himself around her and slid inside. His thick length opened her as she let her legs fall apart to welcome him in. Bodies rubbing, lips kissing.

Luke murmured gentle words against her mouth as he rocked, slow and deep. Each motion deliberate and needy as if he was—

As if he was coming home.

Kelli fought to keep the tears from rising, but it was too perfect, too beautiful.

He slowed. Paused, deep inside her, his fingers brushing moisture from her cheek.

"Kelli? You okay?"

She nodded, catching his fingers in hers and pressing them to her lips. "I'm perfect. Don't stop. Please don't stop."

He adjusted their grip, placing their joined hands on the mattress at head level then returning to the slow, gentle strokes that made her feel as if he was loving every inch of her, connected beyond the physical.

Tears still fell, but Kelli was willing to admit they were good tears. They were about family and having a home, and while she couldn't say the words yet, they were about being in love.

Because she loved Luke. She probably always had, and it had taken finding a surprise grandfather to know that no matter what happened at Silver Stone, *Luke* was home.

She was going to have to find a way to tell him that.

"Kelli," Luke whispered. "You feel so right. You're just—"

She opened her eyes and stared into his face.

"Love me," she ordered, pretending it wasn't demand and wish and a dream and a promise all at that same time.

His fingers tightened on hers, and he stroked harder, a little quicker. Then he slid a hand between their bodies and touched her just right, and she broke. Like the frozen waterfall, she came apart, falling into pieces, held in his arms.

Ready for the spring to make her world new. No matter what that looked like, she could make it through this. She knew she could.

Especially if Luke was holding her.

~

HE DEALT with the condom quickly, then gathered her against him. Their naked bodies ended up twined together as if they were trees that had been planted in the same spot.

She fell asleep in his arms, tears still marring her face.

How was it possible for everything to change so completely and yet feel as if this was the way his life was always meant to be?

Luke adjusted position so he could stroke wisps of hair off Kelli's face, staring down at her with that bigger-than-life sensation in his chest.

All his life, he remembered simply doing the next thing. He'd done that as a young man, growing up under the firm tutelage of his father. He'd learned all the tasks required to keep the machinery running and how to care for the animals at Silver Stone ranch.

Between his father and Ashton, Luke knew he'd had strong masculine examples during his growing-up years. He'd seen his oldest brother deal with heartbreak until finally falling in love with the perfect woman. He'd seen Walker push through fear and worry to end up rock solid with Ivy, the years they'd been apart erased as if they'd never happened.

During all that time, Luke had done the next thing. Gotten up in the morning, done his work. Trained the horses, dealt with customers. He'd enjoyed himself, even had a sense of pride, but there'd always been that edge of following by rote.

It wasn't that he couldn't wait to get up in the morning, he just did. It wasn't that he couldn't wait to work with the horses. Although he enjoyed his tasks, he didn't have any urgent desire that made him eager to start. Even his relationship with his ex-fiancée had been more about expectations than a true desire for connection.

The only thing—the *only* common thread of joy over the past years—was the woman lying in his arms. A woman who, when he'd surprised her at the falls with momentous news, had been more concerned about his comfort than her own.

Kelli was the one perfect element in his life, and now that he truly thought it through, she was the only irreplaceable part as well.

It had taken him until now to figure that out.

She was the reason he was eager to get up and head out to train the horses, because her unending enthusiasm and excitement spilled over into his life with joy. Her jokes and her crazy habits, like leaping from high surfaces, or eavesdropping at the most awkward times—he knew *what* to expect from her, but never when to expect it.

She brought spontaneity into his world, whether they were working together, fighting with each other, or now during this brief time, driving each other wild with sexual antics.

There was nothing habit-like when it came to Kelli. She was so much more than that.

As he stared down at her, long lashes resting against her cheeks, it hit him as solidly as the ground had smacked him when he'd been bucked off Chili Pepper—

He loved her. Completely and utterly. It was the most wonderful thing to realize while simultaneously shooting ice along his spine.

Because all of those men in his life? His father, his brothers, his friends? They'd all taught him how important it was to be able to choose what he wanted.

There was no way Kelli could do that now. Choose him, that is.

She had a whole new world open before her, and it wouldn't be right to force her to stay. Not right now. Not until she'd had the chance to spread her wings and step into Timothy Carlyn's world.

Did he want her to go away? Hell, no. And in spite of the pain inside him as he struggled to do the right thing, he knew there was no way he could let her go. Not forever.

But right now? She was so overwhelmed, she probably had no idea exactly what it meant to be linked with Timothy Carlyn. To be able to have the resources and connections he did.

Luke needed to let her go temporarily to experience that. To let her show off her talents in a place other than Silver Stone if she wanted. He had no right to keep her by his side where he'd finally—*finally*—figured out he wanted her.

Their breathing had slowed. Once again she surprised him, eyes sliding open to stare into his face. "You're thinking so loudly I can hear it."

Her fingers rose to his face then past, stroking through his hair then down his neck, over and over in a smooth circle.

"It's been a big day. Lots to think about," he admitted.

Her lips curled upward. "It's late enough we can give it a rest until tomorrow. Go to sleep, Luke."

"Bossy," he complained, although that was *exactly* what he wanted. Kelli in his life, bossing and teasing and tormenting him.

She placed a hand to his chest and pushed, sending him to his back. Even as she moved she was waking up, mischief sliding across her features. "Seeing as we're very conveniently naked, maybe what you need is a little help relaxing."

Certain parts of his anatomy were fully on board with that suggestion, tightening and hardening as she undulated her hips over him. "If you're tired—"

Kelli raised one brow. "You're not seriously turning down sex, are you? That's not the Luke I've gotten to know over the past weeks."

He didn't like her relegating their time together to simply sex. "You don't need to do anything you don't want to," he admitted. "It's been a difficult day."

She nodded thoughtfully. "It has been, and I was definitely thrown for a loop earlier. But something about coming back here helped center me. I appreciate that. I appreciate *you*."

Kelli pressed her lips to his, the front of her body making contact with his naked chest. There was no denying what she wanted. It was clear in her kiss, in her touch, and the motion of her body.

Luke couldn't say no. And he wasn't missing a moment of now, since he didn't know what would come tomorrow. Maybe he was going to have to say goodbye to her temporarily while she headed out to experience new things.

But as he sat up to join her, body and spirit, he committed again that if she did go, it would only be for a short while. While she branched out, he was going to build them roots. He'd make a place for her to come back to, and he was going to do his damnedest to convince her Silver Stone was where she belonged.

He would have to give her room so she'd feel she could leave.

But now? He was going to love her with everything in him. The way he'd always been meant to.

22

Kelli wandered the barn on Sunday, still puzzling through the right thing to do with Timothy Carlyn's astonishing proposition.

It wasn't as if she was going to up and leave Silver Stone. That option was out, but there had to be a way for her to be able to get to know the man more. Not for anything he could give her, but because it was the right thing to do.

Yet just the thought of her grandfather brought back so many memories of time with her mom and everything she'd escaped.

Yeah, her head was a bit of a mess right now, and there was no clear path to follow.

Normally when she felt like this Kelli would've found Luke and spent the morning trailing after him. It was a bit of a shock to realize that in spite of her hard work to hide her attraction all those years, she'd built a lot of habits into her life that revolved around the man.

Talking to him when she was working through a puzzle had been one of them. The noted exception had been her dealing with the abused-women situation, because that had been too close to a part of her world she didn't want to talk about with *anyone*.

She would've talked with him now, only the stubborn man had been mysteriously missing from bed when she woke. There'd been a plate of food in the fridge and the coffee maker set to go at the touch of a button, so he had cared for her before vanishing.

Damn the man. As sweet as that was, what she needed was a lengthy discussion, and he was nowhere to be seen.

She didn't want to talk to Tamara, nor Ashton, and yet the thoughts inside were near to bursting with the urgency to figure this out.

As the day passed, and the next, Luke went from being annoyingly MIA to super-annoyingly out of reach. He came home late and left early, avoiding all conversation because he had "this thing he really needed to get done" at that moment.

He "trusted her judgement" and "was there when she needed him" but then would vanish for hours without anyone knowing where he'd gone.

She was no dummy. Kelli had figured out what was going on —Luke was avoiding her, although she didn't know why.

Unless it was to piss her off, in which case, he was succeeding. In spades.

Kelli marched into the barn on Wednesday afternoon. She'd had another breakfast alone, and the sweet note he'd left had just made her angrier because she wanted him, not a note.

A door slammed in the distance. A moment late Josiah Ryder burst into view, his cheeks flushed and a furrow between his brows. He jerked to a stop when he saw her.

A second later he was smiling and completely in control. "Kelli. Good to see you."

She snorted. "Dude. You are the best liar I've ever met. Oh wait—it's not called lying, right? It's *acting*."

Josiah pressed a finger to his lips. "You're one of the only people in this town I told about my theatre days, so don't blow my cover."

So that's the way he wanted to play it? Kelli decided to let him off the hook this time. Mostly. "Okay, Superman. Only I thought the mild-mannered hero was a reporter by day, not a vet." She peered behind him. "Who pissed you off?"

"No one." He edged past her. "Got to run. Tell Ashton I'll be back tomorrow for a follow-up check on Thunderbolt."

"No prob." Kelli watched him hurry away, amusement rising when she turned to discover Lisa Coleman headed toward her.

It might have been coincidence, the other woman coming from the very direction that Josiah had just escaped from like he'd been pursued by dragons.

The fact Lisa was preoccupied, checking in all the stalls she passed, seemed a teeny bit suspicious, though.

Kelli cleared her throat, and Lisa's head snapped up, her eyes sparkling. "Hey."

"Hey, yourself." Kelli couldn't resist. "Looking for someone?"

"Josiah," Lisa admitted, somewhat reluctantly.

"Something wrong? I mean, I just saw him. I could run and—"

"Don't worry about it, we're good," Lisa's gaze sharpened. "What's up with you?"

So much for keeping the upper hand. Lisa was not one to be messed around with. "I never said anything was wrong."

"Of course you didn't. Now tell me."

Kelli rolled her eyes. "Fine. Luke seems to be avoiding me. Like literally turning heel and going in a different direction to avoid talking."

"Ahh."

Well, that was annoying too. "*Ahh?* That's really all you're going to say?"

"It's less obnoxious than 'Gadzooks, I've got it!' I think Luke is giving you space to figure out what you want."

"What I freaking want is to talk to him about what I want," Kelli complained.

Lisa laughed. "Yeah. But he's being noble or something annoying. Am I right?"

"Could be. I'm not sure since I can't *find* him to ask." Kelli's annoyance was fading, though. "It's not that complicated, I guess. I just want to think it through more. What's the right thing to do?"

Lisa looked thoughtful. "It sounds like such a simple question, doesn't it? You'd think that the right thing would be sitting up on top, visible and bold. Most of the time it's the opposite. The truth hides, not because it's trying to be hard to find, but because it's important enough you need to dig for it. You've got to really want it."

It had been such a short time, and yet Lisa had stepped into the family and joined Silver Stone as if she belonged there, which made sense because she was such an intricate part of Tamara's life.

Only now Kelli wondered...

Kelli looked her over closely. "What do *you* want, Lisa?"

Lisa blinked hard. Then her face lit up, and an enormous smile slid into place. "I knew I liked you for a reason."

Okay. "That's good, but it's not an answer."

The other woman folded her arms and leaned back against the stall boards. "I haven't had a lot of people ask me that, you know. I've had a lot of people tell me what they think I ought to do, and even more tell me what they think I shouldn't do."

"I get a lot of that, as well, but you're not answering the question," Kelli pointed out. "If I stepped over a line or something—"

"Nah, definitely not a line, but it is something I'll admit I've only been thinking about really hard in the last couple of months." Lisa shrugged. "I want to be happy. I think most people do, but usually what made me happy in the past was making *other* people happy. That's not wrong, but going forward, I plan to focus a little bit more on me. Untangle a few of the secrets I've kept not just from other people, but maybe even hidden from myself."

"Deep."

"Very. I think I'll end up on a journey of discovery, because I don't know what tomorrow should hold. There's an awful long time between now and forever. I want it to matter. Whatever I do. I want it to matter to others, but especially to me."

Doing what mattered. Doing what truly would make Kelli happy.

It was like being hit with a brick wall. Or the time she'd taken a kick right in the solar plexus, flying through the air and reeling from the impact of hoof and earth. "You're not as simple as you like to make others think, are you?" Kelli teased with a smile to soften the words. "I'm glad you want to be happy."

"I'm glad you understood that everything I just rambled off boils down to that one truth."

The man-door of the barn swung open, and Lisa motioned with her head to where a tall figure was marching toward them. "It appears he's come out of hiding. If your one truth is like mine, you want to be happy too. I have a feeling that someone *else* truly wants the same thing, especially with you."

"Yet it feels like he's doing everything possible to make it easy for me to leave," Kelli complained.

"Men." Lisa stared heavenward for a moment, and then her face lit up almost dangerously. "Bet you twenty bucks he starts an argument with you over something stupid before—"

"Lisa Coleman, I told you no more bets regarding my relationships." Kelli pressed her fists to her hips and glared at the other woman, holding her mouth pursed long as she could before breaking into laughter.

Luke was nearly upon them. Lisa backed away, tossing Kelli a wink. "Fine, I won't take your money. I still think you'll end up in the tack room before too long. Because I know what happens when you guys finish arguing and move to making up."

"Kelli?" Luke stepped around Lisa, who wiggled her fingers before taking off with a skip in her step.

Kelli slipped into Chili Pepper's pen. "I'll be out in a second."

"I'll wait."

She had nothing to do. Not really, but the moment to collect her thoughts helped. Kelli pressed her forehead against Pepper's. Speaking in the barest whisper as she gathered her courage. "Maybe you can share a little of your stubbornness to make sure I do this right."

The mare snorted, ruffling Kelli's braids, and she laughed, squeezing Chili Pepper affectionately before crawling out of the pen and closing the gate behind her.

Luke uncurled himself from the wall he'd been leaning against and stepped toward her. "We need to talk."

~

LUKE HAD TRIED to stay away. Really, he had, but it had been growing steadily more impossible. Even riding that morning for a couple of hours had done nothing to still the damn jumping beans in his gut.

He'd stopped on the hillside where his mom and dad were buried, but the only thing that had reminded him of was how fully they'd lived their lives. Every single day until they were gone, they had laughed and loved and given generously to the family.

He might've told Kelli she had to make her own decision and that whatever she wanted, he would support her, but part of his promise was a lie.

If she chose to go away, he was going to die inside. He didn't want her to leave him.

While he'd been daydreaming, Kelli had wandered into the

empty stall beside Chili Pepper, rake in hand as she smoothed the hard-packed earth floor. Working while they talked, the way they had for years together.

But this time, he took the rake from her hands and leaned it against the wall, needing her full attention. "Your grandpa called. He wants your phone number, and I wanted to find out from you first if that was okay. He'd like to come out to the ranch this weekend."

She gave a quick nod before a look of incredulousness spread over her face. "This is not going to go away when I blink, is it?

He shook his head. "No. It's real."

"Of course, you can give him my number. It's good for him to be able to have a way to get in touch—" Her eyes widened like dinner plates, and she swore softly. "Oh my God, he still thinks we're engaged, doesn't he?"

His spine stiffened. "Yeah."

Her face twisted, and her nose wrinkled. "I wonder what he'd say if we told him the truth."

Fuck his good intentions. Luke's heart pounded so hard he felt it in his throat. "You really don't want me that much?"

Her expression turned to sheer confusion. "What?"

"You're willing to simply give me up."

"What are you—?"

"What if it wasn't a lie?" Anger rose along with a sense of out-of-control futility, and he dragged a hand through his hair, pacing away. Pacing back. "I don't have anything I can do to prove to you that I'm worth it. There's nothing I can give up to show that you're worth everything to me. You've got money now, and you've got connections. We don't need each other anymore the way we did heading out to the gala. But if you're not with me, at my side, it's all worthless."

Words spilled from him like a Chinook wind assaulting the icy cold of winter. Relentless, heated and unstoppable.

Kelli's eyes had grown wider and her jaw hung open, but no sound came out.

Which was fine, because he was nowhere near done.

"Maybe it's wrong, but I don't give a rat's ass about Silver Stone if you're not by my side every morning when I wake up." His volume increased, and he crowded toward her. "Hell, I'll move to Kentucky if that's what it takes so I can hold you in my arms every night. If that's where you feel like you have to be."

"Whoa, boy." Kelli's arm shot out against his chest, and she leaned into him, catching him off guard enough that his feet tangled and he tipped backward into the wall of the pen. That was the only reason she could have used her slight weight to pin him in place.

Now she glared at him, staring up with so much determination he totally understood how she controlled the horses.

"You had a few too many cups of coffee this morning, Luke Stone. You need to slow the hell down."

"How can I calm down when you plan to leave me?" God, he sounded as if he was begging her to stay, which wasn't far from the truth.

A furl formed between her eyes. Fire and heat glared back at him. "You promised not to make assumptions, so back up and *shut* up for a minute."

"But I—"

Her glare intensified, and he slammed his lips together, suddenly aware he really had been spewing at the mouth without his brain engaged.

Then she let him have it with both barrels, at just as high a volume as he'd used a moment earlier. "Why would you have to give something up to prove yourself? Isn't the point of caring for someone that you do things for them instead of *not* doing things for them?"

He waited until he was certain he was allowed to speak. "I guess."

"I know you've cared for me as a friend for years. I'm pretty sure you've cared about me these past weeks since we became lovers. I *think* that's what all this talk about holding me in your arms at night and waking up with me in the morning is about."

"What if I want more?"

She folded her arms over her chest. "Maybe you should ask me if that's what I want, if it's what you want. Do you really think I won't believe you if you say you want more?"

"Why are you arguing with me, woman?" Luke snapped.

"Because you started it," Kelli shouted.

"You asked what your grandpa would say if he found out we weren't really engaged."

"It was a rhetorical question, jackass."

"Not to me." The only thing that registered in his brain from the last few minutes was her saying *you should ask me.*

Which is why he dropped to his knees in front of her and caught her hands, staring up at her right there in the horse stall as he held on tight to keep her from escaping.

As he held her because he couldn't let go. "Kelli James, marry me."

She was back to being speechless, mouth open, staring at him as if he'd lost his mind. She was quiet for so long, fear curled in his belly.

Had he'd totally misread *everything*?

"Why?" There was so much hope on her face. "And it better not be because it's logical for you and I to be together."

And it finally—*finally*—sank in what he'd been missing.

"Dammit, Kelli. This isn't about logic, it's about how much I fucking love you and need you—"

Kelli threw herself at him. She wrapped her arms and legs around him as she peppered his face with kisses, laughter pooling around them. His knees ground into the dirt as he clutched her close.

She pulled away far enough to catch his cheeks in her palms, amusement decorating her expression. “This is a little disturbing. That we’re here, in a stall, and you’re proposing.”

“There is no manure present, and right now the only word I want to hear from you is *yes*,” Luke muttered.

“I don’t really have to answer, do I?” Kelli took a deep breath and let it out slowly. “I love you too.”

That was the part he’d forgotten before, but damn if she just didn’t keep on being perfect for him. “That’s been there for a long, long time, even when I was too stupid to say it. I love you,” he repeated, pushing everything inside him into the words. “I think I always have.”

“I’m very lovable,” she pointed out.

He laughed as he picked her up, kissing her hungrily as he pressed her against the wall of the pen.

On the other side of the wood, Pepper nickered, and Kelli laughed against his lips. “She says congratulations.”

“I believe you.”

Only Luke didn’t need a horse, or anyone else, as a witness to what he wanted next.

He carried Kelli across the hall, sliding into the tack room and closing the door. “We need to talk about so many things—”

Kelli’s hands were at the button of his pants, as eager as he was to strip away layers. “Later. Not too much later, but for now I need to make sure I get my twenty bucks worth.”

He stiffened before putting two and two together. “Dammit. Lisa made a bet with you.”

“You should’ve taken me to the hayloft,” Kelli teased, and then her hands were on him, sliding on protection from somewhere, thank God. And they were moving together. Full of life and energy and happiness as she made it very clear that her answer was a one-hundred-percent, fully engaged, Kelli-endorsed, enthusiastically-accepted *yes*.

Her fingernails dug into his shoulders, and her legs wrapped around his hips as he cupped her ass and moved her against him. Together in this place where they'd been a million times.

And while he didn't know what was going to happen in the future, somewhere along the line, whether it was here at Silver Stone or at another ranch, he was pretty sure they'd be finding places to make love wherever they ended up.

"I love you." He whispered the words against her ear as they rocked together, physically connected. Her eyes were bright in the dim light shining through the small side window. He said it again, because it tasted so perfect on his lips. "I love you, Kelli James."

"Thank goodness," she whispered back. "Because it's far easier, this loving stuff, when it's the two of us in the same pile of trouble."

23

It wasn't as if everything changed overnight, but in all the really important ways, it did.

Kelli was living in Luke's house. Not because it was convenient to have a place where they could easily fall into bed, but because it was *their* spot. He'd brought all her things from the bunkhouse, which barely made a dent in the spacious new living quarters.

Having her stuff in a drawer next to his put a smile on her face every time she realized it.

This was real. This was not just a feverish dream where things would escalate to heat and pleasure, but it was moment by moment, day after day for a long line of days that would lead into a year.

Years. Always the next thing, and she was pretty fine with that.

Tough moments poked their head into her perfect happiness, but they were made easier because Luke was there, by her side.

Like now. Timothy Carlyn stood on the doorstep, hat in hand as he waited to be invited inside.

Kelli hesitated briefly before opening her arms and offering a hug, emotion squeezing her as tightly as his arms before her grandpa patted her on the back awkwardly and turned to shake Luke's hand.

She spotted the moisture in the older man's eyes.

They settled in at the new dining room table, the broad wooden surface shone to a high gloss. It contrasted sharply with the randomly shaped chairs she and Lisa had scrounged from the local thrift shop the day before.

Luke sat in the chair next to her, his grin widening. "Go ahead and tell me *I told you so*."

Her grandpa lifted a brow in inquiry.

Kelli laughed. "It's not that entertaining. I just told Luke since we have the second house on the Silver Stone land, it's only fair we host some of the family dinners. That required a table and chairs, and"—she gestured with a hand toward him—"we already have a reason to be thankful for a place to sit."

He nodded firmly. "Luke's got himself a bit of a treasure in you, my girl."

Luke wrapped his arm around her shoulders, pulling their bodies together. "I couldn't agree more."

This meeting should have felt more worrisome, having Mr. Carlyn—her *grandfather*—there. Knowing what a difference he could make, in so many ways, but Kelli had already decided what was most important to her.

Luke had agreed, and no matter what happened, they were in this together.

Kelli took a deep breath. "We've talked about your invitation. We'd be very happy to come visit your ranch, but this is home. We're needed here, and this is where we'll spend most of our time."

"But we want you to know that you're always welcome," Luke added. "And there's nothing to say that Kelli can't visit you on her own sometimes. Occasionally."

Her grandfather laughed. "Not too often, though, if I'm hearing this right."

Kelli's cheeks were flaming. "There's a lot of work to be done," she began before caving and admitting the truth. "And we're two people in love who don't want to spend a lot of time apart."

Around her shoulders, Luke's arm squeezed tight, as if he couldn't stop himself. As if he was never going to let go, and Kelli was just fine with that.

Timothy Carlyn held up a finger then reached into his pocket to pull out an envelope. "I forgot. Dean wanted me to make sure that you got this. Yes, we rushed the testing, but it's proof that you really are my granddaughter. Not that I ever had a doubt, but any naysayers can take their complaints elsewhere."

Kelli nodded, not sure if she was brave enough to do the next part. But she'd spoken with Luke about, and it seemed right.

Hard, but very right.

She spoke quickly, before she lost her nerve. "When you want, I'll give you all the details I know about my mom if you'd like to try and track her down. To be clear, I'm not at all interested in a reunion, but that doesn't mean you shouldn't have the chance to find her."

Her grandpa caught her fingers in his rough hand and squeezed them tightly. "My concern right now is you. We've got a lot of years to catch up on. I don't expect it to happen overnight, but I hope you'll let me enjoy your company as much as possible."

Kelli's world got fuller and more hopeful by the moment. "Of course. Like Luke said, you're always welcome here. It's not much, but Luke suggested we could set up a spare room here for you when you'd like to stay."

Grandpa Timothy, as she'd have to work on thinking of him as, looked pleased as punch at that announcement. "And I know it's a lot to expect, but I really hope I can be involved in your wedding."

The dancing beans in her stomach switched to a two-step.

"We need to set a date, but we'd be honoured to have you participate," Luke said softly.

That was another thing that was real. Really engaged, *really* planning on spending the rest of their lives together.

Really becoming a permanent member of the Stone family.

Luke and Grandpa Timothy got to talking about bloodlines and the upcoming trip down to Kentucky. Kelli tossed in a few comments here and there, but mostly she listened, her gaze travelling back and forth between the two men. One from her unknown past, the other definitely her future, in a way that she'd never dared dream.

When her grandpa left, Luke tucked his arm around her, and she turned to him and kissed him as sweetly as she could.

He pulled away, a twinkle in his eyes as he smiled. "I'm not complaining one bit, but what was that for?"

Kelli slipped her fingers into his and held on tight. "Because all those years ago when I first caught a glimpse of you, I never dreamed this day would come. You looked so amazing up on your horse. You worked hard yet never complained. Just did what needed to be done, always with encouraging words for everyone around you. And even after all those years that I watched you and thought about how amazing you were, and how much I admired you—that feeling inside me just keeps growing as if I tapped into an artesian spring, and it's flooding everywhere."

He tugged her against his body, holding her firmly in place as he grinned at her. "I'm glad. It's good to know I'm not the only one getting in over my head."

"Definitely not."

A COLD SNAP SET IN. Winter darkness lay across the deep drifts and filled their time outdoors with icy cold hands and clouds that formed around their heads every time they breathed.

But inside the barns it was warm. And inside the house, in front of the fire, Kelli and Luke spent hours talking about everything under the sun. Her mom, his parents, their hopes for the future.

Talked, and kissed, and talked some more.

"I still want to know how you ended up at Silver Stone," Luke said when they took a break from the kissing part.

"Gossip," Kelli informed him. "I *might* have been eavesdropping."

He snorted. "Really? I'm shocked."

She stuck out her tongue briefly before continuing. "When I ran away, I hopped on a bus to Calgary. I planned to stay in a hostel for a bit while I checked the want ads for work somewhere in Alberta. I had that I.D. that said I was eighteen, so it didn't seem like it was going to be that difficult. I knew how to ride and how do chores—been doing them for years on the ranch where we lived."

"You definitely knew what you were doing, right from the first time I saw you," Luke agreed.

"I like animals," she said with a shrug. "I was cheap labour, but I was good."

"You are *great*," Luke insisted before interrupting her story with more kissing.

Her head was spinning slightly by the time he let her up for air, and his grin said he knew exactly what he did to her. "Silver Stone? After the bus station?" he prompted.

She nodded, falling into the memories. "There were a bunch of cowboys milling around the bus stop when I arrived on the red eye. Some of them were worse for wear after a night out at the bar. They were discussing if they should head down to Silver Stone without the guys who were still sleeping it off."

Luke's eyes went wide. "Uncle Frank's crew that didn't show up."

"The same. They weren't looking forward to explaining to anyone why they were short-handed. One of them mentioned they'd be branding, which I knew how to do, so I took a chance and got a ticket for the bus they were waiting for. Slipping into one of the trucks Silver Stone had sent was easy—there were other short-term workers from other ranches waiting at the Heart Falls bus stop, so I just acted like I belonged. The rest is history."

"Cocky teenager," Luke said with affection.

"Yup," she agreed. "Aren't you glad?"

"Very glad," he returned.

It was good to finally get to share the story with him.

There were other conversations. Food likes and dislikes, movies and music. Kelli learned more about what made Luke tick on a deeper, more intimate level…

After all the years they'd spent around each other, it was incredible how much they had to talk about that was new and fresh, coming from their changed perspective of being in love.

A different level of discussion on topics they had never really touched on until falling in love changed everything.

Kelli stared up at him from her position lazing on her back. Luke teased a hand over her ribs, and pleasure rose as he caressed her skin, firelight reflecting over them.

"What about kids?" he asked.

"Eventually. I like them, obviously, considering how much I adore Sasha and Emma. But I don't think Tamara and Caleb are planning on having more, so it's not as if we need to rush."

"I'm good with that," he agreed, "Although, let's not wait too long."

Kelli snickered. "Yeah, I guess we shouldn't wait *too* long, or you'll be too old to—"

He covered her mouth with his and stopped her teasing in the best possible way.

The only item weighing her down was the same issue they'd faced back when all this began. And while Caleb didn't walk around with a storm-cloud face anymore, it was obvious he still had things on his mind.

Had the finances improved enough because of their work to get Silver Stone back on track?

February was passing quickly. Plans were underway for a trip to her grandpa's. They were juggling dates because Ivy and Walker were getting married in March, and Tamara's due date was in April. The whole ranch buzzed with excitement.

Including, it seemed, her phone. Kelli looked down with delight to see a message from Diane.

Diane: *I can't wait.*

Kelli wasn't sure what was going on, but she went with it: *okay?*

Diane: *get out. You mean he didn't tell you yet?*

Kelli: *I assume this means Luke is in trouble*

Diane: *calling*

A moment later the phone rang, and Kelli answered instantly. "I don't know what you're talking about, so spill the beans."

Diane's familiar sweet tones slid into her ear like warm honey. "Maybe I'm not supposed to say anything. I'm going to ruin the surprise."

"Consider this like two presents. I get the surprise *now* of you telling me what's going on, and then I get to enjoy whatever it is that you're going to tell me about."

A low laugh bounced back. "You know your trip to visit your grandpa, and can I just say again how freaking exciting it is that Carlyn is your grandpa? Anyway, he gave us a shout, and Jack and

I will be there, so we can get caught up while you visit. He said you didn't want to be gone from home too long, so this way we get to catch up and spend time together and still get you home."

Wow. "That is incredible."

Out of nowhere a rush of emotion and what was suspiciously like tears flooded her eyes. Kelli fought for control while Diane babbled in the background for a minute before finally getting suspicious.

"Kelli, what's wrong?"

She wasn't sure if voicing it would make the dream vanish. "This doesn't happen in real life. All this goodness. Finding friends like you and Jack, finding out I have a grandpa who is interested in me and cares about me. Falling in love with Luke—it seems too perfect to be true."

"Oh, honey. You're right. Maybe this doesn't happen to everybody, but it's definitely happening to you. You deserve it. Now you need to take both hands, hold on tight and enjoyed the ride."

Kelli wiped away tears, working hard to pull herself together.

It was too late to hide her emotional outburst from Luke, though. He was already pulling away from where he was talking to some of the hands, concern on his face as he made his way toward her.

She hurriedly finished her call. "I don't know if I deserve it, but I'm definitely sticking in the saddle for as long as I can. Thanks. Thanks for coming into my life and being a good friend."

"It's only going to get better," Diane promised. "I've gotta run, but I can't wait to see you, darlin'. Chat soon."

She hung up after blowing a kiss, and Kelli put away her phone in time to lift her face to Luke's to accept his kiss.

Luke's fingers under her chin held her steady as he examined her carefully.

It was there in his eyes. It was there in his touch.

The way he felt about her—they'd been saying it on a steady

basis, the *I love you* business, but as much as she needed and wanted to hear the words, the truth was there each and every moment.

In every touch.

"Everything okay?" he asked

"I've got you," Kelli said honestly. "Everything's perfect."

~

IN EARLY MARCH, they gathered in the ranch house kitchen.

The signs of preparation for Ivy and Walker's big event the next day filled the room. But in spite of the busy timing, Luke was grateful when Caleb had brought the four brothers together before the wedding to share the good news.

Luke stared down at the figures in front of him, relief and joy rushing his system. "Please tell me I'm reading this right."

Walker spoke first. "That was my response too, but it's real. Damn if you and Kelli didn't come through for us."

"The contacts you made at the gala helped. A lot," Caleb agreed. "But, Walker, we wouldn't have lasted this long without what you did for us back in the fall. That was enough to get us through the breaking point."

"And Nemo. And Kelli—" Luke had been floored to find out that she'd gone back to the lawyer and made a few changes regarding her shares of Nemo's earnings. "She didn't have to split her shares with the other women."

"You think you could stop her?" Walker asked with a laugh. "The three of them are calling it the Silver Heart fund."

Every time Nemo earned a stud fee, a portion now went into a joint bank account to be used for whatever the three women of Silver Stone deemed was needed. And all of them, Tamara, Ivy and Kelli, had voted to keep the percentage going straight back into ranch operations for the time being.

Kelli had arranged that with the others before he'd even

proposed. She'd already decided to help save Silver Stone. To keep it going for the family she'd chosen.

Luke collected himself before he broke down.

Dustin had his hands on the tabletop, and he stared at them. "Caleb said I was a part of it too, and I'll agree, but it would be a mistake to not recognize how *much* you all stepped up." He lifted his eyes and looked at them each in turn. "I don't know how, but I promise that someday I'll find a way to make a real difference, too."

Caleb laid a hand on his shoulder. "This was the whole family, including you, Dustin, and I'm not just saying that. We worked together and this time, we came out on top. It's Ashton, and the hands. It's Tamara and the girls doing what they could when they could."

Outside the window, a long-muzzled grey face poked up and peered in at them as if wanting to be let in on the meeting. The goat's debonair bowtie tilted saucily to one side. It appeared Sasha was determined to keep replacing the things as fast as the creatures could lose them, and this one was festive red in honour of the wedding.

Dustin snickered. "Fine. We all contributed, but if you try to tell me that the goats had anything to do with this, I'm going to worry about you."

"Dustin, I'm shocked. Don't you feel they're an important part of our family?" Luke teased as he rose to his feet and peeked out the window. Dammit. He gestured for his brothers to join him. "It's not only Meany. All three of them are out, and if we don't get them now, they'll probably show up in the middle of your wedding, Walker."

"That would go over well," Walker muttered, pulling on his coat and reaching for his hat.

"The girls would love it."

"Don't go putting ideas into their head or they'll want the

goats to be ring bearers," Dustin warned. "Right now Sasha is plotting to tie a pillow on Demon's back."

"No goats, and no dogs. And it appears our family meeting is over, called on account of goats," Caleb drawled. "But the good news is Silver Stone's got plenty of family meetings in her future."

They headed outside, the crisp cold air and beautiful blue sky making it clear that, even while they chased the goats, they were home.

When a rope dropped around his torso, snapping tight and trapping him in place, Luke glanced over his shoulder unsurprised to find he'd been hogtied by his favourite cowgirl in the world.

"I heard there were wild animals running loose, so I figured I should help round them up." Kelli tugged the rope, guiding him closer to her horse.

"Round them up and brand them?" Luke teased.

Her eyes slipped over him in appreciation. "Well, it seems only right since branding is what got me started here at Silver Stone. I only want to put my mark on one particular wild beast, though."

Luke stood next to her now, staring up as she loosened the rope, coiled it, and hung it from her saddle. "Trust me, Kelli. You've already put your mark on me. Heart and soul. Now and forever."

She tipped back her cowboy hat, sliding her foot from the stirrup and gesturing for him to join her. "Come on, cowboy. This kind of branding requires privacy."

"I like the sounds of that."

He mounted behind her. The two of them snuck a final glance toward where the rest of the family, Caleb, Walker, Dustin and now Lisa, had been joined by Sasha and Emma.

Tamara leaned against the goat pen gate, her coat stretched hard over the swell of her belly. Ivy was beside her, bundled up in her bright blue coat, the two of them laughing as the three goats leapt everywhere, almost, but not quite in range of their pursuers.

Luke wrapped his arms around Kelli as she tugged the reins and headed toward his house—*their* house. Leaning forward to put his lips by her ear. "So. How exactly does this branding business work?"

She twisted until he could see her smile. "Well, I'll get the fire roaring, open the grate, and wait until the brand is glowing red-hot. You can decide if you want it on your right butt cheek or your left—"

He squeezed her around the waist. "Leave my butt out of it."

Kelli laughed out loud then leaned harder against him. "Then again, maybe kisses will be involved. Long, slow and very heated kisses."

He hummed in approval. "That sounds like my kind of branding."

Silver Stone was still theirs and would be for years to come. Kelli was part of his family, in more ways than one. They had a grandpa to visit, friends to spend time with, but over all that, the deepest sensation riding Luke was one of peace.

He held on tight to the woman who was the perfect bride, and the perfect partner, and the perfect *just Kelli* for him.

Together they rode toward the future.

EPILOGUE

Christmas Eve, just over one and a half years later

Ginny Stone was finally home. And that home, Silver Stone ranch, was bedlam.

She'd arrived just in time for dinner and found the house full to the brim. Which was perfect, in a way. She didn't want any bells and whistles made over her arrival and with so many people milling about, both friends and family, there was no chance one of her older brothers would attempt to haul her into a deep conversation about long-term goals before she'd had a chance to get her head on straight.

The loud and joyous meal was followed by time with her nieces as they enthusiastically caught her up on everything they'd done over the past month since her last brief visit. When she finally convinced them to fall asleep, Ginny joined the rest of the grownups still in the house and helped get the tree in place and decorated, with presents tucked underneath for the surprise of Christmas morning.

The only down-side of the evening was being informed that

her usual room in the basement was already taken. In fact, *all* the usual places were occupied.

Tamara was very apologetic about it, but had a solution. "Would you mind crashing in one of the horse trailers? The one next to the south barn is clean, and there are bedsheets in there." She made a face. "I'm not sure if anyone got around to actually making the bed, though."

"I can handle that," Ginny promised. She laid a hand on her sister-in-law's arm. "It's okay. I'm *family*. You don't need to guest me up."

Tamara wrapped her in a big hug. "I'm very much looking forward to getting to know you better."

"Me too," Ginny said honestly. "Plus, we need to reminisce in Caleb's presence about how you took him to the ground the first time you met."

The burst of laughter from Tamara was heartfelt, and Ginny's optimism returned. Maybe this coming back to the family fold would be easier than she'd hoped.

But she was glad to be able to slip away a few minutes later. Away from the rumble of laughter and the sheer presence of people, and back into the quiet of the winter night. Ginny grabbed her backpack from her truck and wandered slowly, taking in all the visible changes to the place she'd grown up but been away from for years.

The trailer Tamara had sent her to sleep in was a newer one, parked neatly beside the south barn. The three goats in their nearby pen watched her with wild curiosity, and Ginny saluted as she passed. "As you were, fellow mischief-makers."

She opened and closed the trailer door as quietly as possible. No use in letting the goats know they had neighbours, or the hellions would find a way to break out and come haunt her in the night.

The trailer smelled strangely good. She'd expected the air to be slightly stale, so the unusual scent was both a relief and a mystery. Bergamot? Coffee? Those two for sure, but something else familiar that she vaguely remembered...

Tired enough to simply want to crash, Ginny stopped in the small living space to get ready. She stripped off her pants, removed her bra from under her top, leaving only her oversized tank to sleep in.

"Be free," she mumbled softly, taking a deep breath and enjoying the lack of pressure on her shoulders from the bra straps. Big boobs were a pain at times, literally. "I crack me up."

Her eyes had adjusted to the pale glow coming in the window from the yard light, so she didn't bother with turning on the overhead light. She shuffled toward the bedroom area, suddenly wary when a strange, out-of-place sound rumbled her direction.

Ginny cautiously peered around the corner.

Holy shit.

The bed indeed had sheets as Tamara had told her, but they were messed up, scrunched into semi piles over the long muscular form of a man. He was face down, his butt on prime display. The edge of fear that had swept in vanished.

Ginny knew her mystery man.

Lying before her was Tucker Stewart, nephew to Silver Stone's long-time foreman, her older brother Luke's companion in crime during the summers while they were growing up, and her own personal kryptonite.

What she should do was back away and find somewhere else to sleep.

What she did was stand motionless for far, far too long, simply staring.

Time had only made him more delicious. His face was mostly scrunched into the pillow, but his lips were visible. Strong and full, they were parted slightly, a soft rumble only an uncharitable person would describe as a snore escaping him.

She didn't need to see his eyes to remember the pale blue shade. Didn't need to see him awake to be able to recall his all too brief smiles, always accompanied by a spark in his eyes, as if he were astonished that she'd pulled an expression from him other than his usual gruff visage.

Nope, memory painted plenty of pictures for the parts she couldn't see. The parts she could? *Holy mother.* Tucker had packed on muscle in the four years since she'd seen him last.

Triceps defined even in sleep, his visible forearm was dusted with a faint layer of light brown hair. His big hand pressed to the mattress where his strong fingers were splayed as if ready to cup her breast.

His big, *talented* hands. Ones Ginny had enjoyed feeling him run all over her. Broad shoulders that she'd dug her nails into as they'd shot together toward a sweaty, dirty, overwhelmingly pleasurable peak.

The curve of his hip teased her, one thigh pulled up to protect more delicate body parts. The hollow of shadow that hid his groin made her smile and lift her focus to the star of the show. His ass, the sheet shoved far enough aside to showcase every muscular dip and the straight row of dots scarring his right butt cheek.

Which is how she'd recognized him. *Ahem.*

She'd not only enjoyed seeing his naked ass up close and personal before, but she'd been there when her older brother Luke had given Tucker that scar. Twelve years old and pretending they were hosting a magical duel, Tucker had reacted to Luke's *spell* with determination, throwing himself backward only to unknowingly land full force on a rake.

He was no longer that youngster. Nor the teenager whom she'd followed after like a love-struck puppy. Not even the serious young man who she'd finally convinced she was grown up enough to know what she wanted—which included wild, vigorous sex with him.

Long lean lines, bare skin she wanted to touch. She must have made a noise because he woke. His body tightened, which did wonderful things to his ass.

He rolled. Ginny forced her gaze off the tempting bits—*parts. That was* not *a bit*—coming into prime display, shifting to meet his eyes.

Tucker blinked, then blinked again, as a dark smolder twisted into place.

"Ginny Stone. Well, well, *well.* Merry Christmas to me."

New York Times Bestselling Author Vivian Arend invites you to Heart Falls. These contemporary ranchers live in a tiny town in central Alberta, tucked into the rolling foothills. Enjoy the ride as they each find their happily-ever-afters.

The Stones of Heart Falls
A Rancher's Heart
A Rancher's Song
A Rancher's Bride
A Rancher's Love
A Rancher's Vow

ABOUT THE AUTHOR

New York Times and USA Today bestselling author Vivian Arend loves to share the products of her over-active imagination with her readers. She writes contemporary, western, and light-hearted paranormal romances. The stories are humorous yet emotional, usually with a large cast of family or friends, and a guaranteed happily-ever-after. Vivian lives in British Columbia, Canada, with her husband of many years—her inspiration for every hero and a willing companion for all sorts of adventures. Find out more at www.vivianarend.com.

Made in the USA
Middletown, DE
25 January 2022

59502973R00170